Judge & Jury

James Patterson
AND
Andrew Gross

WARNER BOOKS

NEW YORK   BOSTON

Warner Books
Hachette Book Group USA
1271 Avenue of the Americas
New York, NY 10020

Visit our Web site at www.HachetteBookGroupUSA.com

Printed in the United States of America

This Warner Books edition is published by arrangement with Little, Brown and Company, 1271 Avenue of the Americas, New York, NY 10020.

First International Trade Edition: July 2006
10 9 8 7 6 5 4 3 2 1

ISBN-13: 978-0-446-69814-6
ISBN-10: 0-446-69814-8

Raves for James Patterson

"PATTERSON KNOWS WHERE OUR DEEPEST FEARS ARE BURIED . . . THERE'S NO STOPPING HIS IMAGINATION."　　　　　—*New York Times Book Review*

"THE MAN IS A MASTER OF HIS GENRE. We fans all have one wish for him: Write even faster."　　　　　—Larry King, *USA Today*

"WHEN IT COMES TO CONSTRUCTING A HARROWING PLOT, AUTHOR JAMES PATTERSON CAN TURN A SCREW ALL RIGHT."　　　　　—*New York Daily News*

"JAMES PATTERSON KNOWS HOW TO SELL THRILLS AND SUSPENSE IN CLEAR, UNWAVERING PROSE."　　　　　—*People*

"PATTERSON HAS MASTERED THE ART OF WRITING PAGE-TURNING BEST-SELLERS."　　　　　—*Chicago Sun-Times*

"JAMES PATTERSON WRITES HIS THRILLERS AS IF HE WERE BUILDING ROLLER COASTERS. He grounds the stories with a bare-bones plot, then builds them over the top and tries to throw readers for a loop a few times along with way."　　　　　—Associated Press

"A MUST-READ AUTHOR—A MASTER OF THE CRAFT."　　　　　—*Providence Sunday Journal*

"THE PAGE-TURNINGEST AUTHOR IN THE GAME RIGHT NOW."　　　　　—*San Francisco Chronicle*

"JAMES PATTERSON ALWAYS DELIVERS A FASCINATING, ACTION-PACKED THRILLER."　　　　　—*Midwest Book Review*

"PATTERSON IS A MASTER."　　　　　—*Toronto Globe & Mail*

The novels of James Patterson

FEATURING ALEX CROSS

Mary, Mary

London Bridges

The Big Bad Wolf

Four Blind Mice

Violets Are Blue

Roses Are Red

Pop Goes the Weasel

Cat & Mouse

Jack & Jill

Kiss the Girls

Along Came a Spider

THE WOMEN'S MURDER CLUB

The 5th Horseman (and Maxine Paetro)

4th of July (and Maxine Paetro)

3rd Degree (and Andrew Gross)

2nd Chance (and Andrew Gross)

1st to Die

OTHER BOOKS

Maximum Ride: School's Out — Forever

Beach Road (and Peter de Jonge)

Lifeguard (and Andrew Gross)

Maximum Ride

Honeymoon (and Howard Roughan)

santaKid

Sam's Letters to Jennifer

The Lake House

The Jester (and Andrew Gross)

The Beach House (and Peter de Jonge)

Suzanne's Diary for Nicholas

Cradle and All

Black Friday

When the Wind Blows

See How They Run

Miracle on the 17th Green (and Peter de Jonge)

Hide & Seek

The Midnight Club

Season of the Machete

The Thomas Berryman Number

For more information about James Patterson's novels, visit
www.jamespatterson.com

This book is dedicated to the Dana-Farber Cancer Institute and all those who contribute to this worthy cause.

The authors would also like to thank Kevin Palardy, Mary Ellen Murphy, and especially Anne Heausler Dupont. Thanks to Jim Kingsdale, whose travels to Patagonia were illuminating.

Prologue

THE WEDDING

One

MY NAME IS NICK PELLISANTE, and this is where it started for me, one summer out on Long Island at "the wedding of weddings." I was watching the bride celebrating at the head of the dance line as it festively wound through the tables. *A conga line.* I groaned. I hated conga lines.

I should mention that I was watching the scene through high-powered binoculars. I followed as the bride slung her ample, lace-covered rear end in every direction, toppling a glass of red wine, trying to coax some bowling ball of a relative who was scarfing down a plate of stuffed clams up into the procession. Meanwhile, the grinning, affable groom did his Gowanus Expressway best just to hang on.

Lucky couple, I thought, wincing, thinking ten years down the line. *Lucky me, to get to watch. All part of the job.*

As special agent in charge of section C-10, the FBI's Organized Crime Unit in New York, I was heading up a stakeout of a wiseguy wedding at the posh South Fork Club in Montauk. Everybody who was anybody was here, assuming you were into wiseguys.

Everybody except for the one man I was really looking for.

The Boss. The *Capo di tutti capi*. Dominic Cavello. They called him the Electrician because he had started in that trade, pulling off construction scams in New Jersey. The guy was bad, terror-level-red bad. And I had a slew of warrants on him, for murder, extortion, union tampering, and conspiracy to finance narcotics.

Some of my buddies at the Bureau said Cavello was already in Sicily, laughing at us. Another rumor had him in the Dominican Republic at a resort he owned. Others had him in Costa Rica, in the UAE, even in Moscow.

But I had a hunch that he was here, somewhere in this noisy crowd on the South Fork Club's beautiful back deck. His ego was too large. I'd been tracking him for three years, and I expect he knew it. But nothing, not even the federal government, was going to make Dominic Cavello miss his closest niece's wedding.

"Cannoli One, this is Cannoli Two," a voice deadpanned in my earpiece.

It was Special Agent Manny Oliva, whom I'd stationed down on the dunes with Ed Sinclair. Manny grew up in the projects of Newark, then got himself a law degree at Rutgers. He'd been assigned to my C-10 unit straight out of Quantico.

"Anything on the radar, Nick? Nothing but sand and seagulls here."

"Yeah," I said, dishing it back, "ziti mostly. A little lasagna with hot sausages, some stuffed shrimp and parmigiana."

"Stop! You're making me hungry down here, Nicky Smiles."

Nicky Smiles. That's what the guys I was close to in the unit called me. Maybe because I was blessed with a pretty nice grin. More likely it was because I'd grown up with a bunch of these wiseguys in Bay Ridge, and my name ended in a vowel. Plus, I knew more about La Cosa Nostra than just about anyone else in the Bureau, and I was offended by what this scum had done to the reputations of all Italian Americans: my own family, friends of mine who couldn't have been more law-abiding, and, of course, myself.

So where the hell are you, you sly sonovabitch? You're here, aren't you, Cavello? I swept the binoculars along the dance line.

The procession had snaked all the way around the deck by now, past all the juiced-up goombahs in tuxedos with purple shirts and their high-hairdo wives busting through their gowns. The bride sidled up to a table of old-timers, padrones in bolo ties sipping espresso, trading old tales. One or two of the faces looked familiar.

That's when the bride made her mistake.

She singled out one of the old men, leaned down, and kissed him on the cheek. The balding man was in a wheelchair, hands on his lap. He looked feeble and out of it, as if he were recovering from an illness, maybe a stroke. He had on thick black-rimmed glasses, no eyebrows, like Uncle Junior on *The Sopranos.*

I stood up and focused the lens on him. I watched her take him by the hands and try to get him up. The guy looked like he couldn't pee upright, and he could barely wrap his arms around her, never mind get up and dance.

Then my heart slammed to a stop.

You arrogant sonovabitch! You came!

"Tom, Robin, that old geezer with the black glasses. The bride just gave him a kiss."

"Yeah," Tom Roach came back. He was inside a van in the parking lot watching pictures sent from cameras planted in the club. "I got him. What's the problem?"

I took a step closer, zooming in with the lens.

"No problem. *That's Dominic Cavello!*"

Two

"THIS IS A GO!" I barked into the mike attached to my shirt collar. "Target is a bald male in black glasses, seated in a wheelchair at a table on the left-hand side of the deck. It's Cavello! He is to be treated as armed and likely to resist."

From where I was, I had a firsthand view of the next few minutes of action. Tom Roach and Robin Hammill jumped out of the van in the parking lot and headed for the entrance.

We had manpower, backup all over the place — even agents posing as bartenders and waiters on the inside. I had a Coast Guard cutter half a mile offshore, with an Apache helicopter that could be mobilized if necessary.

Not even Dominic Cavello would turn his brother's daughter's wedding into a firefight, right?

Wrong.

A couple of hoods in light-blue tuxedos were taking a smoke break outside when they spotted my team coming out of the van. One headed back inside while the other blocked their approach. "Sorry, this is a private affair. . . ."

Tom Roach flashed his shield. "Now it's open to the public. *FBI.*"

I zoomed back to the other wiseguy hurrying out to the wedding party on the deck. He ran up to the crippled old man in the wheelchair.

I was right! It was definitely Cavello! But our cover was shot.

"We're blown!" I yelled, fixing on the commotion on the deck. "Everybody close in on Cavello! Manny, you and Ed stay put and cover the dunes. *Taylor,*" I called out to an agent posing as a waiter, "wait for Tom's crew."

Then Cavello jumped out of the wheelchair, suddenly the healthiest guy in the world. Steve Taylor put down his serving tray and pulled a gun from under his jacket. "*FBI!*" he yelled.

I heard a shot and watched Taylor go down and stay down.

Chaos erupted. Guests were scurrying around the deck, some shrieking, others ducking under tables. A few of the well-known mob bosses were hurrying toward the exits.

I refocused on Cavello. He was hunched over, slinking through the crowd, still in disguise. He was making a path toward the stairs leading down to the beach.

I took out my Glock and hopped off the ledge I'd been perched on. Then I ran for the clubhouse along the shore road.

Judge & Jury

I stayed near the white clapboard clubhouse, then ran in the restaurant's front door and through to the deck. I could still see Cavello. He had peeled off his black glasses. He shoved an old woman out of his way and leaped over a wooden fence — then he was running toward the dunes.

We had him!

Three

"MANNY, ED, he's headed toward you!"

I saw where Cavello was going. He was trying to get to a helicopter up on the point, obviously *his* helicopter. I pushed through the crowd, shoving people out of the way. At the edge of the deck, I looked down.

Cavello was stumbling over the grassy dunes, making his way along the beach.

Then he ducked behind a tall dune, and I lost sight of him.

I shouted into the radio, "Manny, Ed, he should be on you any second now."

"I got him, Nick," Manny squawked.

"*Federal agents,*" I heard Manny shout through the radio.

Then there were shots. Two quick ones — followed by four or five more in rapid succession.

My blood turned to ice. *Oh, Jesus.* I leaped over the fence, then ran down the dunes toward the beach. I lost my footing and fell to one knee. I righted myself and hurtled in the direction of the shots.

I stopped.

Two bodies were lying faceup on the beach. My heart was pumping. I ran to them, sliding in the sand, which was stained dark with blood.

Oh, dear God, no.

I knew that Manny was dead. Ed Sinclair was gurgling blood, a gunshot wound in his chest.

Dominic Cavello was fifty yards ahead, holding his wounded shoulder but getting away.

"Manny and Ed are down," I yelled into the mike. "Get help here now!"

Cavello was running toward a helicopter. The cabin door was open. I took off after him.

"Cavello, stop!" I shouted. "I'll shoot!"

Cavello looked back over his shoulder. He didn't stop though.

I squeezed the trigger of my gun — twice. The second bullet slammed into his thigh.

The godfather reached for his leg and buckled. But he kept going, dragging the leg, like some desperate animal that wouldn't quit. I heard a *thwack, thwack, thwack* — and saw the Coast Guard Apache coming into sight.

"That's it," I yelled ahead, aiming my Glock again. "You're done! The next shot goes through your head."

Cavello pulled himself to an exhausted stop. He put his hands in the air and slowly turned.

He had no gun. I didn't know where he'd thrown it, maybe into the sea. He'd been close enough. A grin was etched on his face despite the bullets in his thigh and shoulder.

"*Nicky Smiles,*" he said, "if I knew you wanted to be at my niece's wedding, all you had to do was ask. I woulda sent you an invitation. Engraved."

My head felt like it was going to explode. I'd lost two men, maybe three, over this filth. I walked up to Cavello, my Glock pointed at his chest. He met my eyes with a mocking smile. "You know, that's the problem with Italian weddings, Pellisante, everybody's got a gun."

I slugged him, and Cavello fell to one knee. For a second I thought he was going to fight me, but he just stood up, shook his head, and laughed.

So I hit Cavello again, with everything I had left in me.

This time, he stayed down.

Part One

THE FIRST TRIAL

Chapter 1

IN HIS HOUSE on Yehuda Street in Haifa, high above the sky-blue Mediterranean, Richard Nordeshenko tried the King's Indian Defense. The pawn break, Kasparov's famous attack. From there Kasparov had dismantled Tukmakov in the Russian Championship in 1981.

Across from Nordeshenko a young boy countered by matching the pawn. His father nodded, pleased with the move. "And why does the pawn create such an advantage?" Nordeshenko asked.

"Because it blocks freeing up of your queenside rook," the boy answered quickly. "And the advance of your pawn to a queen. Correct?"

"Correct." Nordeshenko beamed at his son. "And when did the queen first acquire the powers that it holds today?"

"Around fifteen hundred," his son answered. "In Europe.

Up until then it merely moved two spaces, up and down. But . . ."

"Bravo, Pavel!"

Affectionately, he mussed his son's blond hair. For an eleven-year-old, Pavel was learning quickly.

The boy glanced silently over the board, then moved his rook. Nordeshenko saw what his son was up to. He had once been in the third tier of Glasskov's chess academy in Kiev. Still, he pretended to ignore it and pushed forward his attack on the opposite side, exposing a pawn.

"You're letting me win, Father," the boy declared, refusing to take it. "Besides, you said just one game. Then you would teach me . . ."

"Teach *you*?" Nordeshenko teased him, knowing precisely what he meant. "You can teach *me*."

"Not chess, Father." The boy looked up. "Poker."

"Ah, *poker?*" Nordeshenko feigned surprise. "To play poker, Pavel, you must have something to bet."

"I have something," the boy insisted. "I have six dollars in coins. I've been saving up. And over a hundred soccer cards. Perfect condition."

Nordeshenko smiled. He understood what the boy was feeling. He had studied how to seize the advantage his whole life. Chess was hard. Solitary. Like playing an instrument. Scales, drills, practice. Until every eventuality became absorbed, memorized. Until you didn't have to think.

A little like learning to kill a man with your bare hands.

But poker, poker was liberating. *Alive.* Unlike in chess,

you never played the same way twice. You broke the rules. It required an unusual combination: discipline and risk.

Suddenly, the chime of Nordeshenko's mobile phone cut in. He was expecting the call. "We'll pick it up in a moment," Nordeshenko said to Pavel.

"But, Father," the boy whined, disappointed.

"In a moment," Nordeshenko said again, picking up his son by the armpits, spanking him lightly on his way. "I have to take this call. Not another word."

"Okay."

Nordeshenko walked out to the terrace overlooking the sea and flipped open the phone. Only a handful of people in the world had this number. He settled into a chaise.

"This is Nordeshenko."

"I'm calling for Dominic Cavello," the caller said. "He has a job for you."

"Dominic Cavello? Cavello is in jail and awaiting trial," Nordeshenko said. "And I have many jobs to consider."

"Not like this one," the caller said. "The Godfather has requested only you. Name your price."

Chapter 2

New York City. Four months later.

ALL ANDIE DEGRASSE KNEW was that the large, wood-paneled room was crowded as shit — with lawyers, marshals, reporters — and that she'd never been anywhere she wanted to get the hell out of more.

But it was the same for the other fifty-odd people in the jury pool, Andie was quite sure.

Jury duty — those words were like *influenza* to her. *Cold sore.* She had been told to report at 9:00 a.m. to the federal courthouse in Foley Square. There she filled out the forms, polished her excuses, and killed an hour leafing through *Parenting* magazine.

Then, at about eleven thirty, her name was called by a bailiff, and she was herded into a line of other unfortunate people with unsure, disappointed faces and up to the large courtroom on the seventh floor.

She looked around, trying to size up the rest of the fidgeting, kibitzing group squeezed into the bull pen. This was definitely not where she wanted to be.

The scene was like a snapshot taken on the number 4 Lexington Avenue train. People in work uniforms — electricians, mechanics — blacks, Hispanics, a Hasid in a skullcap, each trying to convince the person on either side that he or she didn't belong there. A couple of well-to-do types in business suits were punching their BlackBerries, demonstrating in the clearest possible way that they had something far more important to do with their time.

Those were the ones Andie had to worry about, and she regarded them warily — the prospective jurors who had their time-tested, A-number-1 alibis honed and ready to go. Bosses' letters. Partners' meetings. Travel schedules, deals going down. A cruise to Bermuda that was already fully paid.

Of course, Andie hadn't exactly come empty-handed.

She had put on her tight red T-shirt with the words Do Not Disturb emblazoned across the chest. It was the tackiest thing she owned, but we weren't talking *fashionista* here.

We were talking *adios* — excused. Even if it was on the grounds of being thought an airhead or a bimbo.

Then there was the single-mother thing. That was legit. Jarrod was nine, and he was her best buddy as well as her biggest handful these days. Who would pick him up from school, answer his questions, help him with his homework, if she couldn't be there for him?

Finally, there were her auditions. Her agent at William Morris had scheduled two for this week alone.

To amuse herself, Andie counted the faces of people who looked intelligent and open-minded and didn't seem to be conveying they had somewhere else to go. She stopped when she got to twenty. That felt good. They only needed twelve, right?

Next to her, a heavyset Hispanic woman knitting a pink baby's sweater leaned over. "Sorry, but jou know what kinda trial dis is?"

"No." Andie shrugged, glancing around at the security. "But from the looks of it, it's something big. You see those guys? They're reporters. And did you notice the barricades outside and those cops milling around? More uniforms in this place than in an *NYPD Blue* wardrobe closet."

The woman smiled. "Rosella," she said amiably.

"I'm Andie," Andie said, extending her hand.

"So, Andie, how jou get *on* dis jury, anyway, jou know?"

Andie squinted at her as if she hadn't heard right. "You *want* to get picked?"

"Sure. My huzban say you get forty dollars a day, plus train fare. The woman I work for, she pay me whichever way. So why not take the cash?"

Andie smiled and shrugged wistfully. "Why not?"

The judge's clerk came in, a woman with black glasses and a pinched, officious face, like an old-time schoolmarm. "All rise for Judge Miriam Seiderman."

Everyone pushed themselves out of their seats.

"So, Rosella, you want to know how to get *on* this thing?" Andie leaned over and whispered to her neighbor as an attractive woman of around fifty, with touches of gray in her hair, entered the courtroom and stepped up to the bench.

"Sure."

"Just watch." Andie nudged her. "Whatever I do, do the opposite."

Chapter 3

JUDGE SEIDERMAN STARTED OUT by asking each of them a few questions. Name and address. What you did for a living. Whether you were single or married, and if you were, if you had kids. Highest level of education. What newspapers and magazines you read. If anyone in your family ever worked for the government or for the police.

Andie glanced at the clock. This was going to take hours.

A few of them got excused immediately. One woman announced she was a lawyer. The judge asked her to come up to the side of the bench. They chatted a few seconds, and she let her go. Another man complained that he'd just served on a jury up in Westchester. He'd only finished up last week. He got a pink slip, too.

Some other guy who was actually half cute announced he was a crime novelist. In fact, another woman in the jury pool held up his book. She was reading it! After he finished up,

Andie heard him snicker, "I don't have a prayer of ending up on this thing."

Then, Judge Seiderman nodded Andie's way.

"Andie DeGrasse," Andie replied. "I live at 855 West One eighty-third Street, in the Bronx. I'm an actress."

A few people looked back at her. They always did. "Well, I try to be," she said, qualifying. "Mostly I do proofreading for *The Westsider.* It's a community newspaper in upper Manhattan. And regarding the other question, I *was,* Your Honor, for five years."

"Was what, Ms. DeGrasse?" The judge peered over her glasses.

"*Married.* The nuclear option, if you know what I mean." A couple of people chuckled. "Except for my son. Jarrod. He's nine. He's basically a full-time occupation for me now."

"Please continue, Ms. DeGrasse," the judge said.

"Let's see. I went to St. John's for a couple of years." What Andie really wanted to convey was, *You know, Your Honor, I dropped out in the fourth grade, and I don't even know what* exculpatory evidence *means.*

"And let's see, I read *Vogue* and *Cosmo* and, oh yeah, *Mensa.* Charter member. I definitely try and keep up with that one."

A few more chuckles rippled around the courtroom. *Keep it going,* she said to herself. *Push out the chest. You're almost off this thing.*

"And regarding the police" — she thought for a second — "none in the family. But I dated a few."

Judge Seiderman smiled, shaking her head. "Just one

more question. Do you have any reason or experience that would prejudice you against Italian Americans? Or render you unable to reach an impartial verdict if you served on this trial?"

"Well, I once played a role in *The Sopranos*," she replied. "It was the one when Tony whacks that guy up at Meadow's school. I was in the club."

"The club?" Judge Seiderman blinked back, starting to grow short.

"The Bada Bing, Your Honor." Andie shrugged sheepishly. "I was dancing on one of the poles."

"That was *you?*" a Latino guy cracked from the first row. Now a lot of people were laughing around the courtroom.

"Thank you, Ms. DeGrasse." Judge Seiderman suppressed a smile. "We'll all be sure to check out the reruns when they come around."

The judge moved on to Rosella. Andie was feeling pretty confident she had done her job. She felt a little guilty, but she just *couldn't* be on this jury.

Now, Rosella was perfect. A juror's dream. She'd cleaned house for the same woman for twenty years. She'd just become an American citizen. She wanted to serve because it was her duty. She was knitting a sweater for her granddaughter. *Oh, you're a lock.* Andie grinned to herself. Rosella hit every question out of the park. She was like a juror commercial!

At last the judge said she had just one question for the jury at large. Andie's eye checked the clock. One fifteen. If she was lucky, she could still catch the Broadway number 1 and pick Jarrod up at school on time.

Judge Seiderman leaned toward them. "Do any of you know the name, or have you been associated with in any way, Dominic Cavello?"

Andie turned toward the stolid, gray-haired man seated in the third row of the courtroom. *So that's who that was.* A few people murmured. She glanced at Rosella, a little sympathetic now.

These people were in for one scary ride.

Chapter 4

I WAS SITTING in the second row, not far from the judge, during the jury questioning. Security marshals lined the walls, ready to go into action if Cavello so much as scratched his nose. Most of the marshals knew I was the one who had taken Cavello down and that this case was personal for me.

It was driving me crazy waiting to have the opening arguments begin, to have the first witness take the stand.

We got Miriam Seiderman as the judge. I'd had her on trials twice before, and she always seemed to bend for the defendants. But she was thorough, fair, ran a tight court. We could have done a lot worse.

I was thinking this looked like a pretty decent pool of jurors. A couple of them were downright entertaining.

There was a Verizon guy with a New England accent who said he had three town houses in Brooklyn he'd fixed up and that he was bagging the phone company job anyway, so he could care less how long the trial ran.

And a crime novelist who someone in the jury pool recognized. In fact, she was actually reading his book.

Then the woman in the third row. The actress and single mom. She was feisty and cute, with thick brown hair with reddish streaks in it. There was some writing on her T-shirt — Do Not Disturb. Kind of funny.

Once or twice, Cavello glanced back at me. But most of the time he just sat there, hands joined, staring straight ahead.

A couple of times, our eyes met. *How ya doin', Nicky,* his smile seemed to say, like he didn't have a worry in the world, a guy about to go away for life.

Every once in a while he huddled with his attorney, Hy Kaskel. *The Ferret,* he was called. Not just because he made a living representing these bums, but because he was short and barrel-chested, with a hanging nose, a pointy chin, and thick, bushy eyebrows you could brush your shoes with.

Kaskel was a showman, though, among the best there was at his job. The Ferret had gotten two mistrials and an acquittal in his last three mob trials. He and his team just sat there sizing up each juror on a large poster board, taking notes. The Verizon guy. The MBA. The author.

I glanced up at the actress again. I was pretty sure she thought she was out of here. But sometimes that's what you need on a jury, someone who can cut through the bullshit, break the ice.

"Ladies and gentlemen." Sharon Ann Moran, the judge's

clerk, got everyone's attention. The defense and the prosecution had finalized their selections.

I was thinking, just give me twelve jurors smart enough to see through the bluster and bullshit, twelve jurors who won't be intimidated.

One by one, the judge announced the names. Twelve jurors and six alternates. She told them to come up and take a seat in the jury box.

The crime writer was in. Shocked. So was the Verizon guy. And the Hispanic housekeeper, the one who was knitting for her granddaughter.

But the biggest surprise was the actress. *She was in, too!* I never saw anyone so stunned. I think everyone in the courtroom was holding back a smile.

"Ms. DeGrasse, Juror Number Eleven, you can take a seat in the jury box," the judge told her, amused herself. "You got the part, dear."

Chapter 5

THE GLASS ELEVATOR of the Marriott Marquis rose higher and higher above Times Square. Richard Nordeshenko watched the glittery bustle of the street grow distant and small below. *Good riddance.*

"First time to the Marriott, Mr. Kaminsky?" a chatty, red-capped bellhop asked as the elevator rushed them to the forty-second floor.

"Yes," Nordeshenko lied.

Truth was, he had made the rounds of all the fancy hotels near Times Square. The area held a particular attraction for him. Not the lights or the nocturnal amusements, in which he took no part. *It was the crowds.* In the event something went wrong, all he had to do was duck into the throng any time of day or night.

"Kiev, right?" The bellhop grinned at him. It wasn't a question, more like a statement of fact. "You're from the

Ukraine, right? Your accent. It's sort of a game with me. Twenty floors, that's usually all I need."

"Sorry." Nordeshenko shook his head. "Czech." Inside, he was angry with himself. The chatty bellhop had nailed him. Maybe it was just the jet lag, but he had let down his guard.

The elevator opened, and the bellhop motioned Nordeshenko down the hall. "Close." He smiled, with a shrug of apology. "But — what is it you say here? — no cigar."

He'd been traveling for eighteen hours straight, stopping in Amsterdam on a Dutch passport, then in Miami on a business visa to the States. On the flight, he had put on Chopin and Thelonious Monk to relax, and had beaten a chess program on his computer on level eight. That made the voyage bearable.

That and the comfort of the first-class seats on Dominic Cavello's account.

"Room 4223 has a wonderful view of Times Square, Mr. Kaminsky." The bellhop opened the door to his room. "We got the View restaurant and lounge. Your gourmet Renaissance restaurant on the mezzanine. My name's Otis, by the way, if you need anything during your stay."

"Thank you, Otis." Nordeshenko smiled. He pulled out a bill. He pressed it into the bellhop's hand. Otis had fingered him, reminded him he could not be too careful.

"Thank *you*." The bellhop's eyes lit up. "Any sort of entertainment you need, you just let me know. The bar upstairs stays active until about two. I know some places that open up after that, if that's what you like. The city that never sleeps, right?"

"*Velký jablko.*" Nordeshenko replied in perfect Czech.

"*Vel-ký jab-lko?*" The bellhop squinted.

"The Big Apple." Nordeshenko winked.

Otis laughed and pointed at him, closing the door. Nordeshenko laid his briefcase on the bed. He took out his computer. He had people to contact and things to set up. In the morning it would be all work.

But in the meantime, the bellhop wasn't too far off about something else.

He did have his own brand of entertainment planned for tonight.

Tonight, he was going to play poker — with Dominic Cavello's money.

Chapter 6

"YOUR ANTE." The dealer nodded toward him, and Norde-shenko tossed a fresh hundred-dollar chip into the center of the table.

He was in a fashionable poker club in a town house on the upper East Side. The large room had a high, coffered ceiling and tall palladian windows with embroidered gold drapes drawn. All types seemed to be there. Attractive women in evening gowns, amusing themselves at the small-stakes table. The usual gambler types in dark glasses who seemed to be playing for everything they were worth.

It was well after one in the morning, and the four tables were still going strong.

Nordeshenko sipped a Stoli martini as the dealer dealt him two downward cards. He was playing in what they called a freeze-out. A $3,000 buy-in had bought him $10,000 in chips. Winner takes all.

At ten o'clock there had been eight around the table. Now it was down to three: Nordeshenko; Julie, an attractive woman with straight blond hair in a tight-fitting pantsuit; and someone Nordeshenko had nicknamed "Cowboy," an annoying, finger-tapping fool in a Western hat and aviator shades who, hearing Nordeshenko's accent, insisted on calling him Ivan.

Nordeshenko had been patiently waiting to find himself alone with him in a hand all night.

He peeked at his hole cards. An ace and a queen, on suit. He felt his blood perk up a bit. When the betting came to him, he tossed in a $500 chip.

Before, when Nordeshenko had come to New York, he would go to a Russian club in Brooklyn and play chess, sometimes for a thousand dollars a game. He could hold his own, but he soon developed a bit of a reputation, and that brought attention to him — and attention was always unwanted. Now poker was his thing.

Julie, who had the fewest chips at the table and was playing cautiously, called, but Cowboy, rubbing his palms together, pushed a stack of ten greens to the center of the table. "Sorry, sweet pea, but these cards just won't let me sit still."

Nordeshenko held an image of what it might be like to spear this buffoon through the windpipe, which he could do with a sharp thrust of his hand. He thought about raising back, the cards warranted it, but elected, as did the blonde, just to call.

"Well, aren't we all nice 'n' cozy," Cowboy crowed, tilting back his chair.

The dealer flopped three cards: a six, an ace, and a nine. That gave Nordeshenko aces, almost surely the high hand. He bet $3,000.

Julie hesitated, tapping her polished nails on the table. "Oh, what the hell." She finally smiled. "It's only the rent money, right?"

"Well, the rent just got raised a little, darlin'," Cowboy said, pushing in another $5,000 in chips.

Nordeshenko looked him in the eye. This asshole was making it very difficult. *What could he possibly have?* He had watched him chasing cards all night.

"What's *your* ticket say, Ivan?" Cowboy fiddled with his chips. "You still on this train, or time to get off?"

"Maybe one more station." Nordeshenko shrugged, looking toward Julie.

"All in," she said, flipping her cards and pushing the balance of her chips into the pot.

Four spades. Nordeshenko had been right. He had read her trying to make a flush. He still had high hand. And the Cowboy was bluffing.

The dealer turned over a queen of diamonds. Nordeshenko didn't even flinch. Now he had aces and queens.

Julie winced. She hadn't made her flush.

"Well, what'ya say we just put a little more coal in the burner and see what the river brings?" Cowboy cackled loudly, pushing the rest of his chips into the center — $10,000.

Murmurs went up from the people watching. It was clear this would be the final hand. The winner would take the entire $30,000 buy-in.

Cowboy stared at him, not smiling now. "You stickin' around, Ivan, or what?"

"*Miraslav*," Nordeshenko said.

Cowboy took off his shades. "Huh?"

"My name is Miraslav," Nordeshenko said, meeting the bet.

The dealer turned over his last card, the river. A deuce of hearts.

Julie groaned.

Nordeshenko knew his aces and queens should be a winner. He couldn't even imagine what the asshole Cowboy had. He counted out twenty hundred-dollar bills and tossed them outside the pot as a side bet.

Then, amazingly, Cowboy countered with a $5,000 raise of his own. Nordeshenko was stunned.

"Ivan, still with us?" Cowboy tilted back in his chair, clucking unpleasantly.

Nordeshenko reached in his jacket, counted out $5,000 in hundred-dollar bills, and laid them in the center of the table. This was no longer just an amusing diversion.

"Aces and queens." He flipped over his hole cards.

"Oooh." Cowboy blinked, as if stunned.

But then he grinned. "This is gonna hurt, Ivan."

He flipped over his hole cards. Two more deuces. The last card had given him three. Nordeshenko felt as if he'd fallen off a cliff. The moron had been pushing the pot the whole way with just a pair of twos.

Cowboy leaped up, ooo-eeing like a donkey, raking in his chips. Nordeshenko thought he'd like to wipe the grin off the fool's face. But just as quickly, the irrational urge subsided.

Not tonight. He had work to do in the morning. Important work. Whatever he had lost tonight was just a fraction of his fee.

"You know what they say, Ivan," Cowboy said, stacking his winnings, "sometimes it's better to be lucky than good. No hard feelings," he said, stretching out his hand.

Nordeshenko stood up and took it. The imbecile was right about one thing: he'd been lucky tonight. Luckier than he would ever know.

The Israeli was going to let him live.

Chapter 7

IT WAS AFTER EIGHT O'CLOCK that night when I finally made it back to Casa Pellisante.

Home for me was the same rent-controlled apartment in the Hell's Kitchen section of Manhattan on Forty-ninth and Ninth I'd lived in for the past twelve years. I had a view of the Empire State Building from my study window and could kick back on the roof after work with a cocktail, looking out on the red sunsets over Jersey City. On weekends, I could step out the front door right into the Feast of St. Ignatius or a West Indian parade, or grab a beer at an Irish bar sitting next to some Westie I once put away.

I also had Ellen Jaffe there.

Ellen was a hotshot anesthesiologist over at St. Vincent's, with wavy auburn hair, a small button nose, and long, slim runner's legs that were a joy to behold. We'd met at a clambake thrown by a friend of mine and been together for the past two years.

Ellen was pretty, smart as a whip, and just as dedicated to her career as I was to mine. That was a problem. I worked days — and half the nights, lately, preparing the case. She was taking doctoral classes at Cornell Medical and doing her hospital rotations at night. We used to spend entire weekends together in bed. Now we could barely find a night to be in the same room and watch TV.

She said I was fixated on Cavello, and she was probably right. I shot back that she must be having an affair with Dr. Diprovan — Diprovan being the solution of choice when putting people under these days.

Whatever it was, it was killing me how things were sliding downhill between us. But you either fight for it or you don't, and lately, neither of us was fighting a lot for anything.

So I stopped at Pietro's on the way home and picked up an order of the best *amatriciana* in New York — Ellen's favorite. She didn't work Monday nights. Let's not call it a party, but it would be the first quality time we'd spent with each other in at least a week.

Add to that a bouquet of sunflowers from the Korean grocer up the block. I had also left Ellen a message on the machine to set the table.

I turned the key in the front door and saw the table in the dining alcove set for one.

"Buonasera, signorita."

"Nick?" I heard Ellen call from the bedroom.

She came out of the bedroom in her navy Burberry windbreaker and running shoes, knotting her long brown hair. Not exactly the fantasy I had in mind. "I'm sorry, Nicky. I was going to leave a note. Benson just called. They're on overload tonight. They need me in."

"Diprovan again." I sniffed, trying to hide my disappointment, placing the food and flowers on the kitchen counter. Ellen's cat, Popeye, brushed against my leg. "Hey, Pops."

"I can't help it, Nick." Ellen's eyes went to the flowers. She smiled, making the correct connection to a meadow in the Chianti District outside of Siena, an amorous urge we couldn't hold back a couple of summers ago.

"Jeez, what'd you get fired or something?"

"Just a little carried away, I guess."

"No." She shook her head and sighed as if to say, *Nothing's going right for us, lately.* "Not carried away. I'm sorry, Nicky. They're waiting on me. I can't even put these in a vase."

"No sweat." I shrugged. "Actually, they were for me."

Ellen had these red glasses on that I found sexy as hell for some reason. Her small breasts peeked from under a tight-fitting top. I found myself getting aroused. Foolish. Maybe it was just this momentary feeling that I was free from the anticipation of the case. Or the sense that I had to do something . . . for us. I don't even know. As she tossed a few things in her purse, I put my hands on her shoulders.

"Nick, I *can't.* I'm AWOL." She tensed against me. "I gotta go. Hey, I almost forgot. How'd it go today?"

"Well." I nodded. "We got a decent jury. Everybody's ready. Let's just hope Cavello and his lawyers don't pull any fast ones."

"Nick, you've done everything humanly possible, so stop killing yourself. Manny would be proud." She gave me a soft kiss on the cheek, not what I had in mind, but it made me smile.

"Tell Diprovan hello."

"*Nick* . . ." Ellen shook her head, unamused. She turned back in the doorway. "I'm sorry about the dinner. It was a nice thought." Then she looked at the sunflowers on the counter. "You're such a romantic."

Chapter 8

FOR A WHILE I just stood there. Popeye, my new dinner partner, purred against my leg.

I guess, like some spurned high school kid, I was hoping that Ellen might have second thoughts and come back. I had this feeling that the weight of our relationship was suddenly hinging on a hope no stronger than that.

But there was no sound on the stairs. No saving key in the door. I was thirty-eight, head of a major anticrime task force, a big shot in the FBI, and here I was scooping out a container of pasta meant for two — a stranger in my own home.

The silence was suddenly orchestral.

I went into the bedroom and took off my tie and jacket, then checked in the study for a fax. There was a long brick wall covered with bookshelves. Most of the books were from my days at school, and there were a few of Ellen's medical texts. The desk was piled high with briefs from Cavello's trial. On the wall there was a large framed black-and-orange banner:

PRINCETON 1989 IVY LEAGUE FOOTBALL CHAMPS

I had bones that still ached just thinking of those days.

I took the pasta and some wine into the living room and sat there with my feet propped up on an old steamer trunk that acted as a coffee table. I picked up the book I'd been reading, Clinton's *My Life,* and found the page where I'd left off, on the Camp David Middle East peace talks. I thought about turning on the Knicks game. After a few minutes I lifted my eyes without reading a single page.

Did I love her? Was this going to work? Ellen was terrific, but right now we were just going in different directions. And this trial wasn't going to help.

Are you going to fight for this, Nicky?

I reached for Popeye. "C'mon, you look like you could use a date."

I grabbed my old college alto sax from the corner and, with Popeye in hand, went up to the roof. This was where I worked it out sometimes.

It was a cold, clear night. The stars were out over Manhattan. The Empire State Building was lit up red, white, and blue. Across the river, Jersey City might've been Paris, it so dazzled with lights. So I sat there, a few days before the most important trial of my life, Ellen's cat purring at my feet, and played.

Clarence Clemons's riff from Springsteen's "Jungleland."

A clunky version of Coltrane's "Blue Train." I came to the conclusion that there was a hole in my life, and no matter how long I put Cavello away for, I wasn't going to fill it.

You either fight for it or you don't, Nick. You fought for everything. So why won't you fight for Ellen Jaffe?

Chapter 9

I TOOK MY PLACE in the front of the courtroom on Monday morning. My blood was pounding. It always did on the first day of a trial, and this one was *huge*.

The lawyers for both sides filled up the first two rows of the courtroom. Joel Goldenberger was the government's lead prosecutor. He was younger than he looked, maybe thirty-three, tall, self-assured, with light, bushy hair and an agreeable smile. But inside he was a fighter, a real believer. Everyone was talking about him as a future star in the Justice Department. He had already won three well-publicized Wall Street trials.

On the other side sat Hy Kaskel, paging through his notes. The Ferret stood no taller than five five in lifts, with short boxer's arms, but he resembled his nickname in every way when it came to discrediting a witness. Today he wore a dark navy pinstripe suit and striped club tie, a pair of fancy gold cuff links peeking through the sleeves.

In the front row of the gallery I saw Cavello's family. A plump, pleasant-looking woman in a plain but tasteful suit, needlepointing away. And a grown daughter, with wavy, long blond hair, sitting loyally by her mom. Security at the courthouse was tighter than I'd ever seen it before. Hell, I was probably responsible for half of the fuss. Every bag was being opened, every juror's pass double-checked, every press credential checked back against a photo ID. Armed cops were manning the barricades all over Foley Square.

Cavello was being brought through an underground passageway from the Manhattan County Jail two blocks away, where he was being held in his own wing on a maximum security floor. From there, he was transported to the seventh floor in a guarded elevator.

I only wished we had sequestered the jury. This was the biggest organized crime trial in years. But the judge wanted to make a name for herself. Miriam Seiderman had her eye on the state supreme court. She had assurances from the lawyers, from the defendant himself. She wanted the trial conducted in the open light of day.

The door finally opened near the rear. A buzz of anticipation rippled through the air.

Two burly-looking marshals led the defendant inside. Cavello's hands were cuffed in front of him. He was dressed in a brown checked sports jacket and a restrained olive tie, his graying hair nicely trimmed. He didn't look like the animal everyone was expecting. More like a normal, everyday citizen you might see riding next to you on the train.

Cavello took a look around and nodded, as if impressed with the crowded room. The marshals took him to a chair next to his lawyer. They freed his hands. Kaskel leaned over and whispered something in Cavello's ear that made the defendant smile. Our gazes met for a second. His eyes lit up, and he smiled again as if to say, *Good to see you here, Nicky. You really think you can beat me?*

Sharon Ann Moran, the judge's clerk, stood. "All rise."

Through the side door, Judge Seiderman entered the room. She was a smallish, attractive woman with graying hair, a pleasant face, and a tastefully short skirt beneath her judge's cloak. This was the biggest case of her life, too. She took her seat behind the bench and motioned everyone down.

"Mr. Goldenberger, is the government ready?"

"We are, Your Honor." The prosecutor stood and nodded.

"Mr. Kaskel?"

"Yes, Your Honor. The defendant is ready too, and eager to prove his innocence." The Ferret arched his eyebrows. He looked like he was itching for a fight.

"Then, Ms. Moran" — the judge nodded to her clerk, who headed over to the jury room — "you can bring in the jury now."

Chapter 10

ANDIE DEGRASSE was fifteen minutes late that morning. That morning of all mornings. How could it have happened? Well, easy . . .

First, Jarrod couldn't find his math book. Then the IRT was backed up, signal switches down. Then, when she finally reached the City Hall station, the two blocks to the courthouse were barricaded off, all because of this damn trial.

It took her fifteen minutes just to get herself through security. A heavyset female guard in a blue blazer went through her purse like it had al Qaeda emblazoned on the buckle. They checked her cell phone like it was a WMD. Finally, Andie said, "You know that big Mafia trial up on the seventh floor?" The security guard nodded. "Well, it's not starting without me."

By the time she had burst through the jury-room doors, everybody was sitting around the large conference table, looking nervous and tense.

"Sorry." Andie sighed loudly, acknowledging a few familiar faces. "You don't even want to know."

"*Ms. DeGrasse*," Sharon Ann announced, checking off names, "it's really good you could make time for us in your busy schedule."

Already in trouble. Andie sat down sheepishly. She found herself next to Rosella, the Hispanic woman she had been next to during jury selection.

"That leaves only Mr. O'Flynn." Sharon Ann looked at the list, unamused.

A couple of men were reading or doing crosswords. Two of the women had brought paperback novels. There were bagels and muffins and coffee on the table, courtesy of the judge.

"Here," Rosella said, passing her the tray.

"Thanks." Andie smiled, delighted to shift the attention off herself. She took a muffin in a napkin. "No latte, I see."

There were a few chuckles. She looked toward Sharon Ann for at least a hint of a smile. The clerk was as tight as a drum this morning.

The door swung open, and in burst John O'Flynn, red-faced and sweating profusely. "Jeez, guys, it's like a jungle out there, a zoo. The L.I.E. at rush hour. Unbelievable."

"O'Flynn," Sharon Ann confirmed derisively, "I was starting to think I was going to have to put out an APB on you. Nine-thirty tomorrow, Mr. O'Flynn." Sharon Ann tapped her pencil.

"Aye, aye, ma'am." O'Flynn saluted. He plopped himself on a chair next to Andie.

"Nine-thirty tomorrow?" Hector, a cable guy, groaned. "You mean this trial's gonna last that long?"

"Eight weeks, Mr. Ramirez," Sharon Ann replied. "Something better you have to do for the next two months?"

"Yeah, maybe earn a living," the cable guy replied glumly.

Sharon Ann went to the door. "I'm going to check on how things are going. I want to remind you to observe the judge's instructions not to talk about the case."

"Sure." Everybody nodded. It took about two seconds after the door had shut for that to change.

"This Cavello guy" — Winston, the mechanic, still in his work clothes, looked around at the others — "I was reading up on him. Sounds like a pretty creepy dude."

"Murder, extortion, cramming body parts into the trunks of cars. It has a way of blocking the digestion," chortled Marc, the crime novelist.

Rosella put down her yarn. "My huzban's a little scared. He said, 'Whazzamatter, Rosie, you can't get yourself on a nice traffic dispute for a few days? You gotta get on with this wacko mobster?'"

"Hang on," Andie interrupted, "you heard the judge. We don't actually know he's wacko yet. We have to wait until we hear the *evidence* to determine he's wacko."

A few people laughed.

"More to the point" — Andie looked around the table — "what about the fact that these mob guys know all our names and where we live?" A few jurors nodded, each with the same look of concern.

The door to the courtroom opened. There was a hush. Andie had the feeling everybody's eyes were warning her.

Then Sharon Ann was standing there, her narrow gaze

centered directly on Andie. "In my office," she said. Her "office" was one of the two bathrooms, which the other day had been designated for private conversations.

"Huh?"

"*In my office, Ms. DeGrasse,*" Sharon Ann ordered her.

Slowly Andie rose and, with a roll of the eyes, followed the dour court clerk into the cramped bathroom.

"Don't think I don't know what you're up to, Ms. DeGrasse," Sharon Ann snapped as soon as the door had closed.

"W-what I'm up to?" Andie stammered. "I didn't say anything that everyone in that room hasn't already thought to themselves."

Even her sister, Rita. It had been the first thing out of her mouth. *Doesn't it make you a little worried? I mean, they know you, Andie. It's Dominic Cavello. They know where you live.* You didn't need to be a mother to be worried. Just *human.* The whole selection process had been right out in the open. "Listen, Sharon Ann, I . . ."

"You've wanted off this thing from the very beginning." Sharon Ann cut her off. "I'm not having *anyone* poisoning this jury. You got your wish — you're history, lady."

Chapter 11

ANDIE RETOOK HER SEAT back in the jury room, blushing, a little embarrassed and hurt. A few minutes later the door to the courtroom opened again, and she found out just what the judge's clerk meant.

Sharon Ann stuck her head in. "We're not quite ready yet." Then she pointed a finger toward Andie, motioning her up. "Ms. DeGrasse . . ."

A flutter of nerves went down Andie's spine.

"Can you come with me, please? And you can bring your things."

Andie slowly got up, flashing a resigned look around the table. She was gone!

She followed Sharon Ann into the courtroom, which, to her surprise, was hushed and packed. And all eyes seemed to be centered on her. She felt really embarrassed now, like she was being publicly marched into the boss's office and fired — just for speaking her mind.

Sharon Ann led her through a side door in the courtroom behind the judge's bench. A marshal was guarding the hallway. Sharon Ann motioned flatly. "Go in. She's waiting for you."

Andie stepped inside the large, book-lined room. Judge Seiderman looked up from behind a desk covered with papers.

"Ms. DeGrasse." She peered over her reading glasses. "It's come to my attention you seem to have a bit of nervous stomach of the mouth."

"I beg your pardon?"

"You have trouble keeping your mouth shut, don't you?" The judge looked at her sternly. "It might've been amusing during jury selection, but now. . . . We're about to start an important trial, not a theatrical audition. I can't afford any troublemakers on this jury."

Andie stood her ground. "If you're talking about what I said in there, I actually thought it was a pretty legitimate question."

"*What,* Ms. DeGrasse?" Judge Seiderman looked up impatiently.

"Everyone heard our names during selection. And where we live. If we're married or not. Or have any kids. Anyone in their right mind would be concerned. Certainly, people have raised questions."

"*People?*" The judge arched her brows.

"I don't know. My sister. My mother. When I told them I was on this case. That can't exactly be a shock to you."

"Why we opted for how we conduct this trial is the court's business, Ms. DeGrasse. All you have to know is that if we thought there was the slightest danger to the jury, I assure you it would be our first concern." Judge Seiderman sat back. She took out an official slip and reached for a pen. "You've wanted off this trial from the beginning, haven't you?"

"I guess. Maybe last week, but . . ."

"But what? I'm about to give you your wish."

Andie's heartbeat accelerated. Last week she would've killed to hear those words. But over the weekend she'd begun to have a change of heart. She started to see this as a chance to do something decent, something good. She hadn't done a whole lot before to help people. Never served in the armed forces or the peace corps. Never volunteered for much in the community. Basically, she'd had Jarrod — that was it. And over the weekend, it all kind of settled on her.

"It's true. I did feel that way," Andie said. "But if it's all the same, I came here this morning to serve."

The judge stopped writing. She gazed up at Andie, a little surprised by what she'd heard.

"You think you can be a positive force on this jury, Ms. DeGrasse? And not cause any trouble?"

Andie nodded. "Yes, if you let me get back in there, I think I can."

Christ, Andie, all you had to do was keep your mouth shut, and you'd be gone.

Judge Seiderman put down her pen. She took a long, evaluating look at Andie. "Okay, why not? It's your right to serve." The judge summoned her clerk. "Ms. Moran, would you mind showing Juror Number Eleven back to the jury room."

"Thank you, Your Honor." Andie smiled.

Heading back to the courtroom, Sharon Ann held the door. "Well, I'm certainly surprised you're still on this jury."

"Yeah." Andie shook her head in disbelief. "That makes two of us."

Chapter 12

"ON THE MORNING of August sixth, 1993," U.S. Attorney Joel Goldenberger began, "Samuel Greenblatt, a happily married sixty-two-year-old building contractor, was brutally murdered outside his home in Union, New Jersey." The prosecutor pointed to a photographic enlargement resting on an easel. It depicted a smiling, slightly balding man with his wife at his sixtieth birthday party.

The jury stared at the face.

"A car pulled up as Greenblatt left for the office that morning. Two men in caps and sunglasses jumped out and shot him, *multiple times,* as he stepped onto the street. The victim looked at his killers and muttered, '*Why?*' Then he called out, 'Frannie,' the name of his wife of thirty-seven years. Then, to make sure they had finished the job, one of them stood over Mr. Greenblatt's dying body and calmly put two more rounds into his head. After the gunmen drove away, the first one to find the body was his youngest son, a senior at Rutgers. Members of the jury, you're going to be hearing a lot about Samuel Greenblatt during this trial."

One of Goldenberger's assistants passed out graphic police photographs showing the victim's bloodied corpse. One or two women in the jury box squirmed and shook their heads. "Now, no one is claiming Sam Greenblatt was an angel. In fact, he had assisted the Guarino crime family on several union-tampering construction jobs. He had secured bogus contracts for the family through the Local 407, a contracting union the family controlled.

"But what the government *is* saying," the prosecutor continued, gripping the sides of his table, "and what will be repeatedly backed up by the words of several key witnesses, is that the defendant, Dominic Cavello, gave the direct order for Mr. Greenblatt's execution. That the very killers were chosen by Mr. Cavello and rewarded by him — with money and promotions in the organization to which they all belonged. And what was the motive for this killing? Why did Mr. Greenblatt need to be eliminated? Because Mr. Cavello and his cronies believed they were the subject of a state law enforcement investigation, an assumption that turned out to be false. They simply *thought* Mr. Greenblatt could do them harm."

The prosecutor stepped away. He placed his hands on the jury box. "But the killing didn't end there. Contrary to the movies, mob hits don't always go according to plan. What you're going to hear is that this murder spawned a series of killings, *three,* in fact — all ordered by Mr. Cavello with the goal of covering up the first one.

"You're going to hear of union tampering and construction fraud. Of extortion. Loan-sharking. You're going to hear, above all, that Mr. Cavello was the boss of the Guarino crime family. The Boss of Bosses, in fact, using the Colombian and Russian crime syndicates to do his dirty work, a man whose principal business was to enrich himself at the misery and misfortune of any who stumbled into his way. The testimony you will hear will not be hearsay, as the defense would like you to believe, but facts from people who knew Mr. Cavello personally, who participated in these crimes. The defense will surely tell you that these people are not exactly innocents themselves. And they're right. They are criminals, co-conspirators, killers. By all accounts, ladies and gentlemen, these are bad guys. The defense will say that it is their job to lie and deceive.

"But make no mistake," Goldenberger said as he looked each member of the jury in the eyes, "in their stories you will hear the truth. It will be the preponderance of evidence and detail, all backing each other up, that will convince you that Mr. Cavello was the man giving the orders. You will hear the words he used, hear his reactions. And, under the law, that makes him as guilty of the crimes as if he pulled the triggers himself. I hope you will see Mr. Cavello for what he is, ladies and gentlemen: a vicious, cold-blooded killer."

Chapter 13

LOUIS MACHIA, the prosecution's first witness, stepped up to the stand and was sworn in. Machia had been a loyal soldier in Cavello's crime family. He was tall and broad-shouldered, with thick black hair, and was wearing a gray golf shirt.

With a pleasant smile, he looked around the courtroom at the jurors and the press. Never once did his gaze drift anywhere near Cavello.

"Good morning, Mr. Machia," U.S. Attorney Joel Goldenberger said as he stood up.

"Morning, Mr. Goldenberger."

"Can you tell us your current address, Mr. Machia?" the prosecutor asked.

"My current address is a federal prison. I'm afraid I can't divulge which one."

"A federal prison?" The prosecutor nodded. "So, for the sake of the jury, you've been convicted of a crime?"

"Many crimes. Under the terms of my 509 agreement, I admitted to all sorts of them."

"Can you describe these crimes for us? What you pleaded guilty to?"

"*All* of them?" The gangster chuckled. "That would take a lot of time."

Several people in the courtroom laughed out loud. The jury, too. Even Judge Seiderman put a hand in front of her face to conceal a smile.

"How about we start with just the major ones, Mr. Machia?" Joel Goldenberger grinned as well. "The highlights, if you will."

"The *highlights* . . ." Machia bunched his lips. "Well . . . murder. *Two* murders, actually. Attempted murder, assault with a deadly weapon, breaking and entering, loan-sharking, drug trafficking, auto theft . . ."

"That'll do, Mr. Machia. You're right, there is a lot to choose from. So it's fair to say you've been breaking the law for a long time?"

"Pretty much since I learned to use a fork." Louis Machia nodded thoughtfully.

"And these crimes," the prosecutor said, "these are all things you've planned and executed entirely on your own?"

"Sometimes, Mr. Goldenberger, if I catch your drift. Other times I was told to do them."

"Told?"

"Ordered, Mr. Goldenberger." The gangster took a swig of water. "By the family."

"The *family*." Goldenberger stepped toward the witness.

"Is it safe to say that for the past twenty years or so you've been a member of an organized crime family?"

"Very safe, Mr. Goldenberger. I was a soldier. In the Guarino family."

"The Guarino crime family. Your Honor, with your permission, I'd like to show an exhibit to the jury."

One of the assistant prosecutors put a large poster board covered with small photographs on an easel in front of the jury. It showed a pyramid-like family tree of about fifty faces. On the bottom, *soldiers;* on the level above that, *captains;* and on the highest tier were the leaders. That's where Cavello's face was displayed, above the heading *Boss.*

"This is a current depiction of the Guarino crime family, is it not, Mr. Machia?"

The witness nodded. "Yes. At the time of my convictions."

"And that's your face there, is it not, to the left, among those listed as soldiers?"

He smiled affably. "It's an old picture. Not my best. But yes, that's me."

"Sorry, Mr. Machia, next time we'll be sure to update it. What I want to know is if you were *always* a soldier in this family, Mr. Machia, or did you have to work your way up the ranks?"

"Everybody's got to work their way up. I got in by my uncle Richie. I started doing little jobs. Picking up some cash, stealing a car. A B and E."

"By 'B and E,' you mean 'breaking and entering'? A burglary?"

"Yes, that's right, Mr. Goldenberger. Maybe knocking someone's head clear, so they'd see the light."

Again, a few snickers trickled through the courtroom.

"And then you graduated," Goldenberger pressed on. "I mean, from petty stuff, like knocking people's heads clear, to some of the more serious crimes you've admitted to. Murder, attempted murder, drug trafficking . . ."

"I graduated." Machia nodded. "Only thing I *ever* graduated," he said with a crooked smile.

"Please just answer what the government asks you, Mr. Machia," said the judge, leaning over.

"Thank you, Your Honor." The prosecutor went back to his notes. "So I want to get back to the way in which you were promoted, Mr. Machia. From an associate to a soldier. If I'm not mistaken, I believe it's called being *made,* right?"

"You mean like the ceremony? It was at Melucchi's on Flatbush Avenue. In the back. They have a private room there. I never even knew. They asked me to drive one of the captains. Frankie Stamps. We called him that because there were two Frankies, and Frankie Stamps was into mail fraud. I figured it was just a meeting. Every one of the captains was there. Mr. Cavello, too."

"By Mr. Cavello, you mean Dominic Cavello? The defendant? He was there? At that meeting?"

"Sure he was there. He was the Boss."

"We'll get back to that later," the prosecutor said, letting the word *boss* resonate over the courtroom. "But I'm actually more interested in what got you to that ceremony."

"What got me to the ceremony?" Machia shrugged. "It was a Lincoln, I think."

This time, full-out laughter spread throughout the court-room.

"I meant, what did you do to make yourself worthy, Mr. Machia?" The prosecutor pushed through the laughter. "In order to be promoted."

"Oh, that." Machia sat back and reached for his water. He took a long drink. "I killed Sam Greenblatt in front of his house."

Chapter 14

A HUSH SETTLED over the courtroom. Everybody felt it. Andie DeGrasse couldn't believe what she'd just heard.

One minute this guy's making a joke, a regular guy. Then he admits to blowing someone away. She'd never heard anyone speak so casually about killing someone. Like he had to run an errand and pick up something at the store.

"You're admitting you killed Mr. Greenblatt in front of his home?" Joel Goldenberger looked just as shocked as everyone else.

"I already admitted that, Mr. Goldenberger. To the police and to the FBI. I wasn't exactly proud of it, but that's how you get ahead in this game."

The prosecutor stepped back, letting the full effect of Machia's testimony settle in. Andie recalled the crime pictures, the bloody scene. "Can you describe for the jury how that particular job came to be?"

"All right." The witness took a deep breath. "I worked for Ralphie D."

"Ralphie D.," the prosecutor interrupted. "You mean Ralph Denunziatta, right?" He pointed to a round, heavy face higher up in the family tree. "He was a lieutenant in the Guarino crime family?"

"That's him." Machia nodded. "We called him Ralphie D. because —"

"We got it, Mr. Machia. Because there was another Ralphie."

"Ralphie F."

"Ralphie Fraoli." The prosecutor pointed to another face on the other side of the board.

Machia scratched his head. "To tell you the truth, Mr. Goldenberger, I never actually knew what Ralphie F.'s last name was."

The laughter grew heavier now. This would be good comedy if it wasn't so deadly serious.

"So your boss, Ralph Denunziatta, contacted you?"

"He said the family needed this thing done. For the Boss."

"And by 'this thing done,' it was understood he meant a job, a hit? It meant you had to kill someone?"

"It was understood what he meant, Mr. Goldenberger."

"And by the Boss" — the prosecutor faced the witness again — "you took that to mean . . . ?"

"Dominic Cavello." He pointed in the direction of the defendant. "They said a favor had to be done. There was this guy in New Jersey who was causing problems. Not a protected guy, just a regular civilian."

"And how did you feel about taking care of this, Mr. Machia? You knew that it meant killing somebody."

"I knew what it entailed, Mr. Goldenberger." Machia glanced over toward the jury. For a second, Andie's blood ran cold. She felt his eyes were fixed on her. "Ralphie told me how they had it all planned out. It would be a cinch. So I mean, I got this friend of mine to steal a car."

"By your friend, you're referring to Steven Mannarino?" asked the prosecutor. He stepped back to his table and held up a large picture of a chubby, grinning kid with bushy hair in a Giants football jersey, maybe eighteen.

"Yeah, Stevie." Machia nodded. "We'd known each other since we were kids."

"So Mr. Mannarino was to steal the car?"

"And some plates. It was decided the easiest place to hit the guy would be at his house when he came out for work in the morning. What do they call that kind of street that ends in a circle?"

"A cul-de-sac," the prosecutor said.

"Yeah, cul-de-sac. We had several cars around, patrolling the area. Checking for cops. Tommy Moose was in one — Tommy Mussina. Ralphie reported directly to him. We did a dry run two days before. We tailed the mark. This Jewish guy. He kissed his wife good-bye at the door. Seemed like an all-right guy."

"But you were willing to go through with it anyway?" the prosecutor asked.

Machia shrugged, taking a long sip from his water bottle. "Not like you have a lot of choice, Mr. Goldenberger. I seen guys put away for turning down a job. You don't go through with it, you could be next. Besides . . ."

"Besides *what*, Mr. Machia?" the prosecutor urged him on.

"It was a favor for the Boss, Mr. Goldenberger. You don't turn that down."

"And how did you know this, sir?"

"Ralphie said it was for the Electrician."

"And by 'the Electrician,' he meant *who*, Mr. Machia?"

"Objection!" Cavello's attorney stood up with a scowl. Andie looked at O'Flynn; they already had a name for the lawyer in the jury room. *The Eyebrow.*

"Sorry, Your Honor," the prosecutor apologized. "So by 'the Electrician,' Mr. Machia, you *understood* that Ralphie D. meant *who*?"

"Dominic Cavello. The Electrician, that was his name. Ralphie worked for Tommy. Tommy worked for the Boss."

The prosecutor nodded, clearly pleased. "So you knew this hit was for the Boss, meaning Mr. Cavello, wholly because Ralphie D. *said* this to you?"

"*That,* and the other thing." Machia shrugged.

"What other thing, Mr. Machia?" The prosecutor turned, his voice rising.

There was a pause. Louis Machia settled back in his chair. For the first time, Cavello's eyes lifted toward the witness. Machia took a couple gulps of water. Then he put the bottle down.

"Those cars I spoke of, Mr. Goldenberger, driving around. Dominic Cavello was in one, too."

Chapter 15

THEY BROKE FOR LUNCH, and Andie spent it outside in Foley Square. It was cold, but still pretty nice for November. She ate a tuna wrap on a ledge, going over some proofreading for the neighborhood newspaper she worked for part-time. She made an entry in her trial notebook, too — and underlined it: *Cavello was there!*

At two o'clock, they all filed back in. Louis Machia was still on the stand.

"I want to pick up where we left off, Mr. Machia." The prosecutor stepped back up to the stand. "What happened after Samuel Greenblatt's murder?"

"After the murder?" The witness thought a moment. "I was promoted, Mr. Goldenberger. I was made a soldier, like you said."

"I think that was several weeks afterward," the prosecutor corrected him. "Maybe a month?"

"Twenty-seven days." Machia smiled. "To be exact."

There were a few more chuckles from the gallery. From Goldenberger, too. "Clearly, that was an important day in your life, Mr. Machia. But I was referring more to the days *immediately* after Sam Greenblatt's murder."

"Oh, that." Machia shook his head as if he'd been thwacked in the face. He took a sip from his water bottle again. "We ditched the car. We were all supposed to meet up at Ralphie D.'s diner later, in Brooklyn."

"And did that go smoothly, Mr. Machia?"

"*That* part, Mr. Goldenberger, yeah. We left the car at Newark Airport. Stevie tossed the plates into a marsh off of I-95. We were all high fives and celebrating. Good things were going to happen."

"But that wasn't the case, was it? What did happen?"

The dark-haired mobster chortled disgustedly, shaking his head. "I guess after we shot Mr. Greenblatt and pulled away from his house, someone, one of his neighbors maybe, must've got a glimpse at the plates."

"Someone spotted you? And how did you end up realizing that?" the young prosecutor pressed.

"'Cause later that night, around seven, the cops came to my house. I wasn't there, but my wife and kids were. They asked to see her car."

"*Her* car?" The prosecutor looked confused. "Why would they ask to see your wife's car, Mr. Machia?" It was clear Goldenberger knew the answer but was adroitly leading the whole courtroom there.

"Apparently, the plates the neighbor had picked up as we drove away were registered to *her.*"

There was an audible gasp throughout the courtroom.

"*Your wife,* Mr. Machia? You previously told us Steven Mannarino was supposed to steal plates for the hit."

"I guess he did." Machia scratched his head. "From my house."

Andie glanced toward O'Flynn, down the row. They both double-blinked, as if making sure they had heard right.

Chapter 16

JOEL GOLDENBERGER'S EYES were wide. "This is your best pal, Mr. Machia. You're telling me he stole the plates for this hit from *you?*"

"I said we had known each other since we were kids, Mr. Goldenberger. He was my oldest, not my best, friend, and he wasn't the smartest guy."

Snickers of disbelief erupted. Andie glanced up and could see Judge Seiderman hiding a smile again. Finally, when the courtroom calmed down, the prosecutor shook his head. "So, Mr. Machia, go on."

"After my wife called me, I called Stevie up and said, 'Stevie, what are you, fucking nuts?' *Sorry,* Your Honor. Anyway, what he told me was that his mom had found the stolen plates and threw them out and he'd panicked. He only lived down the block, so he knew our place like his own. I guess

70

he found my wife's plates in a box on the side of our house and figured, who would ever know?"

There was a stunned silence for a few seconds — the sound of total disbelief. Then the prosecutor continued. "So what happened when the cops came to your house?"

"My wife told them someone must've jumped the fence and stolen them."

"Your wife's a pretty quick thinker, Mr. Machia."

"Yeah, and she was pretty damn pissed, too." He shook his head and smiled.

This time, no one could hold back. Andie figured everyone had the same image: the gangster's wife coming after him with a frying pan. She put a hand over her face and averted her eyes. She caught a glimpse of Cavello. He was smiling, too.

"And so the cops were satisfied with that explanation? That someone else must've taken the plates?"

"I don't know if you would call it *satisfied*. I had a record. It wasn't exactly hard to pin me as someone who hung around the family."

"This couldn't have gone over very well with Ralphie D."

"I would call that an understatement, Mr. Goldenberger. Everybody was pissed as hell. I met up with Stevie later that night, and he was saying stuff like 'I know I screwed up, but if something comes from this, I'm not going alone.' Crazy stuff. Stuff he knew better than to say. He was just worked up."

"And how did you respond?" the prosecutor asked.

"I kept saying, 'Christ, Stevie, you can't say things like

that. People are gonna hear.' But he was nervous. He knew he screwed up. I never saw Stevie act like that."

"So what did you do?"

"*Me?* Truth was, Mr. Goldenberger, I had my own situation to worry about. I told Ralphie, don't listen to the guy. He won't do anything stupid. He's just freaked out, that's all."

"You told Ralphie about Stevie?"

"I had to, Mr. Goldenberger. If he got nabbed and started to talk, he could bring us all down. But I needed to get myself an alibi, too. I had this knee thing in those days. I needed surgery. So I went right into Kings County Hospital up to this doctor I knew, that *we* knew — he owed us some money — and I told him, you cut me open right now and the tab is clean. But I need the records to say I've been in here since this morning."

"Let me get this straight, Mr. Machia. You got a doctor to falsely admit you into a hospital to provide an alibi for killing Samuel Greenblatt?"

"Yes."

"And he agreed?"

"Well, I had a gun to his head, Mr. Goldenberger."

Andie couldn't believe it. The laughter got wild.

"So, getting back to Stevie Mannarino, Mr. Machia, your lifelong pal." The prosecutor took a few steps toward the witness. "You told Ralphie D. you would cover for him. What'd Ralphie say?"

"He said not to worry. He'd talk it over with the Boss. He said they'd get him somewhere where he could lie low for a while, 'til it all blew over. He told me just to focus on myself, get better. I was in this leg brace. Truth was, I was a little nervous I was never coming out of that hospital myself, if you know what I mean."

"So what happened?" Goldenberger went over and picked up Steven Mannarino's picture. He held it there for the jury to fix on. "Tell the court, Mr. Machia, what became of your pal?"

"I don't know." Louis Machia shrugged. He reached for the water bottle and cleared his throat. "I never saw Stevie again."

Chapter 17

IT WAS ALMOST FOUR. Judge Seiderman looked around the courtroom. She stopped the questioning. "Mr. Goldenberger, I think that's a good spot to leave off for today."

She cautioned the jury not to discuss the case or read the papers. Then they all filed back into the jury room. A few of them hurried off for trains, saying hasty good-byes.

Andie packed up her bag and put on her sweater. "See you tomorrow, everyone. I have to pick up my kid. Anyone taking the IRT?"

A woman named Jennifer said she was, and together they hurried over to Chambers Street and hopped the Broadway number 1 uptown. Jennifer, who sold advertising in the city, got off at 79th, and Andie continued on uptown, to the walk-up brownstone on West 183rd Street overlooking the George Washington Bridge, where she and Jarrod had lived for the past four years.

Andie got out at the 181st Street station and walked down a couple of blocks to 178th to pick up Jarrod at Sandra's. Sandra's son, Eddie, was in Jarrod's fourth-grade class at Elementary School 115.

"Hey, Ms. *Law and Order*," Sandra said, laughing as she opened the door. "You get a part?"

"I got a sentence." Andie rolled her eyes. "Eight weeks."

"Yikes!" Sandra exclaimed. "I got 'em to do their homework, at least part of it. They're in Edward's room. Playing *Desert Ambush*." The two women stuck their heads in.

"Mom," Jarrod crowed, "check it out. We're on level six."

"Well, I'm afraid we're going to have to level six it out of here. Mom's beat."

Out on Broadway, she and Jarrod headed back to their apartment. Dinner was in their future, and she didn't feel like cooking.

"So, what are we up for, mister? Nachos? Deli? I got forty bucks from the U.S. government that says dinner's on me."

"They gave you forty bucks?" Jarrod seemed impressed. "So, what's the trial about, Mom? Anything cool?"

"I shouldn't say, but it's about this Mafia guy. We heard these lawyers talk. Just like on *Law and Order*. And I got to meet the judge. In her office."

Jarrod came to a stop just in front of their building. He cried out, "Mom!"

Their car was parked on the street, a ten-year-old orange Volvo wagon. Sluggo, they called it, because it didn't go very fast and looked like it had taken quite a few punches. They kept it on the street. The local cops always cut them slack.

Someone had smashed the entire front windshield in.

"Oh my God," Andie gasped. She hurried up to the station wagon in disbelief.

Shards of splintered glass were all over the pavement. Who would do such a thing? She'd kept it on the street for years. Everyone on the block knew it. Nothing like this had ever happened. She placed a hand on Jarrod's shoulder.

Then Andie felt a knot tighten in the pit of her stomach. She thought of Cavello sitting there in the courtroom with his calm, indifferent stare. Like he had it all under control. And the stories Louis Machia had told. He had murdered for Cavello. Something like this was child's play to the mob, wasn't it?

"Mom, what's wrong?"

"Nothing, Jarrod." She pulled him close.

But he didn't believe her any more than she believed herself. All they would have to do is follow you home.

Maybe they had.

Chapter 18

RICHARD NORDESHENKO had a very good plan, which was why he was sitting in a fashionable bistro on the upper East Side, watching an attractive, middle-aged woman from the relative safety of the bar.

There were three others with the woman at her table, talking and laughing. The place was jammed with an affluent, successful-looking crowd. The two men with her wore nicely tailored suits, expensive dress shirts, gold cuff links. She seemed to know the other woman in her party quite well. The conversation was lively, familiar. The wine flowed. How nice for all of them.

Nordeshenko had followed the woman home from court that day. To her lovely town house in Murray Hill. After she went inside, he stopped on the street directly in front of the red wooden door. No guards. That's how they did things here. And the lock was a Weiser; it would be no problem. He saw the wires from a security system connected to the phone line. That was no problem, either.

"Mr. Kaminsky." The pretty hostess at the restaurant stepped up to him and smiled. "Your table is ready now."

She seated him precisely where he had requested: at the adjoining table to the woman he had followed. It didn't bother him to be so close. She wouldn't know him; she would never see his face again. He had done this kind of thing countless times.

In the beginning, it was the Spetsnaz Brigade, special forces, in Chechnya. There he had learned how to kill with precision and without any remorse. His first real job had been a local bureaucrat in Grozny who had stolen several pensions. A real pig. Some of the victims had approached him to get even, and they paid him a sum he would not have earned in six months of waiting around to get blown up by the Chechen rebels. He was ridding the world of filthy scum. He could easily justify that. So he killed the bureaucrat with a firebomb placed in his speedboat.

Next, it was a policeman in Tashkent who was blackmailing prostitutes. He'd gotten a royal fee for that. Then a mobster in Moscow. A real big shot; impossible to get close to. He'd had to detonate an entire building, but it was just part of the job.

Then he started offering his services to whoever would pay his price. It was the time of perestroika, capitalism. And he was just a businessman. He'd hit the big time.

He stared at the fashionable woman again. Too bad. She seemed successful, and even likable. He knew exactly how it would go from here. It would begin with something small. A *message*, something that would fester in her mind. Soon, she'd be shitting bricks.

There would be no trial.

The woman shifted in her chair, and a blue cashmere sweater draped over the back fell onto the floor.

A waiter moved in, but Nordeshenko beat him to it. He reached down and picked it up.

"Thank you so much." The woman smiled warmly at him. Their eyes met. Nordeshenko made no move to avoid them. In a different world, she was probably someone to admire and respect. But this was his world now.

He handed back the beautiful sweater. "My pleasure." He nodded slightly in return.

And it was. He had looked into the eyes of many of his victims before he acted.

Your life is about to become hell, Miriam Seiderman.

Chapter 19

"MR. MACHIA, my name is Hy Kaskel," the Eyebrow said as he stepped away from his chair the following morning. "I'm going to be asking you some questions on behalf of my client, Mr. Dominic Cavello."

Andie DeGrasse opened her notepad to a new page, sketching in a caricature of the defense attorney, his eyebrows flashing. She had decided to keep what had happened yesterday afternoon to herself. What could she prove? At this point she didn't want another scene with Sharon Ann about "poisoning the jury."

"I'm familiar with your client, Mr. Kaskel," Louis Machia replied.

"Good." The diminutive defense attorney nodded. "If you please, will you tell the jury just how you know him?"

"I'm just acquainted, Mr. Kaskel. I've been around a table with him a few times. He was there the night I got made."

"Around a table." Cavello's attorney theatrically mimicked him. "Do you consider yourself a close friend of Mr. Cavello's? Has he, say, invited you out to dinner?"

"Actually I *have* gone out to dinner with your client, Mr. Kaskel." The witness grinned. "It was after Frank Angelotti's funeral. A lot of us went out. But as for the other stuff, no. I was just a soldier. That's not the way it worked."

"So you've never heard Mr. Cavello give any orders on behalf of the Guarino crime family? He never said to you, for instance, 'I need a favor from you, Mr. Machia,' or 'I want Samuel Greenblatt killed'?"

"No, Mr. Kaskel, not quite that way."

"That was left to other people to explain to you. Like Ralphie D., whom you mentioned, or this other Tommy character . . . the one with the funny name?"

"Tommy Moose."

"Tommy *Moose.*" The defense attorney nodded. "Sorry."

"That's all right, Mr. Kaskel. We all have funny names."

Peals of laughter erupted through the courtroom.

"Yes, Mr. Machia," the defense attorney said, "but what I was driving at is, you never actually heard my client suggest it would be a good thing if this Sam Greenblatt was killed, did you?"

"No, not directly."

"You heard that from Ralphie D., who, you say, spotted him driving around somewhere in New Jersey in a car."

"It wasn't *somewhere* in New Jersey. It was down the block from where Mr. Greenblatt was killed."

"By *you,* Mr. Machia, just to be clear."

"Yes, sir." The witness nodded. "By me."

Kaskel scratched his chin. "Now, you describe yourself as a longtime member of the Guarino crime family, isn't that right? And you've admitted to doing a lot of bad things on behalf of that family."

"Yes," the witness answered. "To both."

"Like . . . killing people or trafficking in drugs, isn't that right?"

"That's correct."

"What kinds of drugs did you traffic in, Mr. Machia?"

Machia shrugged. "Marijuana. Ecstasy, heroin, cocaine. You name it."

"Hmmph," the lawyer snickered to the jury, "you're quite the entrepreneur, aren't you? You've owned a gun, haven't you, Mr. Machia?"

"Yes, sir. I've always had a gun."

"Ever use your gun or threaten the life of someone in connection to those drugs, Mr. Machia?"

"Yes, sir, I have."

"Ever *take* any of those drugs yourself, Mr. Machia?" Cavello's lawyer pressed.

"Yes, I've taken drugs."

"So you're an admitted drug user, a car thief, a burglar, a knee breaker, and oh, yes, *a killer,* Mr. Machia. Tell me, in the course of your longtime crime dealings, did you ever have the occasion to lie?"

"*Lie?*" The witness chuckled. "Of course I lied. I lied all the time."

"By all the time, you mean . . . once a month? Once a week? Every day, perhaps?"

"We always lied, Mr. Kaskel. That was what we did."

"Why?"

"Why would we lie? To keep out of trouble. To avoid getting caught."

"Ever lie to the cops, Mr. Machia?"

"Sure, I lied to the police."

"To the FBI?"

"Yes." The witness swallowed. "When I was first arrested, I lied to the FBI."

"What about your wife, Mr. Machia? Or, say, your mother? Ever lie to them?"

Louis Machia nodded. "I guess in the course of my life I've lied to just about everyone."

"So let's face it, Mr. Machia, what you are is a habitual liar. Basically, you've lied to everyone you know. The people you work with, the police, the FBI, your wife. Even the woman who bore you. Let me ask you, Mr. Machia, is there anything you wouldn't lie about?"

"Yes." Louis Machia straightened up. "*This.*"

"*This?*" Kaskel mocked him sarcastically. "By *this,* I assume you mean your testimony?"

"Yes, sir," the witness said.

"The government's promised you a sweet deal, haven't they? If you tell them what they want to hear."

"If I admit to my crimes and tell the truth." The witness shrugged. "They said they would take that into account."

"By that, you mean reduce your sentence, correct?"

"Yes."

"Maybe even to 'time served,'" the Eyebrow said, wide-eyed, "is that not correct?"

"It's possible." The witness nodded.

"So tell us," Kaskel said, "why should this jury believe you now, when in practically every other instance of your life, you've admitted you habitually lied in order to save your own skin?"

"Because," said the witness, smiling, "it makes no sense for me to lie now."

"It makes no sense?" Kaskel scratched his chin again. "Why?"

"Because if they catch me in a lie I stay in prison. All I have to do to get my sentence reduced is *tell the truth*. How 'bout that, Mr. Kaskel?"

Chapter 20

THEY BROKE FOR LUNCH. Andie went out with O'Flynn and Marc, the crime writer, to Chinatown, a short walk from the courthouse in Foley Square.

For a while, as they picked at appetizers, they exchanged stories. Andie told them about Jarrod, about what it was like raising a kid in the city by herself. O'Flynn asked what it was like to work on *The Sopranos,* and Andie admitted she'd sort of stretched that a little bit: "I was an extra. I exaggerated to get off the trial."

"Jeez." O'Flynn stared at her glassily. "Y'just broke my heart."

"John's been rewinding through five years of reruns trying to pick you out in the Bada Bing." Marc grinned, picking up a piece of bean curd with his chopsticks.

"So what about you?" Andie turned to Marc. "What kind of stuff do you write?"

Marc seemed like a cool guy to her. He had longish, curly blond hair, a bit like Matthew McConaughey, and always wore jeans with his navy blazer and open-necked shirt.

"Couple of okay mystery novels — one was nominated for an Edgar Award. I did some *CSI* and *NYPD Blue* scripts."

"So, like, you're famous," said Andie.

"I *know* a few famous writers," he said, grinning. "Am I making you nervous?"

"Yeah, I can hardly hold my chopsticks." Andie smiled. "Look at them shake."

"So I gotta ask you guys." O'Flynn lowered his voice. "I know we're not supposed to talk, but this Machia guy, what'd we make of him?"

"We make him to be one coldhearted sonovabitch," Marc said. "But he does know how to get a laugh."

"He *is* a sonovabitch," Andie agreed, "but when he was talking about his friend, I don't know, I felt a different side of him starting to come through."

"I guess what I was really asking" — O'Flynn leaned in close — "is, do we believe him? In spite of all the shit he's done."

Andie looked at Marc. Machia was a murderer and a thug. He'd probably done a hundred horrible things he'd never owned up to. But that bit about telling the truth hit home, how he had nothing to gain from lying now.

The writer shrugged. "Yeah, I believe him."

They both looked at Andie. "Yeah, I believe him, too."

Chapter 21

WHEN THE JURY CAME BACK from lunch, a behemoth of a man took the witness stand. He was probably three hundred pounds, and he was one of the least healthy-looking people I'd ever seen.

"Can you state your name," Joel Goldenberger stood up and asked, "and where you currently reside?"

"My name is Ralph Denunziatta," the heavyset man said, "and I currently reside in a federal penitentiary."

Suddenly there was an ear-splitting boom that seemed to shake the entire building.

Everybody jumped or covered their heads. It was under-the-table time. There were several loud cries. One of the marshals made a move toward Cavello. No one knew what was happening yet. I stood up and was about to jump over the railing to protect the judge.

Then the noise came again. From the street. Maybe a demolition explosion, or a truck backfire. Everyone looked around as the nervous gasps in the courtroom diffused.

The only one who hadn't moved was Cavello. He just sat there, looking around, concealing an amused grin. "Don't look at *me,*" he said, and nearly everybody in the courtroom laughed.

The trial resumed. Denunziatta was about fifty, with a couple of double chins and grayish thinning hair; he spoke in a soft tone. Like Machia, I'd gotten to know him well. I was the one who had arrested him. I actually liked Ralphie, if you could like a guy who wouldn't shrug to see you dead.

Joel Goldenberger stepped up to the stand. "Mr. Denunziatta, would you state your position in organized crime?"

"I was a captain in the Guarino crime family." He spoke in a hushed tone, eyes averted.

"Ralphie D.?" the U.S. prosecutor asked.

The witness nodded. "Yes. That would be me."

"You have a college degree, don't you, Mr. Denunziatta?" the prosecutor continued.

"Yes, sir, I do. In business. From LIU."

"But you never got a regular job? You chose to dedicate yourself to a life of crime?"

"That's correct." Denunziatta nodded again. Ralphie's father was one of Cavello's henchmen when Ralphie was growing up. "My father wanted me to become a stockbroker or get a law degree. But things were changing. The family was in some legitimate businesses — restaurants, nightclubs, food distribution — so I got involved with them. I thought I could avoid things, you know, the things everyone talks about — the violence, the dirty work."

"But you couldn't, Mr. Denunziatta, could you?" Joel Goldenberger asked.

"No, sir." The witness shook his head. "I couldn't."

"And one of those things you couldn't avoid was involvement in the murder of Sam Greenblatt?"

"Yes," he said, locking his thumbs.

"And you pleaded guilty to playing a part in that crime, is that not correct?"

"That's correct," the witness said. "I pleaded guilty to murder in the second degree."

"Why, Mr. Denunziatta? Can you describe your actual involvement in Mr. Greenblatt's death?"

He cleared his throat. "Thomas Mussina came to me. He was a captain then. He reported directly to Dominic Cavello. He knew some people who worked for me owed the family a favor. Jimmy Cabrule — he had gambling debts. Also Louis Machia — he was looking to be made. He figured this was an opportunity."

"By 'opportunity,'" the prosecutor stated, "you mean that if Mr. Machia participated in killing Mr. Greenblatt, he would be rewarded with being formally inducted into the family? Is that correct?"

"That's correct, Mr. Goldenberger."

"So, go on, Mr. Denunziatta. Did Mr. Cabrule and Louis Machia carry out this hit?"

"Yes, they did. In front of Greenblatt's home in Jersey. On the sixth of August, 1993."

"You seem to know the date well, Mr. Denunziatta. Were you there?"

"I was in the area," Denunziatta replied.

"*In the area* . . . ?" Goldenberger cocked his head.

"I was in a car driving around the neighborhood, maybe two blocks away. I heard the shots. I saw Louis and Jimmy C. speed by. Louie's friend Stevie Mannarino was driving the vehicle."

"Was anyone *else* driving around the neighborhood, Mr. Denunziatta? At the time Mr. Greenblatt was murdered?"

"Yes, sir." The gangster nodded. "Tommy Moose was driving around. In a gray Lincoln."

"Okay, Thomas Mussina was there. In a Lincoln. Was there anyone else in this car with Mr. Mussina?" the prosecutor asked.

"Yes, there was." Ralphie sucked in a breath. "Dominic Cavello was in the car."

"How could you be so sure, Mr. Denunziatta, that it was Mr. Cavello in the car with Thomas Mussina?"

"Because they stopped and waved to me. A few blocks from the hit."

"But it didn't surprise you, did it, Mr. Denunziatta? To see him, the Electrician, there?"

"No, sir," the witness said.

"And can you tell the jury why?"

"Because Tommy told me they were going to be there the night before. He and Mr. Cavello. He said Mr. Cavello wanted to make sure everything was done just right."

Denunziatta looked up, as if drawn almost magnetically toward the defendant.

Cavello met his gaze with the most chilling, mirthless smile. It had finality to it. Everybody saw it. It was as if the temperature in the courtroom had dropped twenty degrees in a few seconds.

Go ahead, Ralphie, Cavello's smile seemed to say. *Do what you have to do. When this has all played out, I'll find you.*

Dead man walking, Ralphie.

The prosecutor brought the witness back. "So to the best of your knowledge, Mr. Denunziatta, Mr. Cavello knew about Mr. Greenblatt's murder before it took place?"

"'Course he knew about the murder, Mr. Goldenberger. Jimmy wouldn't tie his shoelaces without the Boss's say-so. Everybody knew that. *Cavello ordered the hit.*"

Chapter 22

MIRIAM SEIDERMAN had seen the monstrous look, too. It almost brought the proceedings to a halt, as all eyes went to Cavello.

Up to now the mob boss had been on his best behavior, but she knew he was tethered by a slender thread. The first two witnesses had been damaging. She could read the jury on that. Only a complete fool would think Cavello had nothing to do with Greenblatt's murder.

Yet he just sat there, like he had it all planned out. His life was going down the tubes, and he was above it all: *You can't hold me here. I'm stronger than you. I'm stronger than the whole system. You can't judge me.* It made her shiver.

After trial that day, she met her husband for dinner with a client. Ben was a partner at Rifkin, Sayles, one of the biggest law firms in the city. She listened, tried to laugh. The client,

Howard Goldblum, was one of the most successful real estate developers in the city.

But inside, she was scared. She kept reliving the trial. It kept reverberating through her. Something about that man. That he couldn't be controlled by any system.

She and Ben got home around ten. The alarm was on. The housekeeper had gone for the night. She double-bolted the front door and went upstairs.

She knew she should tell Ben about today. But it was silly, and she wasn't a silly person. She'd been on a hundred trials. She'd seen plenty of brazen criminals who thought they were bigger than life itself. Why was this one different? *He wasn't! To hell with him.*

She watched Ben disappear into his walk-in closet to get undressed, then into the bathroom. She heard him brushing his teeth. She went over to their bed. She pulled off the pillows one by one. Then she stripped down the duvet.

Miriam Seiderman felt her heart slam to a stop.

"Ben! Ben, come out here, quick! *Ben!*"

Her husband ran into the room, his toothbrush in hand. "What is it?"

Under the covers there was a newspaper, folded open to page two. The headline read, GANGSTER STOPS TRIAL DEAD.

She was staring at Dominic Cavello. An artist's sketch. The very moment in the courtroom that had stayed with her all evening.

That look.

She turned to Ben. "Did you put that here?"

Her husband shook his head and picked up the *Daily News*. "Of course not, no."

A chill started to creep down Miriam Seiderman's spine. The house had been locked, the alarms set. Her housekeeper, Edith, had left at four.

What the hell was going on? *This was this evening's paper. Someone had gotten in here tonight!*

Chapter 23

AROUND THAT TIME, in a dimly lit Albanian café in Astoria, Queens, Nordeshenko sat reading a newspaper of his own.

A few customers were at the bar. A soccer game was playing on the satellite, piped in from the home country, and the local boys were drinking and cheering, occasionally shouting in dialect at the screen.

The café door opened. Two men stepped in. One was tall, with ice-blue eyes and long blond locks flowing over his black leather jacket. The other was short and dark, Middle Eastern–looking, wearing a green military jacket over camouflage trousers. The two men took a seat at the table next to Nordeshenko's. The Israeli never even looked up.

"It's good to see you, Remi."

Nordeshenko smiled. Remi was his Russian nickname. From back in the army, in Chechnya. A version of Remlikov, his real name. Nordeshenko hadn't used it in fifteen years.

James Patterson

"So look what the wind dragged in." The Israeli finally folded down his newspaper. "Or maybe the sanitation trucks."

"Always the compliments, Remi."

Reichardt, the blond with the scar under his right eye, was South African. Nordeshenko had worked with him many times. He had been a mercenary in Western Africa for fifteen years and had learned his trade well. He had been taught how to inflict terrible pain when most boys were learning grammar and mathematics.

Nezzi, the Syrian, he had gotten to know while on duty in Chechnya. Nezzi had once participated in a terror raid against the Russians in which a lot of schoolchildren got killed. Nezzi had blown up buildings, shot Russian emissaries, whatever it took. He could construct a bomb from materials one could easily find in a hardware store. Nezzi had no qualms about anything, no ideologies. In this age of fanatics, it made him a dying breed. Refreshing in a way.

"So tell us, Remi" — the South African shifted in his chair — "you didn't bring us out here to watch Albanian football, did you?"

"No." Nordeshenko tossed the newspaper over on their table. Facing them was the courtroom sketch of Dominic Cavello — the same one he had left in the judge's bed just a few hours before.

"Cavello." Nezzi wrinkled his brow. "He's on trial, no? You want us to do a job on him while he's in jail? We could do that, I suppose."

"Have a drink," Nordeshenko said, signaling the waiter.

"I'll have one *after*," the South African said. "And as you know, our Muslim pal here lives the rigorous life of the Koran."

Nordeshenko smiled. "All right." He lifted the newspaper one more time. On the other side was another courtroom sketch, one Nordeshenko had cut out of the paper from the trial's very first day.

Both killers stared at it. Slowly the message started to sink in.

"You want that drink now?" Nordeshenko asked.

Reichardt's look said, *Lunacy*. "This is America, Remi, not Chechnya."

"What better place to break new ground?"

"Ouzo," Reichardt called to the waiter.

"Three," said Nezzi, shrugging.

The drinks came, and over the shouts for the football game, the men slugged them down, wiping their chins.

The South African finally started to laugh. "You know it's true what they say about you, Remi: you'd be fucking dangerous if you ever got mad."

"Shall I take that as a yes, you're in?" Nordeshenko asked them.

"Of course we're in, Remi. It's the only game in town."

"Three more," Nordeshenko called to the waiter in Russian.

Then he picked up the paper, the sketch of the jury disappearing under his arm. They wanted a trial, these stupid bastards, they were going to get one.

They just didn't know the meaning of the *trial* that was in store for them.

Chapter 24

NO ONE WAS ON the witness stand in the courtroom that morning. The press was cleared. The jury was being kept in the jury room. Judge Seiderman stepped in from her chambers and sent a fiery look hurtling toward the defendant in the second row. "Mr. Cavello, I want to see you and both counsels in my chambers, *now*."

As the judge was leaving the bench, she caught my eye. "Agent Pellisante, I'd like you to join us as well."

Our group made its way through the wooden door on the right side of the courtroom to the judge's quarters. Judge Seiderman took a seat behind her desk, glaring. I'd never seen her so angry.

And she was glaring directly at the defendant.

"Maybe I didn't quite get this across to you, Mr. Cavello, but if you think I will ever bow to intimidation or your mob-scare tactics, you have picked the wrong judge and this is the wrong courtroom. Do I make myself clear?"

"Perfectly clear, Your Honor." Cavello stood, staring right back at her.

"But what I particularly don't take to" — Judge Seiderman raised herself up — "is a defendant who thinks he's big enough to toy and interfere with the criminal justice system."

"Can Your Honor explain what it is you're talking about?" Kaskel asked, obviously confused.

"Your client knows precisely what I'm talking about, Mr. Kaskel," the judge replied, her gaze never wavering from Cavello's chuckling eyes.

She reached into a drawer, pulled out the copy of the *Daily News,* and threw it down on her desk. Facing up was a sketch of Cavello's courtroom look at Ralphie yesterday. GANGSTER STOPS TRIAL DEAD.

"This was in my bed last night. *In my bed,* Mr. Cavello! Under my covers. The evening edition broke around seven. My house was completely locked up and alarmed. No one had been inside since four that afternoon. You have an educated guess as to how this got there, Mr. Cavello?"

"I'm not an expert on these things, Your Honor." Dominic Cavello shrugged smugly. "But maybe that's something you ought to take up with your alarm company. Or your husband. Me, I got a pretty good excuse. I was in that prison over there."

"I told you" — Miriam Seiderman removed her glasses — "these proceedings will not be disrupted by intimidation."

I had to give her credit. The judge was going toe to toe

99

with Cavello. She wasn't backing down. "This court has given you every opportunity to have this trial conducted in the open, Mr. Cavello."

"This court is making assumptions that it cannot possibly back up, Your Honor," Hy Kaskel said. "Mr. Cavello has conducted himself by every rule and stipulation both sides agreed to in the pretrial hearings. You can't point the finger at him."

"I am pointing the finger, Mr. Kaskel. And if it's shown in any way that this is tied back to your client . . ."

"It's okay, Hy." Dominic Cavello restrained his lawyer. "I understand how the judge must feel. She has to do what she has to do. It's just that I have friends who feel a certain way as well, and the problem is, they have to do what they think is right, too."

"*What did I just hear?*" The judge's gaze was electric, drilling in on Cavello's eyes.

"I tried to tell you from the beginning, Your Honor," Cavello said, "we're never going to see the end of this trial. What can I tell you? That's just the way it is."

I couldn't believe what I had just heard. Even for a bull like Cavello, to direct such a bold threat at the court was extraordinary.

"Agent in Charge Pellisante," the judge said, never flinching.

"Yes, Your Honor."

"I'm calling a recess for the day. I want the jury sent home. In the meantime, I'll decide how this proceeding is conducted from here on in."

I felt I had to voice my opinion. "The jury should be sequestered, Your Honor. We can no longer take responsibility for their safety. Or even your own. We've mapped out various locations. I can have protective custody in motion as soon as you give the word."

"Nick," Cavello clucked, turning my way, "it's a big city. Hey, maybe you ought to be watching your back, too."

I stepped forward to take a slug at him — but someone behind me, this big, burly marshal, held me back.

"Do it, Agent Pellisante." The judge nodded. "Set the wheels in motion. Sequester the jury."

Chapter 25

AROUND NINE THIRTY that night, Andie was folding towels in Jarrod's bathroom. Her darling son was in his pj's, sitting up in bed with a schoolbook open on his lap, but he was staring off into space.

"Mom, what's a promontory?" he called to her.

Andie came out and sat on the edge of his bed.

"It's like a piece of land that juts out into the ocean."

"Then what's a peninsula?" he asked next, flipping the textbook page.

Andie shrugged. "I guess it's a larger piece of land that juts out into the ocean."

That day, for the first time in a week, she had picked him up from school. The judge had excused them all before noon, and the rumor mills were buzzing. The newspapers and TV commentators were saying threats had been made. Maybe against some of the jurors.

Andie had asked for some time with the judge and finally mentioned how she had found her windshield smashed in two nights before. Judge Seiderman told her it probably wasn't related. But that wasn't exactly making her feel safe and secure right now.

"So, then isn't every piece of land in the world kind of a peninsula?" Jarrod shrugged. "I mean, look at Florida. Or Africa and South America. Doesn't everything stick out into the ocean at some point, Mom?"

"I guess." Andie tucked in his blanket and sat brushing back his soft, light-brown hair.

"Hey," he said, squirming, "I'm not a baby."

"You're my baby, always will be. Sorry, but that's the deal."

Andie's hand stopped abruptly at the sound of the doorbell.

Jarrod sat back up. They both looked at the clock. It was after ten. "Who could that be, Mom?"

"I don't know. But one thing I do know, Einstein." She took the book from him. "It's lights out." She bent and gave him a kiss.

" 'Night, Mom."

Andie went into the hall to answer the bell. She turned the lock and cracked open the front door slightly.

She did a double take.

It was that FBI guy she'd noticed in the courtroom, the nice-looking one. And there was a uniformed police officer with him. No — *two* police officers, a man and a woman.

What were they doing here at ten o'clock?

Chapter 26

HE HELD UP his FBI shield for her to see. "I'm sorry to surprise you, Ms. DeGrasse. May I come in? It's important."

Andie opened the door. The FBI guy was dressed nicely, in an olive raincoat over a brown sports jacket, with a deep-blue shirt and a tie. Her mind flashed to how she must look — in a bright-pink DKNY sweatshirt, with a towel draped over her shoulder. "I wasn't expecting anyone."

"We're sorry to bust in on you like this. I'm Nicholas Pellisante. I'm a special agent in charge of the FBI's Organized Crime Unit. I'm heading up the Cavello investigation."

"I've seen you in court," Andie said. Then, warily, "Isn't there some kind of rule that we're not supposed to be talking to each other?"

"Under normal circumstances, yes." The FBI guy nodded.

"Normal circumstances? I'm not following you. What's happening?"

"The trial procedures are being changed. As a matter of safety, the judge feels — and I agree — it may be prudent for the members of the jury to be removed from their daily lives."

"Our daily lives?" Andie blinked. What did that mean? She ran a hand through her messy hair.

"The judge would like the jury sequestered. I don't want you to be alarmed. There's no specific threat. It's just for your protection."

"My *protection?*"

"Yours and your son's," the agent said.

Now Andie *was* alarmed. "You're saying there have been threats?" Her mind flashed to the windshield of her car. "This is about what happened the other night."

"I'm not saying that," the agent said. "There's an officer outside who can assist you."

"Assist us with what, Agent Pellisante?" A tremor galloped down her spine. "I have a nine-year-old in here. What do I do with him while I'm being protected? Pack him off to boarding school?"

"Look, I know how this sounds, and I know how short notice it is. We'll make provisions that you get to see your son regularly, for the balance of the trial."

"The balance of the trial!" Suddenly the magnitude of this smacked Andie face-on. "We're only in the first week. This isn't exactly what I signed up for, Agent Pellisante."

The FBI guy looked sympathetic, but also helpless to do anything. "I'm afraid it's not a matter of choice."

Her blood was pulsing. She could have gotten off this trial just the other day. "When?" Andie looked up at him.

Then she realized what he had meant by the *officer waiting outside*.

"I'm afraid, right now. What I have to ask you to do now is to go pack some things."

"You're kidding!" Andie stared at him, glassy-eyed. "My son's in bed in the other room. What am I supposed to do with him? This is crazy."

"Is there someone who can take him for tonight? Somebody nearby?"

"I have a sister in Queens. It's after ten o'clock. What do you want me to do, put him in a cab?"

"You can bring him along," the FBI guy finally said. "Just for this evening, though. You'll have to make provisions for him tomorrow."

"Bring him along." Andie smirked sardonically. *"Where?"*

"I can't tell you that, Ms. DeGrasse. Not far. And you will be able to see him from time to time. I promise you that."

"You're serious." Andie ran a hand through her hair again.

At that moment, she saw Jarrod standing in the hall in his pj's. "What's goin' on, Mom?"

Andie went to him and put an arm around his shoulders. "This man is from the trial. He's with the FBI. He's telling me we have to leave. We have to go someplace. Now. Tonight."

"Why?" Jarrod asked, not understanding. "Tonight? Where?"

The FBI guy kneeled down. "We have to do this in order to let your mom do a brave thing. You'd want her to do that, wouldn't you? You'd do something brave, wouldn't you, to protect your mom?"

"Yeah." Jarrod nodded. "Sure I would."

"Good." He squeezed the boy's shoulder. "I'm Nick. What's your name?"

"Jarrod."

"It won't be so bad." He smiled. He winked back at Andie. "You ever ridden in a police car, Jarrod?"

Chapter 27

WHEN I FINALLY MADE IT home, it was after two.

It wasn't easy rousting people out of their homes late at night, scaring the living shit out of them, being unable to level with them. The jurors were all taken in unmarked cars to a motel across the Holland Tunnel in Jersey City. Eight U.S. marshals had them under guard there for the night.

I was exhausted, and I felt like crap for disrupting their lives. But as I turned the key to my apartment at that predawn hour I knew *I'd* sleep a whole lot sounder for having done it, having moved them.

Stepping into the apartment, I was surprised to find the lights on. At first I figured Ellen was on call. *What else was new?*

Then, Popeye didn't come to greet me like he always did. And he wasn't on the couch where he usually slept.

Something was wrong, wasn't it?

It took a second. Then I flashed to the threat Cavello had made against me in the courtroom earlier. I drew my gun.

Holy shit! Jesus, no. I started toward the bedroom. "Ellen! Are you in there? Ellen?"

The hall closet was wide open, and I noticed a few coats were missing. *Hers.* And two suitcases that we usually had stuffed on the top shelf were gone, too. A couple of photos were missing from the console. Her family and stuff.

"Ellen!"

The bedroom lights were on, shining brightly and hard on my eyes. The bed hadn't been slept in. A tray of her scents and body sprays had been cleared out too.

I had this sinking, helpless feeling, like everything was spiraling out of control. I couldn't believe this was happening. "Ellen . . . Ellen?" I called for her again.

Then I spotted a note on the bed, on my pillow. It was written on her medical stationery.

My heart sank as I read the first line.

My big, strong Nick. This is the hardest thing I have ever had to write. . . .

Chapter 28

I SAT DOWN on the edge of the bed, the pillows arranged the way she always liked them, her scent still hanging in the air.

I know this will hurt you. But I just need to be on my own for a while. We both know what was great about each other just isn't there much right now.

Hopefully, this will make you smile: I promise, there isn't anyone else, just this aching feeling that we're not giving each other what we want or need. And right now, I think I need to look into myself awhile and find out what it is I want someone to give me. You are the best, Nick. You are smart and reliable, and sensitive and strong. You're such a good man. And you know what else you're the best at — I don't have to elaborate!!!

You will make some girl a loving partner in life. I'm just not sure it's me. I need this space, Nick. We both need it! If we're honest, as we've always been with each other.

So please don't call me for a day or two. Don't ask me to come back (if you even want me to). Don't look for me. Don't be the cop, Nicky. I need the strength to do this. I'm at a friend's. Popeye is with me. He's already told me I'm a stupid jerk. (You're always the stud, Nick, even with the guys!)

I do truly love you, Nick. Who wouldn't?

I put down the note. There was a PS. *Okay, I lied just a little. Taking the medical boards was harder.*

I picked up a photo of us on my night table taken up in Vermont, skiing. *Goddamnit, Ellen, we could have worked it out. We could have talked at least.*

I made a move for the phone. I went to dial her cell; then I caught myself and stopped midnumber.

She was right. *Lay off, Nick.* Give her what she asked for. We both knew it. *What was great about each other just isn't there much right now. . . .*

I took off my tie and tossed my jacket on the bed. Then I just leaned back on the pillow and closed my eyes.

I wanted to feel crushed, empty. I wanted to go pour myself a scotch or kick a chair like I was supposed to do when things like this happened.

But I couldn't. I couldn't!

Ellen was right. What was great about each other just isn't much there right now.

Ellen was right about a lot of things.

Chapter 29

A BIG BLUE BUS was waiting for the jury in front of the Garden State Inn at 8:00 a.m.

Three court marshals, with their handguns showing, loaded them on. Another heavily armed marshal was waiting inside. Then three police cars pulled up, lights whirring. Their escort. An FBI man was checking names off a roster.

And this was supposed to fill us with a sense of ease, Andie thought as she climbed onboard. *I don't think so.*

Her sister, Rita, had been driven down earlier in a court-assigned car to pick up Jarrod and take him to school. He'd stay with her and his uncle Ray until this mess was over with. Andie was amazed at how well he had handled himself last night. He never let on that he was afraid or even put out. But this morning, he didn't want to leave her, and finally he cried like a little boy. *Her* little boy, her Jarrod.

"You have to do your job, and I have to do mine," she said as she hugged him close and put him into Rita's car, holding back a flood of emotions. "And remember . . . Florida's a promontory, right?"

"*Peninsula*," he corrected her. She waved as they drove away. One thing for sure — he'd have a helluva story to share in school that day.

Rosella plopped herself next to Andie on the bus. All of their nervous, harried faces said this was a whole lot more than anyone had ever bargained for.

"My huzban, he's very upset at what's goin' on. He tells me, the hell with the forty dollars, Rosie, get jourself off that trial. What about jou? Jou must be goin' crazy with jour son?"

"Jarrod's a trouper," Andie said, half believing it. "He'll get by." She turned around to O'Flynn and Hector. "It's the rest of you guys I'm worried about."

There was a lot of bickering, even before the bus left the motel. Understandable. Hector was insisting this was against the law. That they had to give you a chance to get off now. That they couldn't just hold you against your will. A few people argued with him that that wasn't true.

"It's like the Patriot Act." Marc rolled his eyes. "It's for our own protection."

The bus doors finally closed. The police cars in front began to pull out, lights flashing. The driver started the engine, and the big bus rolled forward slowly.

Andie pressed her cheek to the glass, the sight of the

dreary motel, her new home for the next several weeks, drifting away.

She missed just *knowing* she would see Jarrod that night. "I don't think Sam Greenblatt exactly signed up for it either," she finally said to herself.

Chapter 30

I WAS BEAT, bleary-eyed. I'd barely gotten three hours' sleep the night before. I tried to push the situation with Ellen out of my mind as I sat in court that morning. Cavello was flanked closely by two security people now. One more scene in there, and he was gone.

Joel Goldenberger stepped up to the witness stand. "Good morning, Mr. Denunziatta. I'd like to pick up where we left off the other day." He had papers in his hand.

"You testified that you'd been present in the general area at the time Sam Greenblatt was killed," the prosecutor started in, "and that you spotted Thomas Mussina driving around. With someone else in the car. Would you remind the jury who that other person was, Mr. Denunziatta?"

"It was Dominic Cavello," Denunziatta stated.

"Good." Goldenberger nodded and turned a page. "Now, what I want to move on to are the events that took place subsequent to that. Would you say that you and your colleagues were satisfied with how the job was done?"

"I guess at first we were satisfied." Ralphie shrugged. "I mean, we did the job, everyone got away, no one got hurt."

"Other than Mr. Greenblatt, of course."

"Other than Mr. Greenblatt, naturally." The witness nodded with a contrite smile. "It was maybe the day after that, as I recall, that things started to fall apart."

"What kinds of things are you speaking of, Mr. Denunziatta?"

"This guy that was involved in the hit, Stevie . . ."

"Steven Mannarino," Joel Goldenberger explained.

"Yeah. The kid screwed up. It seemed he didn't find clean plates for the getaway car like he was instructed. So he had to scramble." He cleared his throat. "Apparently he located a set in Louis Machia's yard."

"In the yard of his friend, who had just participated in the killing, right?"

"Yes." Denunziatta rolled his eyes.

"So how would you describe Stevie?" the prosecutor asked. "Was he an experienced guy in this sort of stuff?"

The witness shrugged. "He was a good kid from the neighborhood. I think he had asthma or something. He just wanted to be around."

"Be around?"

"He just wanted to be in the club. He wasn't the smartest kid, but Louie liked him. So we let him run errands. The kid would've done anything to get on the inside."

"And this was his chance, wasn't it? His big audition?"

"If it had gone well, who knows?"

"So what happened to Stevie, Mr. Denunziatta? After it came out how he had messed up?"

"At first, Louis wanted to handle it himself. The cops came to his house that night, after someone spotted the plates. But Louie had his own issues to worry about, and Stevie was going around making a lot of noise, like he wanted us to take care of him and get him out of the area. Away from the cops. No one had actually seen him at the scene, but he was scared."

"So what did you do for Stevie, Mr. Denunziatta?"

"I told him I would work it out. I met with Tommy Moose. And Mr. Cavello. We took a walk at the Kings County Mall. I said we needed to get this kid out of town. My uncle Richie had a place in the Poconos. He could've hid out there. Tommy agreed that it seemed like a reasonable plan."

Goldenberger nodded. "So that's where Stevie went then, after the Greenblatt hit?"

"Not exactly," Denunziatta said, and cleared his throat.

"Why? You were in charge of the hit. The person you reported to agreed. No one could pin that the guy was involved, right? Why didn't Stevie end up in the Poconos?"

"Because Dominic Cavello didn't go along with that," Ralph Denunziatta said, looking down.

"He didn't go along with it?"

"No." Denunziatta shrugged. "The Boss said Stevie's gotta go."

"*Stevie's gotta go,*" Joel Goldenberger said. He took a step or two toward the witness. "He said it just like that, Mr. Denunziatta? Those words? 'Stevie's gotta go'?"

"No, not those exact words." Ralphie shifted in his seat. He cleared his throat, twice. "As I recall, his exact words were, 'Cut the fat fuck up and stuff him in a can for all I care. The kid has got to go.'"

Chapter 31

"'CUT THE FAT FUCK UP and stuff him in a can for all I care. The kid has got to go.'"

The prosecutor paused to let the effect of the words fall on the jury. Everyone in the courtroom seemed stunned.

"You heard Dominic Cavello say those words? Give you a direct order to kill Steven Mannarino?"

The witness swallowed uncomfortably and shot a quick glance toward the defendant. "Yes."

A heavy silence settled over the courtroom. All the while, Cavello just sat there with his elbows on the table and his fingers folded together, staring straight ahead as if he hadn't even heard a word. It was like none of this even mattered.

"And Thomas Mussina," the prosecutor prodded, "he agreed with this?"

"What could he do? The Boss had given a direct order."

"So what *did* you do, Mr. Denunziatta? You promised Stevie you'd take care of him, right?"

"I did." The witness reached for some water. "I think he was staying at his sister's. I had someone get in touch with him and tell him to pack a bag and meet us at Vesuvio's, this place we all knew in Bay Ridge. I told him he couldn't say a word to anyone about where he was going. Even to his mother."

"Go on."

"So we met him there. I got Larry Conigliero and Louis DeMeo. Stevie got out of his car with this dumb little travel bag. He asked how long he'd have to be away, and I told him maybe a couple of weeks or so, until it all died down."

"You were lying to him, right? You had no intention of helping him get away?"

"That's correct." Ralphie nodded, taking a swig of water.

"So what happened, Mr. Denunziatta, after Mr. Mannarino got in that car?"

"They drove away. They took him to Larry's garage. They told him they wanted to pick up some tapes there or something, for the drive. Larry told me Stevie never had a clue. He turned around and shot him in the backseat. Then they had to cut him up, like Mr. Cavello said. They wanted to follow his orders just in case. Then they drove him to the Poconos. He's still there today, for all I know."

"So you reported back to Mr. Cavello," Joel Goldenberger said, "that the murder he ordered was done."

"I reported back to Tommy."

"And shortly after that, you became a captain yourself?"

"Yes." He nodded. "After about two months."

"And did Mr. Cavello say anything about why you had been made a captain in such a short time?"

The witness stared across the room. Toward Cavello. "He made a joke that I wouldn't be buying any property in the Poconos anytime soon."

Even now, Cavello seemed to find the line amusing.

"Thank you, Mr. Denunziatta." The prosecutor closed his notes and went to his seat. "One more thing." He turned back. "Did Louis Machia ever find out what became of his buddy?"

Ralphie lowered his eyes. "No, Mr. Goldenberger, Louie never knew what happened to Stevie."

Chapter 32

ANDIE TRIED TO RELAX in her motel room that night, but it wasn't happening.

She found Denunziatta's testimony that day pretty unsettling. The more she heard, the more she was developing an intense hatred for Dominic Cavello, even though she knew she was supposed to remain objective. She lay on her bed, leafing through a *Vanity Fair,* but her thoughts went to Stevie, the trusting wannabe, with his toothbrush and a change of shorts in his little travel bag, thinking he was going to the Poconos to lie low. *Cut the fat fuck up and stuff him in a can for all I care.*

She was feeling so alone. Some detective show was playing low in the background on the TV. She reached for the phone and dialed Jarrod at her sister's.

"Hey, hon," Andie said, brightening already.

"Hey, Mom!" Jarrod answered. It was great just to hear his

voice. Talking to Jarrod always cheered her up. They were buddies.

"How's it going, guy? Auntie Rita treating you okay? She *feeding* you?"

"Yeah. Everyone's real nice here. The food is great."

"So it's not so bad after all, staying with your cousins?"

"I guess. It's just that . . ." Jarrod's voice grew soft. "Why do you have to be there, Mom?"

"Because they're making us stay out here so we can really concentrate on the case. So no one will interrupt us."

"People at school are saying it's so this Mafia guy doesn't come after us. Try to hurt us."

Andie sat up and flicked the TV off. "Well the people at school are wrong, Jarrod. No one's coming after us." It was one thing if *she* had to be out here, totally separated and alone. It was another thing for her nine-year-old to be sucked into this.

She tried to lift his spirits. "Anyway, how many kids get to ride in a police car with a real FBI honcho?"

"Yeah, I guess. That was cool."

There was silence between them for a few seconds.

"Guess what?" she said. "I spoke with the powers that be. They said you can come down here for the night next Tuesday — for your birthday. I hear there's some pretty good Italian food out here in Jersey."

That did the trick. Jarrod was over the moon. "Can I stay over?"

"Yep, Jar, I cleared that, too. They even said they'd ride you back to school in a police car in the morning."

"That sounds great! I miss you, Mom."

"Me too, Jarrod. I miss you more." Andie moved the phone away a little and covered her mouth. She knew her voice was about to crack, and she didn't want Jarrod to hear that.

I miss you more than you'll ever know.

Chapter 33

WE BROUGHT IN three more strong witnesses on Friday and Monday. Each built up the case against Dominic Cavello; each dug the blade in deeper and deeper.

One was Thomas Mussina, the famous Tommy Moose, Ralphie D.'s boss. He was currently in the Witness Protection Program.

Mussina backed up everything that Machia and Ralphie had previously testified: that Cavello had given the direct order to murder Sam Greenblatt; that Tommy was actually driving him around, in his gray Lincoln, just blocks from the scene; that after they heard the shots and saw their guys speeding away, all Cavello did was wipe his hands and say, "So that's done. How 'bout some eggs?"

Mussina also corroborated Denunziatta's story about what happened to Stevie. He used the exact same words: "Stevie's gotta go."

Then he told the jury about a dancer, Gloria, who worked at a fancy strip club Cavello owned in Rockland County, New York. Gloria bragged to one of the other girls that she had squirreled away thirty thousand dollars in cash. Her "I-70 fund," she called it. One day she was going to take her daughter and just drive west, start a new life.

Tommy Mussina told the jury, "When Mr. Cavello heard this he got mad as hell. He thought this chick was stealing from him. So he sent a couple of guys to her apartment. They screwed her, strangled her, and tossed the body in a Dumpster. Luckily the kid was at school."

"They found the money?" Goldenberger asked.

"Yeah." Mussina nodded. "Stuffed inside a suitcase in a closet. Thirty grand, just like Gloria had said. They brought it back to Mr. Cavello."

"Why?"

"He wanted it." Mussina shrugged. "He laughed, said, 'What was once Caesar's belongs to Caesar.' I was there."

Vintage Cavello. Coldhearted and unnecessary. Over-the-top cruel.

"So in the end," the prosecutor said, shaking his head sadly, "did the money turn out to be stolen after all?"

"Nah. She saved it up just like she'd said. Mr. Cavello ended up giving it back to the family as a fund for Gloria's kid. He got a good laugh out of that one. It was the girl's own dough."

Chapter 34

AFTER MUSSINA'S TESTIMONY, the jury members filed into the jury room for lunch. No one seemed particularly hungry. "You see that asshole sitting there?" Hector shook his head angrily. "He barely moves a muscle. Like he's got the world under control. Even *us*."

"Well, he won't have it under control much longer if I have anything to do with it." Rosella crossed herself. "God rest his soul. *In hell.*"

Andie sat down. She glanced at Marc. The writer was just leaning on the windowsill, staring out at lower Manhattan.

"That poor dancer. Some getaway fund, huh? I have a little boy. That could've been me at another time in my life," Andie said.

Marc nodded sympathetically. "*Which* club was it you said you danced at?"

"Very funny." Andie scrunched up her face. But at least

the joke broke the tension. One by one, people began to smile and sit down. They passed out plates.

"After this is over we should all meet. I know this farm in the Poconos," John O'Flynn said, piling cold cuts onto his bread.

Winston, the mechanic, laughed. "Yeah, just watch out for all the large mounds of dirt."

Lorraine let one of her loud, high-pitched giggles go. That set everybody off. It was amazing that after all the grisly testimony they could just kick back and laugh.

"Lorraine," Andie said, "I have a dare for you. We all put ten bucks into a kitty, and the next time the Eyebrow makes one of those ridiculous statements about Cavello being a good citizen, you let rip one of your laughs."

"That would be priceless." O'Flynn cackled. "I'm in. I think even Judge Seiderman would get a charge out of it."

Lorraine must've liked the image, because she let another one loose. Shrill and penetrating. Everybody laughed even louder than the first time.

Andie had to admit that over the past week she had gotten close to these people. Maybe it was the nature of what they were doing. Sharing the same room, hearing the same sick, unsettling testimony.

She looked around the room. "Listen, it's my kid's birthday tomorrow. I arranged for him to come back with us and spend the night. What do you guys say about soda and cake in my room after dinner?"

"Hey, a party," O'Flynn said, nodding for all of them.

"We'll get party hats and noisemakers!" Rosella exclaimed. "Like New Year's Eve. Be a birthday he'll never forget."

"Courtesy of the United States government," Marc said. "They owe us something after all this, right? What's the little guy's name?"

"Jarrod." Andie smiled. "That's great. Thank you, guys. There's just one *other* thing. I kinda promised you'd all bring presents."

Chapter 35

I WATCHED THE JURY file back in for the afternoon session. Minutes later, another star witness was on the stand. He was an ex-mobster named Joseph Zaro, a former union official in the Local 407. The 407 was the contracting union Cavello controlled in New Jersey.

Zaro explained how for years contractors were squeezed for payoffs to get building contracts. How it literally took a hundred thousand dollars in a suitcase dropped at union headquarters if you even wanted workers to show up for the job. Or, if a contractor wanted a mix of union and nonunion labor to save money, that cost you 20 percent of the savings up front.

For years, we knew it was the biggest racket going in New Jersey, and that Cavello was literally skimming millions off the top. We just couldn't catch him.

"How many contracts did you rig for Mr. Cavello?" Joel Goldenberger asked Zaro.

"Dozens. Hundreds?" The witness shrugged. "And there were two other guys like me doing the exact same job."

"The exact same job? Meaning extortion?" Joel Goldenberger pressed him.

The witness shrugged again as if it was the most natural thing in the world. "Yeah."

"And what would happen," the prosecutor asked, "if the contractor refused to pay?"

"Then they wouldn't get no labor, Mr. Goldenberger."

"And if they still refused to pay? Or if they used outside workers?"

"You mean *outside our union?*" the witness asked.

"Yes."

Zaro looked around blankly for a second; then he scratched his head. "You understand, we were talking Dominic Cavello here, Mr. Goldenberger. I don't think I ever recall that happening."

A few people around the courtroom laughed.

Goldenberger smiled, too. "So this was basically a monopoly? Mr. Cavello over there could dictate terms to the entire construction business?"

"There wasn't a building went up in north Jersey, and parts of New York, that Dominic Cavello didn't get a piece of." The witness laughed out loud.

Even Cavello seemed to curl a smile at that one. As if he was proud of his business acumen. We had him dead to rights. Murder. Union tampering. Fraud. You could read it on every face in the courtroom. You could even read it on Cavello's face, beneath the cold stare that seemed to say, *This doesn't bother me at all.*

Now the prosecution had one final witness, one who could testify about an even uglier side of Cavello. One who could drive the nail into his coffin for good.

Me.

Chapter 36

I TOOK THE STAND the next afternoon.

"Please state your name." Joel Goldenberger stood up and faced me. "And what your association is with this trial."

"Nicholas Pellisante," I said. "I'm an SAC in the New York office of the FBI. I'm the head of a unit known as C-10. We oversee organized crime."

"Thank you. And in your role as head of this unit, Agent Pellisante, you are the senior law enforcement agent on the investigation into Dominic Cavello, is that correct?"

"That's correct." I nodded. "Other than the assistant director and the director."

"The assistant director and the director?" Goldenberger cocked his head. "You mean of the New York office?"

"No, Mr. Goldenberger." I paused, then moistened my lips with a sip of water. "Of the entire FBI."

Goldenberger looked impressed. "Those are pretty good

credentials, Special Agent Pellisante. Now, you haven't always held this position, have you, sir?"

"No. Before that I was an agent on the task force for five years. Prior to that I taught a class in criminal anthropology at Columbia. I also worked at the Justice Department in DC for three years. And before that I was in law school."

"And you hold a law degree from where, Mr. Pellisante?"

I played along because this was designed to set me up as even more impressive to the jury. I took another sip of water. "Columbia."

"So you've been investigating organized crime for how many years?"

"Eleven. Five as a special agent. Six as the special agent in charge."

"So it's fair to say, in the course of your experience, you've come across some pretty bad people, isn't that right?"

"The absolute worst. The Colombian drug cartels, Cosa Nostra, the Russian mob. I think I've looked into some of the most corrupt and violent organizations on the planet. My specialty, I guess."

Goldenberger smiled politely. "And in the course of these investigations, how would the defendant, Dominic Cavello, rank in terms of your experience?"

"Rank?"

"In terms of the criminal behavior you've investigated."

I cleared my throat. "Mr. Cavello is the most ruthless and cold-blooded killer we've ever looked into. He's *personally* ordered the deaths of over thirty people we can directly tie him to. He is an evil human being."

"Objection!" Hy Kaskel shot up. I expected that. "The defendant is not being charged with any of these alleged homicides. The government's investigations and pet theories are not of interest to this court."

"Correction, Your Honor." Joel Goldenberger waved. "The government will rephrase. I guess what I'm asking is, does your experience with this man go beyond just your investigation? You've had personal experience, haven't you, Agent Pellisante? You've seen Mr. Cavello's brutality firsthand?"

"Yes." My gaze shifted to Cavello. I wanted him to feel my eyes. I'd waited a long time to say these next words.

"I've personally witnessed Mr. Cavello commit murder. *Twice.*"

Chapter 37

I'D ASSEMBLED HUNDREDS of wiretaps and recorded conversations as part of my testimony, but we just started with *my* story, what I had seen myself.

"Would you describe for this court the events surrounding Dominic Cavello's arrest?" Goldenberger asked me.

I glanced toward Manny Oliva's wife, Carol, who was sitting in the first row. I was glad she was here for this.

"We had been told that Cavello was going to attend his niece's wedding at the South Fork Club in Montauk on July 23, 2004. We had multiple warrants outstanding."

"You had tried to arrest Mr. Cavello before?"

"Yes. Cavello had gone underground, though. He was a threat to leave the country."

"So you staked out the wedding on this tip. Can you describe for the court some of the other agents who assisted you there?"

"Sure." I swallowed back some emotion. I talked about Manny first. "Manny Oliva was my ASAC at C-10 for three years. I took him right out of Quantico. I brought him up through the ranks. He and his wife had just had twin girls."

"And Edward C. Sinclair, he was with you there as well?"

"Ed Sinclair was as exemplary a special agent as we had in the unit," I said. I nodded to his wife, Maryanne, and his son, Bart, in the seats next to Carol Oliva.

"So can you paint the picture for the jury, Agent Pellisante?" Joel Goldenberger placed a blown-up aerial photograph of the scene on an easel across from the jury box. "Agents Oliva and Sinclair are where in the stakeout?"

I walked over and took a pointer. "They were on the beach, outside the club grounds, blocking any escape." I described how Cavello had disguised himself as an old man in a wheelchair. How, as my special agents moved in, he jumped out of the chair, trying to escape. How he shot one of my agents who was posing as a waiter, Steve Taylor.

"He ran down toward the beach. Manny and Ed were in position. *Here.* I radioed ahead that he was headed toward them."

"Can you describe what happened next? I know this is difficult for you, Agent Pellisante, and for the family members of the agents who are present in the courtroom."

"I heard a volley of shots." I clenched my teeth. "I counted five — two quick ones, then three in rapid succession. I ran down from my position over the dunes and saw the bodies in the sand."

There wasn't a sound in the courtroom. I looked away from the easel, and every eye was focused on me.

"Then what did you do?" Goldenberger asked.

"I went over to the bodies." I cleared my throat. "Manny was dead. He'd been shot in the head. Ed was hit in the chest and neck. He was bleeding profusely. I could see he was dying."

"And did you see Dominic Cavello?"

"He was running down the beach, trying to get away. He'd been hit in the shoulder. I could make out what looked to be a gun. He was headed toward a helicopter on a promontory. I radioed for help, and we called in a helicopter from a Coast Guard cruiser offshore to block Cavello's escape.

"Then I went after him and fired my weapon, hitting him in the thigh. In the time I was calling for help he must've hurled the gun into the ocean."

"So you never found a weapon?"

"No." I shook my head. "We never did."

"But you have no doubt who killed your agents, do you?"

"None whatsoever." I shook my head. I looked squarely at the defendant. "Dominic Cavello. There was no one else near Ed and Manny when I heard those shots. And the bullet they removed from Cavello's shoulder was from Ed's gun."

"Just to be perfectly clear" — the prosecutor turned and raised his voice — "do you see the man you chased on the dunes that day? The man you saw running away from the dead agents' bodies?"

"That's him," I said, gesturing toward the second row. "Dominic Cavello."

For the entire trial Cavello had gazed stoically ahead, but now he was focused on me.

And I found out why.

Suddenly Cavello leaped out of his chair. He pulled himself up on the table like some enraged madman. His face was red, the veins in his neck about to explode.

"Fuck you, Pellisante! You son of a whore! You lying piece of shit!"

Chapter 38

WHAT HAPPENED NEXT was total bedlam.

"Lying bastards!" Cavello bellowed in a hoarse, crazed voice. He slammed his fist on the table, sending papers and documents flying.

"And fuck you to this court!" He glared at the judge. "You have no hold on me. You think you have, because you've bribed a few of my old enemies to carry your lunch pails. But you don't have shit. *I have you!*"

The marshals sprang into action. Two of them jumped in and grabbed Cavello by the torso, wrestling him to the ground. People were screaming. A few ran out the exits.

Cavello fought like a berserk animal. "You don't have me, Pellisante! I have *you!*"

A third guard jumped into the fray, and finally they forced the mobster to the floor. Two of them held him down while the third squeezed a set of cuffs over his wrists. He was still shouting at the top of his lungs.

"This court is a joke! A mockery! You'll never convict me no matter how many traitors and wiretaps you have. It's too bad, Nicky — *about your friends!* But whoever killed those scum, I would kiss them on the lips."

"Get him out of here," Judge Seiderman called out from the bench, trying to regain control. "Mr. Cavello, you have lost your privilege to sit in on this trial. You are in contempt. You are barred from this courtroom. Jurors, you will go back into the jury room immediately. Bailiff!"

Pandemonium continued in the courtroom. The jurors looked shell-shocked. Members of the press were already running out of the gallery to call their newspapers.

"Take me out of here! Bar me!" Cavello twisted his face toward the judge. "I don't want to be here any fuckin' longer!" His voice bellowed throughout the courtroom. "Your court is a joke!"

Blood trickled from Cavello's mouth. His formerly neatly groomed hair was tousled and wild. The guards lifted him up and tried to drag him through the side door. They had gotten one leg through when he wildly jerked around, and I saw something I could hardly believe.

The bastard was smiling.

Chapter 39

THE JURORS WERE STILL buzzing about what had happened. Shocked. Blown away. The court officials had rushed them all into the jury room. No one could recall ever seeing anything like Cavello's blowup in the courtroom.

"The asshole just made it easy for us." Hector shook his head. Everyone seemed to agree.

Maybe it just got to him, Andie thought. *His case was shot to hell. He cracked.*

The jury was going to be leaving the courthouse earlier than planned, and Andie hoped Jarrod was already here waiting for her and his special birthday celebration. They were quickly herded into the elevator to go downstairs, where the blue bus would be waiting.

As the elevator hit the lobby, Andie tried to regroup. Jarrod was here! In his Stephon Marbury number 3. Rita was waiting with him in the lobby. As soon as Jarrod saw his mother, he ran up and jumped into her arms.

"Happy birthday, honey!" It was wonderful just to see his happy face and give him a big birthday hug and kiss. Cavello, what had happened in there, didn't matter anymore.

"What's going on, Mom?"

Andie squeezed him double-tight. "Don't worry about it, sweetie."

The bus was waiting right there on the street. Andie and Jarrod climbed on first and made their way into one of the rear seats. Hector and Rosella, who sometimes spoke to each other in Spanish, sat in front of them. O'Flynn squeezed into the row behind them with a rolled-up *Sports Illustrated* in his fist.

"So tell me about school," Andie said.

"Nah." He grinned broadly. "It's my birthday, Mom. No school today, okay?"

"Yeah, okay."

They wanted to get them away from the courthouse as quickly as possible, and that was all right with her. A marshal jumped on, counted heads, winking because there was one more than usual. He slapped the side of the bus, sending it on its way with an "Okay!" The driver started the engine.

Andie looked back at the courthouse. Standing outside the side entrance was the FBI guy, Pellisante. He had set up the whole thing when she came to him with the idea for Jarrod's birthday party.

Thank you. Andie waved at him through the glass. An appreciative, one-finger wave.

He waved back.

Two police cars led the way as the bus pulled out from the curb onto Worth Street. It was a twenty-five-minute trip through the Holland Tunnel back to the motel. A few of the jurors looked around at Andie, wondering when they could break the surprise and sing "Happy Birthday" for this nice-looking boy.

"Hey, Jarrod." O'Flynn leaned over, staring at his Stephon Marbury jersey. "You like the Knicks?"

"I like 'em. I like *Halo* more."

"*Halo?*" It was a popular battle video game. Pretty violent and graphic. O'Flynn grinned at Andie. "Your mom lets you play *Halo,* huh?"

"His mom does no such thing," Andie said. "His aunt, though, that's another story, for another time."

A few of them laughed.

The bus pulled ahead to the corner of Church and stopped at a red light.

Andie looked out the window. She was thinking about the party and when to spring it on Jarrod that everyone knew this was his birthday. She figured they'd wait until they got close to the tunnel, build a little suspense. Rosella had made a colorful banner. HAPPY BIRTHDAY, JARROD. This was going to be so great.

She saw a gray side-paneled van pull up right next to them. APEX ELECTRICAL SYSTEMS. ASTORIA, QUEENS.

Jarrod said, "So, what'ya got planned, Mom? You *always* have a plan."

She was about to give him an answer when she noticed something a little strange.

The driver of the van had jumped out. He was dressed in a navy work uniform, had a baseball cap pulled over his face, long blond hair peeking through. What made it doubly strange was when the guy in the passenger's seat jumped out too.

They both started to run.

Across the busy intersection. Away from the van. When they reached the other curb, they glanced back. Not at the van.

At them! *At the bus.*

"Mom? Are you listening to what I'm saying? Earth to my mother. Hel-lo."

And suddenly she knew! Stabs of terror ripped at her chest.

"Get out of here fast!" Andie screamed to the driver. "Drive away. Now!"

But the light was still red. And they were locked in traffic. Besides, everyone was talking among themselves and not seeing. Jarrod looked up at her strangely and squinted. "Mom?"

"Oh, Jesus." Andie shuddered, unable to take her eyes off the van. She put her arms around Jarrod. She hugged him close to her chest. Something terrible was about to happen.

"Oh my God. No!"

"Mom?"

Chapter 40

I THINK BACK sometimes to that moment — to the very heartbeat before something terrible happened. Something I couldn't stop.

What if I could just reach out my hand and turn back the hands of time? Hold on to the moment for one more second? See what I should have seen?

I would see that smile. Not Andie DeGrasse's, sitting next to her son on the bus as they drove off.

Cavello's smile. In the courtroom, just moments before.

I would know exactly what it meant.

I had followed the jury out of the courthouse and stayed there, watching the bus as it pulled away from the curb.

With Ellen gone, my life was falling apart a bit. So it made me feel good to help the two of them, DeGrasse and her little boy. It made me feel that in all this craziness, I had done something for a change that put some life back. I watched her wave at me, that happy smile. I waved back. *Happy birthday, kid.*

And then the world fell apart! Theirs, and mine.

The gray van pulling up next to the bus at the red light. Then two men, in work clothes, suddenly running out.

Running away.

It took a second for it all to register, even for someone trained to see the worst in any situation. Then all of a sudden it was as clear as day. The whole horrible picture.

I heard myself yelling, "Get out of there now!" I started running toward the bus through traffic. "Get out of that bus!"

Then the van exploded, and the entire street just lit up in this brilliant flash. The recoil threw me back into a mailbox. Intense heat from a block away slammed into my face.

Oh, God, no! No!

All I could do was watch helplessly as the juror bus was engulfed in flames. Then it exploded.

I fumbled for my radio, connected back to the security team at the courthouse. "This is Pellisante. We've got a full-scale nine-one-one. The juror bus just blew up! Corner of Worth and Church. Repeat, the juror bus just exploded! We need full medical support out there now!"

Then I ran toward the bus at full speed.

It was bad. Very bad. Flames raged out of the hulk of the van. Dense gray smoke billowed over the street. People everywhere around me were screaming. Passersby, injured by the blast, were lying dazed on the street. A taxi lay upended and in flames.

I did a quick scan for the two men in work clothes. They

were gone, melted into the bedlam. Dear God, the juror bus was no more than a charred, burning carcass. The entire left side was just a fiery, jagged hole.

I ran to the entrance. The blast had blown it wide open. The heat coming off arm rails felt like a thousand degrees.

Everything was covered in flaming char. The bus driver was dead. Not just dead, decapitated. Oh, God. One of the passengers, an elderly woman who I could picture sitting in the back row in court, had been flung over the driver's back and smashed into the front window. I didn't remember who she was — which juror?

"FBI," I screamed into the thick, diesel-smelling smoke. "Can anyone hear me in there?"

I waited for voices. *There had to be voices. C'mon!* Moaning, shouting, screams for help, some evidence of life.

I shielded myself from the flames as I listened for somebody, anybody.

Nothing came back, no sound. That's what I'll always remember. That's what will always haunt me. *The silence.*

Chapter 41

IT FELT AS THOUGH my heart didn't move a beat. I just stood there listening, praying. *Somebody say something back to me. Shout! Scream for help!*

All I heard was the crackle of flames, and all I saw was the dark gray smoke mushrooming through the bus. The scene was as still and desolate as a bloody battlefield after the fighting was done.

I covered my face with my hand and pushed my way down the aisle. Madness, but I had to do it. It was impossible to see. Somebody, a small woman, had been hurled against a side window and was twisted into a grotesque position. Others had died right in their seats. Clothing was burned off.

I recognized some of the faces. The writer was dead. So was the kindly-looking Hispanic woman who always knitted. Both had been roasted in their seats. Then I saw the red-haired guy who worked for Verizon, O'Flynn.

"Can anyone hear me?" I shouted. Only silence came back from the passengers.

I heard sirens outside. Emergency vehicles had arrived on the scene. Someone else, a policeman, stepped onboard. "Jesus, God." He winced. "Is anyone alive?"

"I don't think so."

I tripped over some kind of mound. It turned out to be the body of the Jamaican mechanic, his clothes charred, his body crisp.

The thick, acrid smoke was starting to get to me. I coughed, pulled up my shirt, and covered my nose and mouth with folds of cloth.

"We better wait for the emergency people," the cop called to me. He was right. There were noxious fumes and fire everywhere. The damned thing could go up at any time. I tried to see the back of the bus. There were no signs of life there either.

Then I heard something. A groan — more like a whimper. *Someone alive?*

"FBI," I shouted, fighting against the fumes. The smoke was blinding. "Where are you? Are you all right?"

I heard the voice again, just a murmur.

"I'm coming."

Then I saw him. On the floor. It was the boy! He was in the fetal position underneath a seat. "Jarrod!" I bent down — I remembered his name. "Jarrod!"

I put my face down to his, as close as I could get. The floor was hot, steaming.

My stomach fell. The little boy was dead. His pink skin

was black with horrible burns. I wanted to retch. I couldn't help bringing up the image of his face just seconds before in the window as his mother waved to me. "I'm sorry, little guy."

Then I heard it again. The whimper, soft and faint. Someone was alive.

I pushed over twisted metal and bodies to the very back of the bus. Vinyl seats and plastic panels were melting in flaming strips. The smoke clung to my skin, like scalding rubber.

I heard it close. "*Jarrod . . . Jarrod.*"

It was Andie DeGrasse. She was pinned beneath a metal support beam. Her hair was black. Her face was covered with blood. Her lips quivered. "*Jarrod . . . Jarrod.*" She kept calling for her son.

"Help is here," I said, bending to her.

She was the only one alive.

Chapter 42

RICHARD NORDESHENKO heard the tremendous blast. At precisely 2:03 p.m., from three blocks away. He felt the ground beneath him shudder, the earth slide. It was done.

He had instructed his limo to wait while he went inside an electronics store and purchased a gift for his son. *World Championship Poker.*

Nordeshenko had heard similar explosions before. The *double* concussion. The ground shaking. Like an earthquake, actually. The store clerk looked confused. Nordeshenko knew what had happened. Nezzi had taken no chances. There was enough C-4 in that van to do the job three times over.

Nordeshenko tucked the package under his arm and left the store. He looked forward to getting home. He had a few gifts for his son: an iPod and the new computer poker program that he knew would delight the boy. And earrings for his wife from New York's Diamond District.

His work here was over, and it couldn't have gone any better.

He had already received a message about his Swiss account. More than two million dollars. There were still a few more payments that had to be made. But he had earned every penny. He would take it easy for a while when he returned home.

"What the hell was that?" the limo driver said, looking back toward Foley Square as Nordeshenko climbed back in the car.

"I don't know. Some kind of explosion. Maybe a fuel line." The scent of gasoline and cordite hung in the air.

They heard sirens. Two police cars rushed past them toward the courthouse, lights flashing.

"Something's happened!" the driver exclaimed, turning on the news. "This is not good."

Nordeshenko looked back and saw a cloud of black smoke rise up above the buildings, coming from directly behind them.

He placed the gift for his son in his traveling case. Two rings came from his cell phone — Reichardt and Nezzi were safely away now.

"Let's go," he said to the driver. "We'll listen on the way. I have a plane to catch."

Chapter 43

SHE OPENED HER EYES very slowly.

She felt no pain. Just woozy and unreal. She was here —
but she wasn't. A leaden pressure was in her chest. Where
was she? What had happened? Tubes were coming out of
her, attached everywhere. She tried to move but couldn't.

Nothing. No power over her own body. Was she paralyzed?
How had it happened?

Then Andie began to panic. Something very heavy and
bulky was blocking her throat. Making her gag. She couldn't
speak because of the obstruction.

A nurse came in. Just the look on the nurse's face told her.
Something terrible has happened. What?

"Andie. Don't try to talk, sweetheart. There's a tube down
your throat to help you breathe. You're in Bellevue Hospital.
You've been in surgery. You're going to be okay."

Andie made herself nod, eyes flicking wildly around the room. The *hospital* room.

Then it started to come back to her.

The jurors' bus. She had been on the bus. A gray van had pulled up. . . .

That's when the panic started to grip her chest again. Her eyes darted anxiously toward the nurse. *What happened next?* She tried to speak again, but could only cough and gag. Her fingers found the nurse's hand somehow. She managed to grab two fingers. She held on as tight as she could.

My son . . . Where is Jarrod?

"Please." The nurse squeezed back. "Try and stay calm now, Andie."

She knew something horrible had happened, something unbelievable. She tried to sound out Jarrod's name, but her air passage was blocked. And her mouth was as dry as sandpaper. *Please, please, my son.*

But something was forcing her to close her eyes, and Andie couldn't fight it.

Chapter 44

WHEN SHE OPENED HER EYES again, someone else was standing there. She blinked sleepily. *FBI. The one with the smile.*

But he wasn't smiling now. Actually, he looked terrible.

Memories of what had happened began flashing in her mind. The bus stopped at a red light. Then the van. The two men running away. She had reached out and tugged Jarrod close to her.

Jarrod?

Her eyes went back to the FBI man. She tried to scream out her son's name. *Please, don't you understand? Can't you read it in my eyes?*

He just looked at her and shook his head. "I'm sorry."

Sorry? she repeated to herself. It took a moment to register. *What is he saying? Sorry for what?*

She felt him place his fingers lightly on her hand. Then a squeeze. His touch told her everything.

It was rushing back at her now. Her panic when she saw the men running from the van. The terrible explosion. Then she was thrown back. She remembered calling Jarrod's name over and over.

Her body spasmed in shock now.

Andie felt something burn a path down her cheek. *This can't be real. This can't have happened.*

The FBI man wiped away her tear.

She still hadn't been told what happened. They didn't have to tell her now. She knew. She could see it in his eyes.

Oh, my poor Jarrod.

Tears began streaming down Andie's cheeks, and she had the feeling that they would never stop.

Chapter 45

THEY DON'T USUALLY ALLOW anyone inside the cell blocks at this time of night, even law enforcement. Tonight, I was on my own.

"Nick, it's late," said Trevor Ellis, who was in charge of the sixth-floor cell block, where witnesses and defendants were held in the Manhattan County Jail. We passed through the electronic doors together. Only the night crew was around.

There was a guard at the desk, checking monitors. Trevor nodded for him to take a break. "I'm okay with Agent Pellisante here. Get some coffee."

"It's official business," I told Trevor. We walked some more, then stopped at the end of the corridor. Cavello's cell was cordoned off, at the very end of the long wing.

"You're sure you want to do this?" Ellis looked at me.

Nineteen people had died this afternoon. Seventeen jurors.

My jurors. One victim was a kid on his tenth birthday. Some things you just have to do — regardless of the risk or the consequences.

"Official business," I repeated.

"Yeah," he said. "You give him some official business for me."

Cavello's electronic cell door clicked open.

He was lying on a cot with his knees drawn up and an arm crooked behind his head. His eyes widened when he saw who it was.

"Nicky," he said, barely hiding that same mocking grin I had seen so often in the courtroom. "Jesus, I just heard. What a mess!" He slowly raised himself up off the cot. "I want to tell you how sorry I . . ."

I slugged him in the face, and he went down.

"Jeez, Nicky." Cavello grunted, rubbing his jaw. He reached for the metal cot post and pulled himself back up, grinning. "Y'know, I heard of hung juries before, but this one takes on a whole new meaning."

I hit him again. Harder. Cavello slammed back against the concrete wall. He still stared at me with a sort of laughing arrogance, an animal savagery behind his eyes. "Your fault, Nicky. What'd you expect? I was gonna roll over and die? You *knew* that. You know me, like nobody else does." He wiped away a trickle of blood with the back of his hand.

I went over and yanked him off the floor by his collar. He was still wearing the same shirt he had on in the courtroom that day.

"You may think you've won, you piece of shit, but I'm gonna dedicate my life to you going down. Nineteen people died. One of them was a ten-year-old kid."

"There was a kid on that bus?" Cavello said, showing mock surprise. "Jesus, Pellisante, you oughta know better than that."

I punched him with everything I had. Cavello crashed into the cell wall again. I couldn't control myself. I'd never hated one person so much.

I heard Trevor Ellis behind me. "Okay, Nick, that's enough."

I ignored him. I pulled Cavello up again and threw him to the other side of the cell. He went into a metal sink and fell to the floor. I went and pulled him up again. There was blood all over his shirt. "They were just doing their duty," I screamed in his face.

"Go on," Cavello mocked. "Hit me. It doesn't hurt. But you got it wrong. I told you. No court can hold me. You say I'm going down." He spat out a glob of blood. "Maybe. But it won't be from you. You see those cameras up there? They got every second of this. You're through. I won't go down. But *you* will, Nicky Smiles."

I hit him again, and Cavello spun backward against the concrete wall. Trevor Ellis and a cell-block guard rushed in behind me. One of them pinned my arms while the other got between me and Cavello. He struggled to his feet again. He was wobbly, holding his side.

"Look at you." Cavello started to laugh. "You think *you* got *me?* You're the one who's through. You're the one gonna be seeing that kid every day for the rest of your life. Me, I'll sleep like a baby tonight."

Trevor and the guard yanked me out of the cell, but Cavello called after me. His words and laughter echoed down the hall.

"Like a baby, Pellisante. You hear that? First day in a month, I don't have to worry about a goddamn trial."

Part Two

RETRIAL

Chapter 46

ELBOWS ON MY DESK, I looked out at the class of twenty-two astonishingly smug and overconfident first-year law students.

"Can anyone tell me why the law permits law enforcement agents to use deceit at the investigative stage, when they're not even sure of a suspect's guilt, but strictly forbids them from lying during the testimonial stage, when they're absolutely sure the suspect is a criminal?"

Five months had passed. I had taken an extended leave from the Bureau, and I'd been teaching a course in criminal ethics at the John Jay College of Criminal Justice since January.

Some leave. I was doing everything I knew just to hold it together. I wasn't sure I'd ever go back, at least not to C-10, not after the beating I had given Cavello in his cell. But who was I kidding? It was more than that. Lots more. The bastard had been right. Since that day, the image of Jarrod's face look-ing out the window of that juror bus hadn't left my mind.

A female student in the second row raised her hand. "It's the means to an end," she said. "*Mapp*, and *United States versus Russell* allow the police to use deceptive procedures to obtain evidence. Without it, they might never make a case. It's deception for the greater good."

"Okay." I nodded, then got up and started to stroll around. "But what if the police have to lie about those procedures during testimony — in order to protect their case?"

In the back row I spotted something that annoyed me. Some kid seemed a lot more interested in a newspaper folded in his textbook than he was in me. I raised my voice. "Mr. Pearl-man, you care to weigh in on this?"

The student fumbled with his textbook. "Yeah. Sure thing. Not a problem."

I went up to him, removing the newspaper from his desk. "Mr. Pearlman here is busy checking his stocks while the Fourth Amendment is under siege. I hope for your future clients' sake you've got a nice family practice in entertain-ment law to go into."

There were a few laughs around the room. Typical suck-up snickers.

I felt a little ashamed, though. Like one of those profes-sorial bullies who gets his rocks off from a big show of power over his class. And that wasn't me. A few months ago I was pushing around one of the most notorious criminals in the country. Now it was just some kid, in law school. *Jeez, Nick.*

"So, Mr. Pearlman," I said, offering the kid an olive

branch, "the Supreme Court case that held that the exclusionary law of evidence was binding is . . . ?"

"*Mapp versus Ohio,* sir. U.S. 643. 1961."

"Nice guess." I grinned. I tucked the newspaper under my arm. "I have stocks, too."

The bell rang shortly afterward. A couple of students came up to go over an assignment or question a grade. Then I just sat alone in the empty classroom.

You're lying to yourself again, Nick. You're trying to run, but you're not fast enough. It wasn't about some kid catching up on the box scores in my class. Or the Fourth Amendment, or police methodology. It wasn't even about this closed, dark corner of the universe I had let myself drift to, pretending I was building a new life.

No. I flipped the paper over on my desk. I stared at the headline. The very one I'd been waiting these past five months to see.

GODFATHER, PART II. In big bold letters.

Unfinished business — that's all it was. Cavello's retrial was scheduled to begin next week.

Chapter 47

SHE WAS DOING her best to recover, but it was hard and lonely. And long. And basically impossible. Yet she was starting to come through it.

For a while her sister, Rita, stayed with her. Andie had suffered a ruptured spleen, a collapsed lung, a lot of internal bleeding, and burns on her legs and arms. But those were the wounds that healed. What hurt a lot more was the pain inside. Every time she looked into Jarrod's room, caught his scent on his books and things, his pajamas, his pillows.

Then there was the anger she felt every single day. Anger that his killers had never been brought to justice. That everyone knew who was behind it — Cavello! And the bastard wasn't even being charged. She even had dreams of finding him in his jail cell and killing him herself.

Then one day she was finally able to put some of Jarrod's things away, pack them into boxes, without crying. Without being too ashamed. She had asked the coroner to cut off a piece of the Knicks uniform shirt Jarrod was wearing that day. She kept it in her purse.

MARBURY

3

She started back toward having a life with the simplest things. Doing her proofreading, seeing a flick. It was like relearning the steps of life all over again. Telling herself it was okay. To *live* was okay.

Over time, she found herself reading the papers again, watching the news. Laughing at a joke on Letterman. One day, she even picked up a copy of *Variety*. A few weeks later, she called her agent.

Then, five months after it happened, Andie found herself standing in front of the doors to a casting studio on West 57th Street. The call was for some Cialis commercial. All it took was looking fortyish and a little sexy — pretty much herself. Her agent said, *Go. See how it feels.*

Standing in front of the studio, Andie had never felt so terrified in her life. It was like the first time she ever went on a casting call. It was too new. It wasn't right. *Way too soon.*

A pretty blond woman stepped out of the elevator behind her. "You goin' in?"

"No, you go ahead." Andie shook her head. A wave of panic swept over her. A tightness pounded in her chest. She needed air.

She didn't even wait for the elevator, just hurried down

the back staircase and onto 57th Street. Her legs felt weak and wobbly. She sucked a deep, grateful breath into her lungs.

This isn't going to go away, Andie. It's always going to be with you. Survivors pull it together. You have to do that, too. A few people passing by on the street glanced at her. She realized how foolish she felt, and probably looked.

Andie pressed herself against the cold concrete of the building and took another breath. She reached into her purse and felt for the little piece from Jarrod's uniform. *You're always going to be with me.*

Andie went back into the building, taking the elevator this time, back up to the third floor. She stood outside the studio again. Clutching her portfolio, she sucked in a breath. *This was hard. This was so damn hard.*

A woman stepped out just as she entered, and the woman had that look of disappointment Andie knew so well. Andie pushed through the doors and walked up to the receptionist.

"Andie DeGrasse. I'm here to read for the part."

Chapter 48

FROM A STAIRCASE across 183rd Street, I bit my lower lip as I watched her coming back home. I don't think she ever saw me, and I wanted to keep it that way. The alternative was too crazy to spend time thinking about.

Andie DeGrasse looked good. She was dressed up and clutching a large black portfolio. On the outside it looked as if she had it all back together. But I thought I knew what must be going on inside her.

I came up this way from time to time, and I wasn't even really sure why.

Maybe I just felt good that someone had come out of this thing alive. A couple of times I even went up and knocked on her door. I'd say hi, or bring something — a little news about the investigation. Basically, stand around a few moments, as though it was an official visit and I had something to say that I couldn't quite put into words. It felt good being connected to somebody. I didn't reach out to people much since the trial.

Maybe I was just kidding myself again. Maybe it was simply Andie DeGrasse. How she was pulling her life back together after what had happened. I envied that. That she never once accused me, though she had every right to — that she never looked at me with blame in her eyes.

Maybe it was simply the knowledge that we shared something — neither of our lives would ever be whole again. That's what I believed, anyway.

So I watched her as she climbed the stairs to her building and unlocked the inside door. She checked her mail and tucked a few envelopes and magazines under her arm, then disappeared from sight. A short while later, the lights went on in her apartment. *What am I, a stalker?* But I knew that wasn't it.

I finally walked across the street. Another tenant stepped out, and I fumbled in my pockets for a second, as if I'd lost my keys, catching the door before it closed.

Her apartment was 2B, on the second floor, facing the street. I climbed the stairs. I remembered the night we took the jury in. For a few seconds, I just stood in front of her door. *What was I here to say?* I had started to knock when it hit me, the feeling of total foolishness, stupidity.

I backed away quickly, heading to the stairs.

That's when the door opened. And I was facing Andie.

Chapter 49

SHE WAS STANDING THERE in a powder-blue sweater over jeans, barefoot, holding a black trash bag in her hand. When she saw me she did a double take. "*Hey.*"

I tried to act just as surprised — because I *was.* "I was dropping something off," I said, holding out the book I'd brought along. "I read this book. I was going to give it to you. I mean, I *am* giving it to you."

"*The Four Agreements.*" She removed it from the manila envelope, nodding. "'Don't take anything personally,' 'be impeccable with your word.' My sister gave it to me. Good choice, Agent Pellisante."

"I'm evolving. And it's Nick." I shrugged.

"Which is it?" she asked. "Evolving, or Nick?"

I smiled. "So, how's it going?"

"I went to an audition today. A Cialis commercial. You know, when the moment hits."

"And how'd it go?"

She smiled. "Dunno, exactly. All I had to do was look forty-ish and sexy. Right up my alley, right? But I read the part. It's the first time. . . . Have to pay the bills, right?"

I gave her a knowing look. Sometimes, I just wanted to reach out and hold her, hoping she would rest her head on my chest awhile. I just wanted to show I cared.

"I don't know — for forty, I think you look great. Honestly."

"Forty-*ish*." She raised an eye with a sharp smile. "Come back in eight years and I'll give you credit for a compliment. In the meantime . . ." Andie leaned against the door frame. "So how's the class you're teaching?"

A couple months back, I had written to her to let her know I'd left the Bureau and started teaching again. I just stood there with my hands in my coat and shrugged. "The highs aren't quite the same as my old job. So far, no one's shooting at me, though."

Andie smiled again. "How about I give you a choice, Nick? You can take the trash down behind the staircase on your way out. Or, if you want, you can come in."

"I'd like to," I said.

"You'd like to *which?*"

I stayed where I was. "You know, the retrial's starting. Jury selection's coming up. Next week."

"I read the papers," Andie said.

"I'm still a witness. The case is strong. They're going to put him away this time."

She stared at me awhile. Her mouth was full and her eyes sharp. Brown. "That's what you came by to tell me?"

"No." What promises could I make that I hadn't already broken? We'd never caught the men who killed her son. We had nothing to tie it to Cavello. "I thought maybe you'd want to come to the trial with me."

She took a step back. "I don't know. I don't know if I can be close to that man."

"I understand." I lifted the trash bag out of her hand. I guess that was a decision. She smiled as if she could see right through me.

"Still the public servant, huh, Nick?"

I gave her a self-deprecating smile. "Evolving."

She smiled.

"Hey, Pellisante," she called, catching me halfway down the stairs. "Next time, you really should think about coming in."

Chapter 50

THE FOLLOWING MORNING I was at my desk. In my office. At home.

I was doing what I always did on the days I didn't teach. What I'd been doing every free day for the past five months: sifting through every piece of information I could find on the case. Every document. Every sliver of evidence.

Looking for some way I could tie the bus blast to Dominic Cavello.

If anyone saw my study, my disheveled desk, they'd probably think they'd stepped into the lair of some obsessive, pathological nutcase. Good God, I had photos taped everywhere. The blast site. The van. The juror bus. Thick binders of FBI reports on the explosive device stacked high. Interviews with people on the street who might've seen the two men in work clothes running away.

More than once I thought I had caught a break. Like when

the stolen New Jersey plates led back to some horse trainer in Freehold who had links to the Lucchese crime family. But that turned out to be coincidence. None of it led anywhere. None of it directly tied to Dominic Cavello or his people.

I was sipping my morning coffee, having to admit that my mind was drifting back to Andie DeGrasse, when the phone rang.

"Pellisante," I answered.

It was Ray Hughes, the agent who'd taken my place at C-10. "Nick" — he sounded happy to catch me — "any chance you're free?"

Sometimes we'd have lunch, and Ray would pick my brain, or I'd pick his. I figured all he wanted was to go over my testimony for the upcoming trial. "I'd hate to miss out on *Ellen*, Ray, but I think I could find my way down to see you."

"Not here. There's a government jet waiting for us. At Teterboro."

If Ray wanted to grab my interest, he had it. The offer of a crummy sandwich at his desk in the Javits Building would have done the trick, too.

"A plane to take us where, Ray?"

The acting head of the Organized Crime Unit paused. "Marion."

I stood up quickly from my desk, coffee spilling over my work notes.

Marion was the federal prison where Cavello was being held.

Chapter 51

ABOUT FOUR HOURS LATER, the government Lockheed touched down at the airport in Carbondale, Illinois. A car was waiting for us and drove us to Marion Federal Prison. Marion was a vast, depressing-looking redbrick fortress stuck in the middle of a marshland in rural southern Illinois. It was also one of the most secure federal prisons in the United States. Although Cavello had yet to be convicted, after what happened in New York, the government wasn't taking any chances.

Warden Richard Bennifer was waiting for us. He escorted us out to the special control units, where Cavello was being held. The only visiting station was a glass-paneled room, with a guard standing by with a Taser and a surveillance camera running at all times. The prisoners here were lifers, level sixes, lost to the outside world for all time. I rejoiced. I was looking forward to seeing Cavello spend the rest of his life in a place like this.

Ray Hughes and Joel Goldenberger remained outside and watched through the one-way glass.

Cavello was already sitting there when I came in. He was dressed in an orange jumpsuit, his feet chained together. He was gaunter and older than when I'd seen him last, and a thin, gray growth clung to his jawline.

He'd been informed the government was here to see him, but the government was here to see him a lot. When he saw it was me he did a double take. Then came a wistful smile, as if he had just found an old friend.

"Nicky!" He tilted back his chair. "Is it a holiday or something? Who's minding the class?"

I sat down across from him, behind the protected glass, and didn't laugh. "Hi, Dom. How's the jaw?"

"Still hurts." He laughed. "Still think of you every time I brush my teeth."

Then he twisted around to the guard behind him. "You watch this guy. Last time he came to see me in jail, I had to take my meals through a straw for months." He wheezed a laugh. "This is the guy that should be in here, *not me.* Anyway, you're lookin' fit, Nicky. Playin' any golf? Retirement looks like it agrees with you."

"They let me come back, Dom, just for a day." I smiled thinly. "To deliver some news."

"News, huh? Good, I don't get much news in here. Jeez, Nick, they got some special downward career spiral planned out for you. You're a messenger boy now. Anyway, I'm glad you're here. I like the company. It's just that, you look a little peaked, eh? Must be that kid, huh? Tell me, how're you sleeping these days?"

I balled my fists tightly. I knew he was trying to make me react again. But this time I just let him go. "I'm going to be sleeping just fine, Dom."

"And how's that gal doing? You know, the pretty one who was on that bus. I heard she pulled through. I tried to send a little money to some kind of fund." He shrugged. "But my lawyer told me that when they heard it was from me, they sent the check back. Imagine. And for once I was just trying to do something nice. How's that for sour apples?

"Anyway, Mr. Messenger Boy, I'm doing all the talking. What kind of news you got for me? I'm all ears."

"We thought you'd want to know. The government's going to be adding two new indictments against you."

"Two *more?*" He sighed theatrically. "Who can keep track?"

"These you will, Dom. They're for the murders of Special Agents Manny Oliva and Ed Sinclair."

Cavello furrowed his brow. "I'm trying to think, do I know them?"

"We have the murder weapon, Dom. A couple of clammers uncovered it. After all these months, there it was, buried in the sand. Ballistics confirmed it. It's the gun that killed the two agents. You're going down for it, Dom. It's a match."

The jocular grin slowly started to fade from Cavello's face, replaced by a look of serious concern. This was a capital offense, and the murder weapon sealed it. "Clammers, huh?

Imagine that. You look like you won the lottery, Pellisante. You wanna let me in on the joke?"

"The joke is I'm going to see you at trial next week, you piece of shit. And here's some other news. It's going to take place at Fort Dix army base in New Jersey. The trial will be closed to the public. Totally secure.

"The jury will be secret and sequestered on the base. This time, you won't be able to get to anyone. We've got you, Dom. U.S. Attorney Goldenberger is waiting outside with the indictments now."

It was my turn to smile. A smile I'd waited more than two years to give him. "How's that for sour apples, Dom?"

Cavello just stared back at me. He scratched his chin. "An army base, huh? Fort Dix. Isn't that where all the explosives are, Nicky boy? Could be a real blast!"

Chapter 52

RICHARD NORDESHENKO stepped up to the immigration booth marked Visitors at JFK. He pushed his passport and visa through the slot.

"Kollich." The black, heavyset immigration agent leafed through his documents. He typed in the name. "Can I ask you to please place your index finger on the pad?"

Nordeshenko complied. He wasn't worried. This time he was Estonian. His name was Stephan Kollich. Pharmaceuticals. As the agent went through his passport, he would find that the travel-weary businessman had been to the United States many times.

The past five months had been trying ones for Nordeshenko. Pavel had been sick. At first it was thought to be the flu. Then it was diagnosed as diabetes, type one. After months of treatment, they finally had it under control. Then Nordeshenko's leg began to worsen. His old Chechen wound, the shrapnel finally taking its toll. These long trips killed him. He shifted uncomfortably. He even had to wear special shoes.

Now he had to do this Cavello job all over again. And he'd done so well the first time.

"Business or pleasure, Mr. Kollich?" the immigration officer asked, double-checking the face in the documents against Nordeshenko's.

"Business is my pleasure," Nordeshenko replied. The officer smiled.

This time it promised to be messy. He would have to put himself on the line, use all the skills he had learned. He already had his plan in motion. Reichardt, the South African, was already here in New York.

Preparation was Nordeshenko's trademark — what he had made his reputation on. And never once had he taken a job that he did not complete.

The immigration agent picked up his stamp. "How long will you be staying in the United States, Mr. Kollich?"

"Only a few days." That was the one thing he would say that was definitely not a lie.

The agent stamped his passport. He folded the documents together and pushed them back through the slot with a nod.

"Welcome to the United States, Mr. Kollich."

Chapter 53

"I'VE GOT NEWS," I said to Andie DeGrasse over the phone.

I wanted to tell her about my visit to Cavello, the new indictments. I wanted to keep the hope alive that if we'd found something on Manny and Ed after all this time, there had to be something out there on the bus explosion. At least that's how I was rationalizing it. The truth was, I'd been thinking about her a lot over the past few days. The truth was, I wanted to see her again.

"You like paella, Pellisante?" asked Andie after I'd given her my news.

"I like paella, sure," I said. On weekends with Ellen, I wasn't above rolling up my sleeves and putting dinner together myself. "In fact, I'd go to heaven for a good paella."

"Then how does tomorrow sound? Around seven? I want to hear about your meeting with Cavello blow by blow."

"Tomorrow sounds good," I said, surprised at the dinner invitation.

"And, Pellisante," Andie said, "prepare to die and go to heaven. My paella's that good."

I hung up, and couldn't stop the smile that was creeping over my face. The first one in quite some time, actually.

Chapter 54

THAT NIGHT I COULDN'T SLEEP. Part of it was Andie, I know. Part was the exhilaration of seeing Cavello out in Marion.

For so long I was sure he was going to get away with the murders of my two close friends. Today had changed all that. On the jet back from Marion I had called Manny's and Ed's wives. I told them that they would see the bastard finally put on trial for the murders of their husbands.

I was wired — awakened! For the first time in months. I was free from the guilt and shame I'd been trapped in since the jury stepped on that bus. It's out there, I told myself, a connection to the explosion. I just had to think outside the box.

That's when it hit me. It was as if the alarm clock had gone off — my brain a little bleary from *ER* reruns at

2:00 a.m. I leaped out of bed and headed into my office, un-stacking one of those towers of FBI documents piled high on my desk.

You're looking in the wrong place, Nick.

The IED. The improvised explosive device. The bomb. That was the key.

I yanked out the FBI forensic report on the explosives. I pretty much had the damn thing memorized by then anyway. The van had been packed with more than thirty pounds of C-4. Enough to do the job ten times over. Getting their hands on that much plastic wasn't like shopping for dry tarp at the local hardware store. *You just have to think of it as antiterror, Nick. Not anticrime.*

My C-10 buddies had gone over every turncoat and in-former on the list, and couldn't scare up a lead pointing to the kind of people Cavello might normally call on for a job like this. It needed coordination much more sophisticated than anything he'd tried before. The technology had first been used by the Chechens.

Why not the Russian mob?

Somewhere in this pile, my Homeland Security contacts had given me books of known bad guys who were thought to be in the country at the time of the bombing.

So I started over again. Leafing through pages of blank faces and names. Andie claimed she'd seen a man with long blond hair under his cap, running away. So why not? What if the hit was set up by the Russian mob?

Sergei Ogilov was still the Boss of Bosses in Brighton

Beach. He wasn't exactly a golfing buddy of mine — I'd put a number of his men away, or had them deported. But he'd probably talk to me.

A long shot maybe, but sometimes they come in.

Like Dominic Cavello's gun had washed to shore.

Chapter 55

MONICA ANN ROMANO was in the middle of the best sex she'd ever had. Not that the list of her lovers was very long. It certainly wasn't. The man she'd met while having an after-work drink with friends was taking her from behind. He was very good, from her perspective anyway. Not like the boring accountants and law clerks she'd been with before, who only lasted a couple of minutes and were as nervous and inexperienced as she was.

"How's that, luv?" he said. "Is it good for you? Does it feel okay?"

"Oh, yes," Monica said, panting. Did she even have to answer? She felt herself about to come. This was the third time.

For far too long Monica had come home from work, made dinner for her sick mother, and slumped into the den with her to watch TV. She was thirty-eight years old. She knew she had put on weight and that no one really looked at her anymore. Until this chance meeting, she had pretty much given up on the idea of ever finding somebody.

And then — *Karl.*

She still found it hard to believe someone so good-looking and well-traveled had come on to her. That in the crowd of attractive female lawyers and legal aides, this tall, blond European with the sexy accent had picked her out. He said he was Dutch, but she didn't really care where he came from. The only thing that mattered was where he was now, about eight inches inside her.

Karl finally rolled onto his back, breathing hard, his body slick with sweat. He reached for her hand. He pulled her close and lifted the hair away from her face. "How was that? Good for you, I hope?"

"Perfect." Monica sighed. "I'd say I'd like to volunteer you for a few friends at the office, but I don't want to share you with anyone."

"Don't want to share me?" He grinned. "You selfish little siren. You know what I say to that?"

"What?" Monica smiled. "You don't want to share me either?"

"I say *this!*"

All of a sudden, he dug his thumb deep into her throat. The spasm of shock and pain straightened her spine. The pain was unbearable.

Karl pulled her right off the bed. Monica's eyes were jumping out of their sockets. *Stop, please, you're hurting me,* she tried to say, but all that came out was an awful garbled sound.

She tried to pull away from him. His grip was immovable. *Why are you doing this?*

"You know what I say to you, Monica?" He brushed back his long blond hair. "I say, I'm glad you liked it, Monica. All our fun and games so far. But now it's your turn to do something for me. Something a little more serious. Something . . . more pleasurable."

Chapter 56

"YOU WORK at the federal courthouse?"

He still had his strong fingers dug into her throat. Monica could barely suck enough air into her lungs to breathe. "Yes." She managed a single word.

"Good answer." Karl nodded. He relaxed his grip a little. "You've been there awhile now, yes? I bet you know everybody. All the other fat cows? All the security personnel?" His fingers squeezed, and Monica's eyes widened, tears streaming down her cheeks. "You *do* know them, don't you, Monica?"

She nodded, her lungs about to explode. *Yes, she knew them.* She saw them every morning and afternoon. One of them, Pablo, always kidded her because she liked Mike Piazza and the Mets, and so did he.

"Good girl," Karl said again, allowing her to take a needed gulp of air. "People trust you, don't they, Monica? You never miss a day at work. You take care of your mother in your little house in Queens. It must be lonely coming home every day, making her din-din, checking her oxygen. Taking the poor woman to the doctor."

Why was he saying this? How did he know everything about her?

With his free hand, Karl reached into the drawer of the bed table and removed something. *What?*

A photograph! He flipped it in front of Monica's eyes. An alarm bell went off in her. It was her mother! Outside their home in Queens. Monica was helping her down the stairs in her walker. What was going on?

"Emphysema?" Karl nodded sympathetically. "Poor lady, barely able to breathe. What a shame, if she had no one to take care of her." His thumb dug into her throat again. Shock waves ran down her spine.

"What do you want from me?" Monica gagged, feeling as if her chest was about to explode.

"You work in the courthouse." His blue eyes gleamed. "I need to get something inside. This will be easy for you. As you Americans say — a piece of cake!"

Suddenly Monica saw what this was about. What a ridiculous fool she'd been to even think he was interested in her. "I can't. There's security."

"Of course there's security." Karl smiled. He clamped his fingers on her throat again. "That's why we have you, Monica."

Chapter 57

ANDIE LOOKED NOTHING short of terrific as she opened her apartment door for me. She had on a zippered red sweater and a pair of faded jeans. Her hair was tied back in a brooch, with a few loose curls dangling down her cheeks. Her eyes were dazzling — and looked pleased to see me. I felt the same way about her.

"Smells like I remember," I said, inhaling a whiff of shellfish with tomatoes and saffron. The paella that was going to take me to heaven.

"At least I won't have to catch you sneaking around outside," Andie said with a smile.

"How about *stakeout*? That sounds a little better," I said, holding out a Spanish Rioja.

"You're staking *me* out? Why?"

"Well, maybe that's what I'm here to talk about."

"Do tell," said Andie, batting her eyelashes and grinning.

I'm sure I just stood there for a second, recalling how she had looked to me in the jury box during the trial, with that crazy T-shirt on, before any of this happened. Our eyes had met a few times back then. I thought we were both aware of it. There had definitely been one or two averted stares.

"I have some appetizers under the broiler. Make yourself at home."

I stepped into the small, nicely decorated living room as Andie ducked back into the kitchen. She had a yellow paisley fabric couch and a coffee table with *Architectural Digest* and *InStyle* on it. A creased paperback, *The Other Boleyn Girl*. I recognized the jazz she had on. Coltrane. I went over to the bookshelf and picked up the CD. *A Love Supreme*.

"Nice," I said. "I used to play a little sax. *Long* time ago."

"What?" she called from the kitchen. "Like in the fifties?"

I came over and took a seat at the counter. "Very funny."

She slid a platter of cheese puffs and empanadas across the counter. "Here, I went all out."

I grabbed a cheese puff with a toothpick. "Tasty." She poured me a glass of Pinot Grigio from an open bottle and sat across from me.

She had a fresh, blossomy scent — lavender or apricot or something. Whatever this was — dinner, a date, just bringing her up to speed on Cavello — I was already enjoying it more than I thought I should.

She smiled. "So, uh, this *is* just a little bit awkward, isn't it?"

"I left the car running downstairs, just in case."

"In case it got weird?"

"In case I didn't like your paella."

Andie laughed. "Bring it on," she said, and tilted her glass. "So I guess this is good news, right?"

"That's right." We clinked glasses. "Cavello is going down this time." Suddenly, talking about my meeting with the gangster didn't exactly seem like the thing to do. All we ever had between us was that awful trial. There was a lull. We both took another sip of wine. Andie smiled and let me off the hook.

"We don't have to talk about it. We can talk about your class. Or what's going on in Iraq. Or, God forbid, the Yankees."

Over dinner, I finally told her more about my meeting with Cavello. I think it made her feel good, knowing the bastard would have to account for something. And the paella was a ten, just the way I liked it.

Afterward, I helped her clean up, stacking dishes in the sink until she made me stop, insisting she'd finish the rest later. She put on a pot of coffee.

Andie's back was to me. We were talking about her acting, when I noticed a photo on the counter. Her and her son. She had her arm wrapped around his neck, smiles everywhere. Love. They looked like the happiest mother and son.

When I looked up, Andie was facing me. "Don't take offense, Nick. But why do you keep coming around here? What is it you want to say?"

I was at a loss. "I don't know."

"You want to say it hurts? I know it hurts." Her eyes were glistening now. "You want to say you wish you could've done something?"

"I don't know what I want to say, Andie. But I know I wanted to come and see you."

And I wanted to just reach out and hold her, too. I don't think I ever wanted to take someone in my arms as much as I wanted her. And I think, maybe, she wanted it, too. She was just leaning there, palms against the counter.

Finally, Andie smiled. "Car's still running, huh?"

I nodded. In the past minute or so, the temperature had risen about a hundred degrees in the kitchen. "Don't take this wrong, but I think I'm gonna pass on that coffee."

"Hey." Andie sighed. "Whatever."

I found my jacket on the chair where I'd left it, and Andie walked me to the door. "Everything was great," I said, "as advertised." I took her hand and held it for a second.

"It's because I feel good around you. That's why I came. You make me laugh. No one's made me laugh in months."

"You know, you've got a nice smile, Nick, when you let it out. Anyone ever tell you that?"

I turned to leave. "Not in a while."

She closed the door behind me. There was a part of me that wanted to say, *screw it, Nick,* and turn around. And I knew if I did, she would still be there. I could almost feel her standing on the other side of the door.

Then I heard Andie's voice. "What's done is done, Nick. You can't make the world come out right just because you want it that way."

I turned and pressed my palm against the door. "I can try."

Chapter 58

RICHARD NORDESHENKO kept his face still as he squeezed his hole cards up from the table. A pair of threes. The player across from him, in a black shirt and cashmere jacket, and with an attractive male companion looking over his shoulder, tossed $2,000 into the pot. Another player after him raised.

Nordeshenko decided to play. He was ahead tonight. Decidedly. Tomorrow his work began. He would make this his last hand, win or lose.

The dealer flipped over three cards: a two, a nine of clubs, and a four. No improvement, it would seem — for anyone. Cashmere Blazer winked to his boyfriend. He'd been pushing pots all night. "Four thousand." Nordeshenko read him for four clubs, trying to make his flush.

To his surprise, the other player behind him raised, too. He was heavyset and quiet, wore dark shades, hard to read.

Despite his large hands he nimbly shuffled his chips. "Four thousand more," he said, leveling off two stacks of black chips into the pot.

The right bet, Nordeshenko thought. Drive the third player out — in this case, him. But Nordeshenko wasn't going to be driven out. He had a feeling. Things had been going his way all night. "I'm in." He stacked a tower of eight black chips and pushed them in.

The dealer flipped over another four. Now there was a pair on the board. The guy chasing the flush checked. The heavyset player was betting now. Another four thousand. Nordeshenko raised him. To his surprise, Cashmere Blazer stayed along.

Now there was more than $40,000 in the pot.

The dealer flipped over the last card. The six of spades. Nordeshenko couldn't see how it helped anyone, but he recalled when he'd been in this exact spot before. His adrenaline was racing.

The man with the boyfriend puffed out his cheeks. "Eight thousand!" The few spectators murmured. What the hell was he doing? He'd been pumping the pot all night. Now he was throwing good money after bad.

The heavyset player shuffled his chips. Nordeshenko thought maybe he did have a pair in the hole. A *higher* pair. Clearly, he read his hand for the best at the table. "Eight thousand." He nodded, making two even stacks of eight black chips. "And eight more."

Now the murmurs became gasps. Nordeshenko made a steeple with his fingers in front of his mouth, then let out a deep breath. Clearly, the heavyset man expected him to fold. And 90 percent of the time, he would've done just that. He was up enough. Why give everything back?

But tonight, he felt this power. Soon he'd put his life on the line. All the money in the world might be meaningless then. That gave him freedom. Besides, he was almost certain he had read the table perfectly.

"Shall we make it interesting?" he asked. "Here is your eight thousand." He looked at Cashmere Blazer. "And yours," he said, nodding to the man in shades, evening out a second column of black chips. Then he made a show of doubling the entire stack. "And sixteen thousand more."

This time there wasn't a gasp — only a hush. A hundred thousand dollars sat in the center of the table!

Nerves were what separated you under fire. Nerves, and the ability to read one thing. Smell it. That's what made him the best at what he did. Nordeshenko stared at the man in shades. *Indecision? Fear?*

Cashmere Blazer sagged back, clearly feeling like an idiot. Better to toss in his cards now without showing them and not be thought a total fool. "Adios," he said.

'You're bluffing," the heavyset guy said, swallowing, his eyes X-raying Nordeshenko through his shades.

Nordeshenko shrugged. "Play and see." He was sure all the man had to do was push in the balance of his chips and he would take the hand.

"Yours." He grunted, flipping his cards upright. A pair of sixes.

Nordeshenko flipped over his lower pair. "You were right."

Shouts went up. The dealer pushed the mountain of chips his way. He had won more than $70,000!

Moreover, he had read every indication, every mannerism, correctly. That was a good sign. For tomorrow.

Tomorrow was when the real game began.

Chapter 59

AT 10:00 A.M., Dominic Cavello was brought handcuffed into Judge Robert Barnett's courtroom.

Four U.S. marshals surrounded him. Several others were spread out at intervals along the perimeter of the room. This was a pretrial hearing, back at Foley Square. Cavello's lawyers had made a motion to suppress all evidence related to the murders of Manny Oliva and Ed Sinclair. They wanted a hearing to determine whether the evidence should be allowed, but I knew the judge would see their request for what it was — a stalling tactic.

Cavello acted his usual cocky self as he was led into the spacious room. He chirped hello to Joel Goldenberger across the way — asked how he was doing, along with the wife and kids. He made a comment to one of the guards about the Mets, how they'd finally put a real team together this year. When he spotted me in the rear, he winked, as though we were old friends. He conveyed the image of a guy about to beat some minor traffic violation, not a person on leave from the isolation unit at Marion who might very well be headed back there for the rest of his life.

The door to the courtroom opened. Judge Barnett stepped in. Barnett was supposed to be a no-nonsense guy. He had been an offensive lineman while at Syracuse and served as a fighter pilot in Vietnam. He didn't give a shit about the press, or free access, or Cavello's lawyers' theatrics. The judge had presided over a couple of Homeland Security cases after 9/11 and imposed the maximum sentence permitted by law on every one. We couldn't have gotten a better judge for this.

He quickly signaled everybody to sit down. "I've studied the motions," he said, adjusting thick black reading glasses, "and I find no merit in the defense's motion to delay this trial any longer. *Mr. Cavello.*"

"Your Honor." The defendant stood up slowly, showing no reaction to the decision.

"You'll be answering the United States government's charges beginning Monday morning, ten a.m. You are entitled, by law, to be present at the selection of your own jury, which will take place in this courtroom. But these proceedings will be conducted totally in secret. No names will be divulged once they are selected. At that point they will be transferred to the Fort Dix army base in New Jersey, where, as you already know, your trial will take place. You will be restrained there as well, as will the jury. The entire trial will be conducted behind closed doors.

"And, Mr. Cavello." The judge stared down at him sternly.

"Yes?"

"I'm warning you only once. Any disruptions — and I mean if you as much as tip over a glass of water unexpectedly — and you will be watching your own proceedings on Court TV. Is that understood?"

"I wouldn't dream of it, Your Honor," Cavello said.

"I didn't ask you that, Mr. Cavello." The judge's voice stiffened. "I asked you if it was understood."

"Of course." Cavello bowed respectfully. "Perfectly, Your Honor."

Chapter 60

THE TELEPHONE WAS RINGING, and Monica Ann Romano froze where she was sitting on the living room couch. She didn't want to answer it.

She already knew who it was. Who else would be calling this late on a Sunday night? She had a crazy thought that maybe if she ignored the ring, he would go away. Everything would go back to how it had been before she had the best sex of her life.

She just sat looking at the phone, letting it ring.

"Would you answer it, please!" She and her mother were watching TV, and the ringing was blocking out the sound.

Finally Monica stood up and wrapped the cord out into the hallway. She noticed her hands shaking. "Hullo."

"Hello, luv." The voice on the other end made her blood freeze.

How had she ever gotten herself into this mess? How had

she been so pathetically stupid as to think he'd be interested in her? She should go to the police. She should hang up on him and call them now. They would understand; they would still trust her at her job. And if it wasn't for her mother, she had told herself over and over, she would. *She would!*

"What do you want?" she answered curtly.

"You used to like hearing my voice, Monica," the caller said. "I'm feeling hurt. What do I want? I want the same thing you do, Monica. I want you and your mother to live a long, healthy life."

"Don't play with me," Monica spat out. "Just tell me what you want me to do."

"All right," he said. He seemed to be enjoying himself. "How about we meet for coffee tomorrow morning before you go to work? The café right across the square, where we met that other time. Say, eight thirty sharp. I'll fill you in on what happens from there."

"This is *it*," Monica said, her stomach knotting. "You promise, just this one thing."

"Be a good little girl, and you'll never hear my voice again. But *Monica*," Karl said in the sort of voice you'd use to reprove a child, "don't get any ideas. I'll do what I said I would. I promise. In fact, if I wasn't so trusting you'll be a good girl, I could do it right now. Come back in the living room. *Come.*"

Monica ran back into the room where her mother was watching TV.

A light shone on the window. Headlights. Then a car horn, three sharp blasts. She began to shake so hard she thought she could hear every bone in her body rattle.

Chapter 61

THAT MONDAY MORNING was the tightest security I'd ever seen for a trial. *Godfather, Part II.*

It was more like a show of force by law enforcement. Dozens of cops, some in armor and riot gear, holding automatic weapons, manned barricades all over Foley Square. The line of prospective jurors stretched out the door, with policemen going up and down, checking IDs, opening bags, leading bomb-sniffing dogs. About a dozen TV vans were lined up and down Worth Street.

Everything was by the book, exactly how I would have done it. Still, with several trials running concurrently, all the lawyers, witnesses, jurors, and staff, there were a thousand things that could go wrong.

Instinctively, I checked the courthouse security room, which was situated on the ground floor. Security staffers were watching monitors of all floors. Entrances, elevators, the basement garage, and the corridor where Cavello was to be transferred to and from the Manhattan County Jail. I tried to tell myself that nothing was going to happen, that everything was going to go off as planned.

I was headed back up to the courtroom, passing by the lobby, when I heard my name shouted. "Nick! Nick!"

It was Andie, restrained by two guards. She was waving. "Nick, they won't let me in!"

I walked over to the entrance. "It's okay," I said to the guard. I flashed my ID. "I'll take responsibility. She's with me."

I pulled her through the jostling crowd. "You were right. I had to be here, Nick. I couldn't stay away. For Jarrod, if not me."

"You don't have to explain, Andie. Just come."

I led her into one of the elevators, pushed the button for the eighth floor. There were a few others on board — a couple of attorneys, a court stenographer. The ride seemed interminable. I squeezed her hand. "Hmmm," she said. Just that.

When the doors finally opened on eight, I pulled Andie to the side and waited for the other people to clear. Then I gave her the hug I wanted to give her the other night. I almost kissed her, too. It took guts to be here. To show her face. But I could feel her heart beating against me. "It's okay, Andie. I'm glad you're here."

I showed my ID to a guard stationed outside the courtroom and escorted her inside. The room was still nearly empty. A couple of marshals chatting, a young assistant district attorney laying out jury forms along the lawyers' row.

Andie looked anxious suddenly. "Now that I'm here, I don't know if I can do this."

"We'll stay over here," I said, placing her in the back row of the gallery. "When he comes in, we'll be together. Maybe we'll wave."

"Yeah, or give him the finger."

I squeezed her hand. "Nothing bad is going to happen. The evidence is even more solid than before. He's gonna arrive soon, and we're going to choose twelve people. Then we're going to put him away until the day he dies."

Chapter 62

MONICA ANN ROMANO suspected what was in the small bundle she was carrying, and it made her want to throw up.

She had taken it from the man she once trusted. Now she walked nervously across the square, showing her federal ID and passing by the guarded police barricades to the courthouse. It was the most nerve-racking thing she had ever done in her life. By a lot.

Finally, she stood in the courthouse employee line. Every bag was being opened. Even the lawyers' and their staffs'. Monica knew who was in the courthouse that day: Dominic Cavello.

"Big doings today, hon," chirped Mike, a lobby guard with a large handlebar mustache, who pulled her through the maze of people and over to the authorized personnel line.

"Uh-huh." Monica nodded nervously. She smiled hello to a couple of familiar faces.

The guy in front of her, a lawyer with a beard and long hair, opened his case. Monica was next. Pablo, who always teased her about the Mets, caught her eye and smiled. Her heart was beating savagely. She felt the weight of the bundle pressing down on her. What if they looked inside?

The lawyer in front of her closed his case, passing through. Now it was just her and Pablo. *Could he hear her heart pounding?* Holding her breath, Monica stepped into the gate.

"How's the weekend, hon?" The guard took a perfunctory peek inside her handbag. "You catch those Mets?"

"Sure I did." Monica nodded, closing her eyes, expecting a loud beep to go off. *Her life to be over.*

It didn't. Nothing happened. She stepped through. Just like every other day. A tremor of relief went through her. *Thank God.*

"See you at lunch," Pablo said. She started to hurry away. Then she heard him call, "Hey, Monica."

Monica Ann Romano froze, and she turned around slowly.

The guard flashed her a wink. "I like your hat."

Chapter 63

THE LAWYERS WERE IN the courtroom. Cavello, too. Judge Barnett gazed out at the nervous group of prospective jurors who had cautiously filed in. "I doubt there's a person in this room who doesn't know why we're here," he said.

Each juror had been given a number. They all took a seat. Every eye seemed to be glancing at the gaunt, gray-haired man who sat with his legs crossed in front of them. Then they looked away, as if afraid to let their eyes linger too long. *That's Cavello,* their faces said.

I turned back to Andie, who only moments before had watched as the bastard was led in. Cavello's handcuffs were removed. He took a look around the courtroom. Cavello seemed to find Andie immediately, as if he knew she would be there. He paused and gave her a slight, respectful nod.

But her gaze didn't waver. It seemed to be telling him, *You can't hurt me anymore.* She wasn't going to give him the thrill of seeing her look scared. She clenched her palms against the railing. Finally she looked away. When she lifted her eyes again, they landed on mine. She gave me a thin smile. *I'm okay; I'm good. He's going down.*

"I also doubt there's a person among you who truly wants to be here," Judge Barnett went on. "Some of you may feel you don't belong here. Some might even be afraid. But, be assured, if called, it is your legal and moral duty to serve on the trial. And twelve of you are *going* to serve — with six more as alternates. What is *my* duty is to remove whatever fear and discomfort many of you may be feeling, given the defendant's last trial.

"Therefore, your names and addresses, anything about your family or what you do, will not be released — not even to the members of this court. Those selected will spend the next six to eight weeks confined to the Fort Dix army base in New Jersey, where this trial will take place.

"I know no one is eager to give up their lives and remain separated from family and loved ones for that amount of time. But the defendant must be tried — that is all our duties. A jury will be decided upon — and he *will* be tried. Anyone who refuses to do his or her duty will be held in contempt of court."

The judge nodded to the clerk. "Now, is there anyone in this room who, due to some commitment or handicap, feels he or she cannot faithfully execute this duty?"

Virtually every hand in the room shot into the air at once.

A ripple of muffled laughter snaked around the courtroom. Even Cavello looked at the show of hands and smiled.

One by one, jurors were called up to the bench. Single mothers. Small-business owners. People pleading that they had paid for vacations or were holding doctors' notes. A couple of lawyers argued they should be excused.

But Judge Barnett didn't buckle. He excused a handful, and they left the courtroom, discreetly pumping a fist or grinning widely. Others glumly went back to their seats.

Finally, about a hundred and fifty people remained, most looking not very pleased.

Cavello never even glanced at them. He kept drumming his fingers against the table, staring straight ahead. I kept thinking of the words he had uttered to me as they pulled me away from his jail cell the day of the juror bus blast.

Me, I'm gonna sleep like a baby tonight. . . . First day in a month I don't have to worry about a trial.

"Mr. Goldenberger, Mr. Kaskel," the judge addressed the attorneys, "I'm sure you have some questions you'd like to put to these good people."

Chapter 64

RICHARD NORDESHENKO had filed unnoticed into the courthouse. It hadn't been difficult to obtain a standard juror's notice from Reichardt, then doctor the date and name to fit his need. He got in line with the other dour-looking jurors. Then, like every job he had ever done, he walked in through the front door.

For a while, Nordeshenko sat eyeing a magazine in the crowded jury room, listening to people's numbers being called. Many of them were nervously muttering what-ifs about getting selected for the Cavello trial. Everyone he listened to seemed to feel they had a foolproof excuse.

Nordeshenko quietly chuckled to himself. *None of them would need an excuse.*

At 10:15 a.m. he checked his watch. Nezzi would be driving the stolen catering van into the underground garage.

Nezzi was the best in the world at this. Still, you never knew what could happen on a job, especially one as complex as this.

Last night, Nordeshenko had written a long letter to his wife and son. He had left it in his hotel room, in the event he did not make it back.

In the letter he admitted he was not exactly the good man they may have always thought he was, and that the things they may be hearing about him were probably true. He wrote that it saddened him that he had had to hide so much from them over the years. But in each life, he added, one is never all bad or all good. What was good about his life was the two of them. He wrote that he loved them both very much, and trying to close with a joke, he told his son that he too had grown to prefer poker over chess.

He signed the letter, *from your loving husband and father, Kolya Remlikov.*

Nordeshenko's real name.

A name neither of them knew.

At precisely 11:40 a.m., Nordeshenko put down his magazine and made his way outside and up to the third floor. It was mostly court and administrative offices. He found the men's bathroom along the elevator bank and ducked inside. A heavyset black man with a large mole on his cheek was finishing up washing his hands. Nordeshenko ran the water, waiting for him to leave.

When the black man departed, Nordeshenko removed the top to the trash receptacle, dug his hand through the balled-up paper towels, and removed the carefully wrapped bundle that he knew was there. Just as Reichardt had said it would be.

Nordeshenko went into a stall and unwrapped the bundle: a Heckler and Koch 9mm pistol, his gun of choice. He checked the magazine and, seeing that it was fully loaded, tightly screwed on the suppressor.

He knew the judge was a stickler for regimen. He always let out his court a few minutes before 12:30 p.m. for lunch. The story went that no lawyer arguing before Barnett wanted to be in the middle of a key point around that time.

Only a few minutes more.

From his pocket, Nordeshenko took out a tiny cell phone. He had checked one at security, just like everyone else, but kept the second hidden away. *No messages.* That meant Nezzi was gone and everything was set now.

He checked the code that would get things started. All that was left to do was to hit Send.

Nordeshenko left the stall and took a last look at himself in the mirror. His heartbeat started to quicken. *Remi, be calm. You know how people will react. You know human nature better than anyone. The element of surprise is with you. Just like it has a dozen times before, everything will go your way.*

With his newly dyed hair, the fake beard, and glasses, the thought passed through him that in the next few minutes he might die as he always feared: *unrecognized.* With someone else's name. The prints would have to be matched, and even then, the trail was blank. Just a sergeant in the Russian army, a deserter. It might be weeks, months, before anyone even knew he was dead.

Of course, and Nordeshenko smiled to himself at this, he might live, too. He cocked the Heckler and stuffed it inside his pocket.

It was like pushing all your money into the center of the table. In this case, a 2.5-million-dollar fee.

You never knew for sure until you turned over the last card.

Chapter 65

DOMINIC CAVELLO was eyeing the courtroom clock too, trying to block out the idle chatter, which he knew, in just moments, would have very little to do with the rest of his life. That was when Judge Barnett would lean into the microphone, no matter who was speaking, and ask if this was a good time to take a break.

And then, as if on cue, at 12:24 p.m. the judge cut in on the prosecutor's questioning. "Mr. Goldenberger . . ."

Cavello felt his pulse start to race. *Sayonara*, he snickered. *Playtime's over. Little Dom here is ready to go home.*

The judge instructed the prospective jurors to reconvene at exactly two o'clock. Slowly, the jury pool began to file out. "Marshals, you may take possession of the defendant now."

Cavello stood up. He didn't give a shit about what was going to happen next. In fact, he'd make their job easy. "Okay, fellas." The same two who had brought him in this morning were taking him back to jail. The broad-shouldered guy with the thick mustache held out the cuffs. "Sorry, Dom."

Cavello put out his wrists. "Not a problem, Eddie-boy. I'm all yours."

He knew their names. He knew a half dozen little things about them. The black guy had been a tank commander in Desert Storm. The one with the bushy mustache had a son who was being recruited by Wisconsin to play football. He snapped the shackles tightly over Cavello's wrists.

"Jeez, guys, can't you give an honest citizen a break? Hey, Hy," he called out to his attorney, "you guys have a nice big steak on me. See you back here at two."

The marshals led him out the side entrance to the elevator in the hall, on the way back to his prison cell, a couple of blocks away. He'd made the trip so many times, he could probably do it in his sleep if he had to.

"You know what the worst thing is about spending the rest of your life in jail?" He winked to the marshal with the mustache as they headed out into the hall. "The food! Especially at that pigsty, Marion. You know the only thing that keeps you going out there?" He nudged him with an elbow. "The death sentence, that's what. The lethal injection." Cavello laughed. "That's the only thing that gives you any hope!"

A third guard, with a radio in one hand, was holding the doors open when they got to the elevator. He barked into the radio, "They're on their way." Eddie and the black guy escorted him inside.

The black marshal pushed U, for *underground*. He knew that if the basement was selected, the elevator wouldn't stop at any other floor, unless it was overridden from inside. The doors closed.

Cavello turned to the black marshal, who never talked very much. "You like pizza, Bo? Black people eat pizza, don't they?"

"Yeah, I like pizza, Dom," the black guard growled.

"Sure, all cops like pizza." Cavello sighed. "Hey, you know what we should do? Screw this jail thing. How 'bout we ditch this baby at the lobby and take a spin out to the old neighborhood in Brooklyn for an hour or two? I'll show you what a real Italian meal is. C'mon, I'll have us all back by two. They won't even know we were gone."

He nudged Eddie as the elevator descended, watching the floor lights start to go down.

"That would be a pisser, wouldn't it, Eddie-boy? The whole free world is out looking for us — and we're just sitting at Pritzie's having a veal and peppers and a beer. So whaddya say?"

The burly marshal grinned. "Sounds like a plan, Dom."

"That's what it sounds like to me, too," Cavello said, following the lights of the floor panel as the elevator descended. "A plan."

Chapter 66

ANDIE WAS WAITING for me out in the hallway. She said that she'd seen enough. She didn't have to be there anymore. I rode down the elevator with her and a couple of prospective jurors to the lobby. There was a little awkwardness between us there. I told her how brave I thought she was to come. She gave me a quick kiss on the cheek.

"Thank you, Nick. It was a good idea."

On my way upstairs, I stuck my head inside the security room for a check on Cavello. He was headed down to the basement now. I watched over the shoulder of one of the agents as Cavello moved in front of the elevator, chatting with his guards. Everything was under control. The security captain was in close contact with all points along the exit route. "The subject's in motion," he reported in.

Suddenly, the ground beneath us rocked. It was like an earthquake! Coffee cups, pens, clipboards clattered to the floor.

"Jesus, something's happened," one of the agents monitoring the screens shouted and pointed. "In the garage! There's been an explosion down there! Holy shit!"

We crowded close to the monitor and watched what happened next in shock. Billowing gray smoke began to block the screen. Then everything went completely black.

A radio report crackled in from one of the units stationed underground. "There's been an explosion down here. The garage is on fire. There may be casualties. I can't make much out. Too much smoke, smoke everywhere."

The captain seized a microphone. "This is Meachem. We have a situation in the garage! Some kind of explosive device has been detonated. I want SWAT, backup, and medical units down there pronto. And I want to know what the hell's going on."

I didn't have to look at the screen. I *knew* what was going on.

The screens kept flashing back and forth to different monitors in the garage, trying to locate a clear view of what was taking place. I grabbed Meachem by the shoulder. "Captain, this isn't about the garage. It's about Cavello! Get all agents on alert. He's on his way down there now!"

I rushed back to the other end of the console and checked the elevator scene.

Jesus, no!

My eyes bulged in horror. I couldn't believe what I was seeing — only I knew it was happening again.

I ran to the door.

Chapter 67

CAVELLO WAS STILL in the elevator, kibitzing with the guards, joking for all he was worth. His eyes angled toward the control panel. The descending lights flashed: 7, 6, 5.

Now!

In that instant he lunged toward the panel, pressing his thumb solidly onto the heat-sensitive square for the third floor.

"*What the hell?*" The elevator jerked to an unexpected stop. The door started to open. The black marshal reached out to rein in Cavello, powerfully pressing him up against the wall. Then someone stepped inside.

The marshal's jaw fell open. "What the —"

The first shot caught him between the eyes and hurled him against the paneled wall. He sank to the floor, leaving a dark-red smear.

The next two shots caught Eddie-boy in the chest. Two

plum-colored circles appeared on his white shirt. The guard released Cavello with a deep groan as he crumpled to the floor. He looked up at the shooter. "I've got kids."

"Sorry, Eddie-boy," Cavello said. Two more silenced thuds ripped into his chest, and the guard went still.

"Hurry," the Israeli snapped, pressing the button for the lobby, then tossing Cavello a pouch. "We don't have any time."

Inside the pouch, Cavello found a dark woman's wig and a raincoat. The Israeli plopped the wig on Cavello's head and draped the coat loosely over his shoulders, doing his best to conceal the fugitive's cuffed hands. He knew they only had seconds, no more, while attention was diverted by the explosion in the garage.

Cavello pressed down the wig. "Is everyone in place?"

"We had better hope so," Nordeshenko said, positioning himself behind Cavello in order to conceal his gun. "You're ready? This is no sure thing."

"Whatever happens," Cavello said, "it beats life in prison."

"Perhaps," said the Israeli.

The elevator doors opened again at the lobby. A couple of people were waiting to board.

"It's broken. Take another," Nordeshenko growled, pushing Cavello past them. Then he and the disguised mobster rushed down the long corridor toward a side entrance onto Worth Street.

Behind them, people had seen the bodies in the elevator. They were screaming. Nordeshenko never looked back. "*Hurry!* Or we both die here. I'm allergic to prisons."

It was about forty yards down the corridor to the security

station, but it seemed like more as they wove through by-standers, ignoring the shouts behind them. Nordeshenko spotted Reichardt and two of Cavello's men posing as press at the entrance. He turned up the collar of Cavello's raincoat and hurried toward them.

Fifteen yards more. That was all.

As they approached, a radio crackled. "Something's hap-pened!" one of the guards shouted. "Close it down, now!"

Reichardt removed a dark metallic object from under his jacket. Then everything went completely nuts. Shots rang out, automatic gunfire in the courthouse lobby. Two guards went down before they had a chance to get to their guns. The last one, a blond woman, fumbled frantically with her holster as Reichardt slammed her against the marble wall with a burst of automatic fire. She hit the floor dead.

Nordeshenko and Cavello were running as they reached the security station.

They heard a shout. "FBI! Everybody get down!"

Nordeshenko took a look and saw a figure at the end of the corridor, arms extended in shooting position, trying to get a shot off through the crowd. *Shit.* He pressed Cavello in front of him. A round whizzed past his face, ripping into the chest of one of Cavello's hoods. Reichardt returned the fire. The noise of the gunfire was deafening. People were scream-ing and scrambling for their lives.

Nordeshenko shielded Cavello with his own body. It was the job. He pushed through the doors. *Outside!*

It was chaos all around them. Cops were running toward the entrance to the underground garage down the block. The detonated bomb had worked well. A cloud of dark smoke rose into the sky.

A young cop came up to them, not sure what was going on. "We're hurt," Nordeshenko said to him. "Look." As the cop leaned closer, Nordeshenko stuck the muzzle of the Heckler into his chest and pulled the trigger. With a groan, the policeman sank to the sidewalk.

A black Bronco screeched to the curb in front of them. The back door was flung open, and Nordeshenko, Cavello, and Reichardt dove inside.

Nezzi was at the wheel. Without coming to a complete stop, the Bronco sped away.

A commercial truck pulled out directly behind them, then suddenly stopped in the street, blocking any pursuit.

At the corner the light was green. They shot onto St. James and drove up two blocks, through Chatham Square, then made a right on Catherine, in Chinatown. They made another quick right on Henry, then Nezzi pulled the Bronco into a vacant lot.

Nordeshenko leaped out, still shielding Cavello's body, and ripped open the sliding door of a blue minivan. He pushed the gangster in. Then he jumped behind the wheel. Reichardt and Nezzi got into a tan Acura parked across the street. The Israeli saluted them.

For the first time, Nordeshenko felt a cautious sense of optimism. No one was following them. No one was shooting either.

The two vehicles pulled away.

A block away, three police cars sped by, lights flashing.

They were going in the opposite direction. Nordeshenko let himself smile. One day they would hold a clinic on this escape.

"Are we free?" a voice from behind asked. Then Dominic Cavello lifted up his head.

"For the moment," Nordeshenko said. "Now all we have to worry about is getting *off* this island."

Chapter 68

I RAN OUT to the street and stood there — staring help-lessly as the black Bronco sped away. There was no way I could stop it. I watched it turn at the corner, melding into traffic, then disappear from sight.

Every muscle in my body seemed to shrink and collapse; I'd never felt more useless in my entire life. Two police cars started after them, having to navigate around some delivery truck blocking the street. But it was too late.

I ran back to the courthouse and flashed my ID at a startled cop, grabbing his radio. "This is Special Agent Nicholas Pellisante of the FBI. Dominic Cavello has escaped from the federal courthouse in Foley Square. He is traveling east on Worth in a black Bronco, unidentifiable plates, headed toward Chinatown. Suspects have fired shots. There are multiple casualties."

A dead patrolman lay crumpled on the pavement. He

looked no older than twenty-five. Stunned pedestrians were rushing out of the courthouse. Most had their hands to their faces. Trying to cover up the shock?

I rushed back through the doors and into the courthouse. EMS techs were already administering to one of the fallen guards. Meachem was there, the captain. He was ashen-faced. Some useless police chatter began to trickle in. I felt the urge to slam the radio up against the wall and watch it shatter.

I didn't know where to go, except back inside the security office. Special Agent Michael Doud was in there. He was in charge of the FBI's on-site security team, and he was already playing back video from the bloody scene in the elevator.

"I saw the getaway car," I told him. "Black Bronco. I couldn't see the plates. There are two security marshals down out front."

Doud took a deep breath. "I've got the mayor's office on the line. And the chief of police. There's an emergency order to block all tunnels and bridges out of Manhattan. Everything's on the highest crisis alert. They shouldn't be able to get off the island."

"Don't bet on it," I said, and gritted my teeth.

I sat down and slammed my fist against a nearby table in frustration. All of a sudden I felt a tremendous draining of strength. What the hell? I placed my hand against my ribs. The feeling was slick and warm.

Jesus, Nick.

I was bleeding like a stuck pig.

Chapter 69

DOUD'S EYES MET MINE. We both looked down at my blood dripping onto the floor.

"Sonovabitch," I said. Then I opened my jacket. There was a wide circle of blood seeping through my shirt.

"Get EMS in here, now!" Doud shouted to one of the security men.

"Good idea." I nodded, sagging back against the wall.

A shout came over the radio. "I think we've got a fix on them." It was the open line to the mayor's crisis center. A black Bronco had been spotted turning off Tenth Avenue, feeding into the entrance for the Lincoln Tunnel, heading to New Jersey.

"We've got the entrance covered," the voice from the crisis center declared. "Port Authority's got SWAT in place there."

Through the phone lines, we were able to patch in a video

feed from the crisis center. Above us, one of the monitors began showing a wide sweep from a camera overlooking the tunnel. The black Bronco was about tenth in line. "There it is!" All of a sudden the camera zoomed in tighter. The traffic was funneling into two lanes.

I held my side, but I wasn't going anywhere right now. I could make out the black Bronco. The same one? It sure looked like it.

"Suspect vehicle has Jersey plates. EVX-three-six-nine," a voice announced over the radio.

For a second I was caught up like everyone else, just hoping we had managed to land on the right vehicle. Then a thought flashed through my mind. I grabbed a microphone off the table.

"This is Special Agent Pellisante. These people likely have automatic weapons and *explosives*. The car could be booby-trapped. Cavello might not even be in there anymore. The SWAT teams should do their best to isolate the vehicle."

My wound was history now. I moved closer to the screen and watched the Port Authority team start circling in, surrounding the vehicle from a distance, letting others pass. It was a tricky assault. There were lots of innocent people around. Hundreds of them.

Black, helmeted figures began to creep into the wide-angled camera view. The Bronco was four rows from feeding into the tunnel entrance. I could see the police teams narrowing in, arms drawn. The Bronco's windows were tinted black. If someone in there was looking out, they had to see the assault force coming.

The Bronco inched up to the first row. A police car suddenly sped up, blocking the entrance to the tunnel.

SWAT personnel were all over the place, crouched low, closing in.

I could see exactly what was happening. The Bronco was surrounded by at least twenty heavily armed policemen.

The Bronco's front doors swung open. I stepped closer to the screen. "Be him," I said, balling my fists. "Be him."

People were coming out of the Bronco, hands in the air. A male dressed all in black. Then a woman, wearing a floppy hat. A small boy. The boy was crying; he grabbed the woman.

"Son of a bitch!" I heard someone say over the radio. The picture didn't need any words or captions, though.

It was the wrong car. We'd lost Dominic Cavello.

Chapter 70

I STAYED IN THE COURTHOUSE security room until the EMS people wouldn't let me be there any longer. A couple of young med techs did their best to treat me, but I wasn't going anywhere until I saw the videotape. The tape of the man in the elevator — the one who had sprung Cavello.

I watched it at least a dozen times.

He was medium height, not especially well built. I couldn't really tell if he was young or old. I looked for any distinguishing marks. He had a beard, which I figured for a fake. Short dark hair, glasses. But this guy knew precisely what he was doing. He never hesitated, not for a second. He was a pro, not just some hired gun. He caught us off guard, even with New York's finest and two dozen FBI agents all around the courthouse.

"Can you zoom in on the face for me?" I asked the security tech manning the video machine.

"Right." A touch of a button, and the camera panned in.

I stood up, moving myself closer to the screen. The film got grainy. It narrowed in to a close-up of the steely, professional eyes as the killer himself stepped on the elevator. Steady and businesslike, efficient. I burned those eyes into my mind. The security tech slowly advanced the film, frame by frame. Suddenly there were gunshots. The two marshals went down.

"Get this over the wires to the NYPD and the crisis control room," Mike Doud directed the techie. "I want this picture out to every bridge and tunnel and every cop on the street."

"It's a waste of time," I said, sagging back against the table. "He doesn't look like that anymore."

Doud snapped at me, obviously frustrated. "You got a better idea?"

"I might. Compare it to the film from Cavello's *first* trial. Go day by day if you have to. Eliminate the beard and the glasses. I'll bet he was there."

The medical people were literally dragging me away now. They had a van waiting. I looked up at the face on the screen one last time. I wanted to make sure I recognized it when I saw him again.

I was sure I was looking at the man who blew up the juror bus and murdered all those people.

Chapter 71

WHEN THE CALL CAME IN I was in the back of an EMS van, rushing me to Bellevue Hospital.

I was stripped to my waist and had an IV in my arm and EKG sensors attached to my chest. The sirens were blaring as we zigzagged through traffic up the lower East Side. I asked for the cell phone in my jacket.

"I just heard," Andie said. Her voice was cracking with disbelief and sadness. "Oh, God, Nick, I just saw it at a coffee shop. It's all over the news."

"I'm sorry, Andie." But I was more than sorry. How many times could I say those words to her?

"Goddamnit, Nick, every cop in New York was down there."

"I know." I sucked in a breath. One of the EMS people tried to take away the phone, but I brushed him aside. The flesh wound in my side wasn't hurting so much now. Nothing cut deeper than the anger and disappointment building inside me.

"The bastard killed my son, and now he's free."

"He's not free," I said. "We'll get him. I know how that sounds, but we'll get him." The hospital was only blocks away. "*I'll* get him."

For a second Andie didn't answer. I didn't know if she believed me, and in that moment, I didn't care. *Because I meant it.*

I'll get him.

I felt as if I might be passing out as I disconnected from Andie with a mumbled "Bye." The van was stopping at the emergency entrance.

I never even told her that I'd been shot.

Chapter 72

RICHARD NORDESHENKO shifted the silver Voyager into the entrance lanes for the George Washington Bridge. The tie-up was massive, and Nordeshenko wasn't surprised. He scanned the radio news channels — they were already all over the story.

Flashing police lights were everywhere. Every single vehicle was being checked, trunks opened. Trucks and vans were being pulled aside, their cargoes searched. Nordeshenko looked up into the sky. Above him, he heard the *whip-whip-whip* from a police helicopter circling above. This wasn't good.

They had already changed cars twice. He had removed the beard and eyeglasses he'd worn in the courthouse. There was nothing to worry over, right? Just be calm. Cavello was safely hidden in a hollowed-out compartment under the rear seat. Even if the Bronco had been located by now, what did it matter? Everything was in order. No one could connect him to the vehicle he was driving now. *Unless they found Cavello.*

The tall steel towers of the bridge loomed about a quarter mile ahead. Police on foot were making their way back toward their car. It was a typical code-red response. SWAT teams and bomb-sniffing dogs. Well-trained perhaps, but with no practical experience.

"What's the delay?" the gruff voice said from the back. "How does it look up there? Is everything okay?"

"Relax, you should be honored. This is all for you."

"It's cramped in here. And hot. It's been over an hour already."

"Not as cramped as the isolation unit of a federal prison, yes? Now be quiet, please. There is one last checkpoint to pass through."

Two policemen wearing armored vests and carrying automatic rifles were coming up to the Voyager. One of them tapped on the window with the barrel of his gun. "License and registration, please. And open the back."

Nordeshenko handed the officer his documents, which showed he was a resident of 11 Barrow Street in Bayonne — and that the van was registered to the Lucky George Maintenance Service in Jersey City.

"Any word?" Nordeshenko asked him. "I heard what happened. It's all over the news."

The officer checking his documents didn't answer. The other flung open the hatch to the back and peered in. All that was visible back there was an industrial-sized vacuum cleaner, a rug-cleaning machine, and some cleaning agents in a plastic tray. Still, Nordeshenko held his breath as the policeman poked around.

Nordeshenko had a pistol strapped to his ankle. On a dry run the day before, he had decided what he would do. Take out the officers. Run back against traffic to the other lane, where cars were still moving. Pull a driver out of any vehicle and get out of there. Cavello was on his own.

"What's that?" one of the policemen barked. He pushed aside the machinery and pried open a compartment.

Nordeshenko nearly reached for his ankle, but didn't. Not yet. His heart stood still. *Take out both of them. And run.*

"There's supposed to be a spare in here," the officer said, "by law. What if this old piece of junk breaks down?" He recovered the compartment.

"You're right, Officer." Nordeshenko slowly relaxed. "I will tell it to my boss. I'll tell him we owe you a free rug cleaning."

The policeman handed Nordeshenko back his license as the cop in back slammed shut the doors. "You don't owe me shit," he said. "Get a spare tire in here, pronto."

"Consider it done. I hope you catch him," Nordeshenko said. He raised the window and started to drive away. Minutes later, as he cleared the security area, traffic picked up pace. They crossed over the bridge. As soon as he saw the sign separating New York from New Jersey, his heart started to slow down.

"Congratulations. We're golden," he called back. "By this time tomorrow you'll be out of the country."

"Good." Cavello lifted himself out of the compartment. "In the meantime, there's been a change of plans. There's something I have to take care of first. A debt I have to pay."

Chapter 73

THEY DROVE WEST to Paterson, New Jersey, on Cavello's instructions — a tree-lined neighborhood of middle-class homes. Nordeshenko pulled up in front of a modest, pleasant, gray-and-white Victorian. It was April, but a Nativity scene was still there from Christmas, center stage in the small front yard.

"Wait in the car," Cavello said, tucking the handgun he had taken from Nordeshenko into his belt.

"This isn't what you're paying me for," the Israeli said. "This is the kind of thing that can get us killed."

"In that case," said Cavello, opening the door and turning up his collar, "think of it as on the house."

He went around the side and pushed open a metal chain-link fence leading to the backyard. He was excited now.

He kept his promises. That's what made him who he was.

People knew, when the Electrician promised to do something, it always got done. Especially this promise.

He walked up close to the house until he came to a porch in back, screened in by wire mesh. Then he stopped. He heard the sound of a TV inside. A children's channel. He listened to the singsong voices and some happy clapping. He saw the back of a woman's head. She was sitting in a chair.

Cavello climbed the porch steps and opened the screen door. He had to laugh. Nobody needed alarms in this neighborhood, right? It was protected. It was protected by *him!* You pull something in this neck of the woods, you might as well keep on running for the rest of your life.

"Rosie, how do you like your tea?" a woman's voice called from inside.

"A little lemon," the woman in the chair said back. "There should be some in the fridge." Then, "Hey, look at the little lamby, little Stephie. What does a little lamby say? *Baaah . . . Baaah.*"

Cavello stepped in from the porch. When the woman in the chair saw who it was, her face turned chalk white. "Dom!"

She was bouncing a baby girl, no more than a year old, on her lap.

"Hi, Rosie," Dominic Cavello said, and smiled.

Panic crept over the woman's face. She was in her early fifties, in a floral shift, with her hair up in a bun, a St. Christopher medal around her neck. She wrapped her arms around the child. "They said you'd escaped. What are you doing here, Dom?"

"I promised Ralphie something, Rosie. I always keep my promises. You know that."

There was a noise from behind them, and a woman walked in carrying a tray with tea on it. Cavello reached out his hand and shot her with the silenced gun, the wound opening where her right eye had been.

The woman fell over, and the tray hit the floor with a loud crash and clatter.

"Mary, Mother of God." Ralph Denunziatta's sister gasped. She hugged the child close to her breast.

"That's one cute kid there, Rosie. I think I see a little of Ralphie, with those fat little cheeks."

"It's my granddaughter, Dom." Rosie Scalpia's eyes were flushed with panic. She glanced at her friend lying on the carpet, a red ooze trickling out of her eye. "She's only one year old. Do what you came here to do, just don't hurt her, Dom. She's Simone's daughter, not Ralphie's. Please, do what you have to do. Just leave my granddaughter alone."

"Why would I want to hurt your little *nipotina*, Rosie?" Cavello stepped closer. "It's just that I owe your little prick-faced brother a favor. And there's nothing we can do about that."

"Dom, please." The woman looked terrified. "Please!"

"The problem is, Rosie, even though I wish your little granddaughter here a long and healthy life, after I square things a little." He leveled the gun in the woman's face. "Truth is, hon, you just never know."

He pulled the trigger, and the top of Rosie's forehead blew

out, sending a spatter of tapioca-like bone and brain over the drapes.

Ralph Denunziatta's little grandniece started to cry.

Cavello knelt down and stuck his finger into the baby's belly. "Don't cry. You're a cute one, aren't you, honey?" He heard the teakettle whistling on the stove. "Water's ready, huh? *C'mere.*" He lifted the child up out of her dead grandmother's arms. She stopped crying. "Thatta girl." He stroked her back. "Come, let's take a little stroll with your Uncle Dom."

Chapter 74

THEY RELEASED ME from the hospital at my own request later that day, with a large bandage over my ribs, a vial of Vicodin, and the doctor's order to go right home and rest.

Truth is, I was lucky as hell. The bullet had barely grazed me. But I still had one hell of a rug burn on my side.

Two agents from Internal Affairs debriefed me after I was treated. They drilled me over and over about the events at the courthouse, from the moment I had seen what was taking place on the security screens to my run out to the lobby. I had discharged my gun. One of Cavello's men was dead. And what was making it particularly ugly was that I wasn't on active duty.

But what was hurting me a lot more than my side was that it had been more than five hours now and there was no sign of Cavello or the black Bronco. We had the escape routes blocked as well as we could. We had Cavello's known contacts blanketed. But somehow, even with the tightest security ever for a trial, the sonovabitch had gotten away.

Against my protests, a nurse had wheeled me down to the lobby at Bellevue, and I stiffly climbed into a waiting cab.

"West Forty-ninth and Ninth," I said, exhaling, resting my head against the seat and shutting my eyes. Over and over I saw the black Bronco speeding away, disappearing into traffic. And me, unable to do a thing. How the hell had they pulled this off? Who was the gunman in the elevator? How, under all that security, had they been able to get a gun inside?

I slammed the heel of my hand into the driver's barrier so hard I thought I broke my wrist.

The driver turned — a Sikh in a turban. "Please, sir, this is not my cab."

"Sorry . . ."

But I wasn't completely sorry. I felt packed in a pressure cooker. My blood surged with this restless, clawing energy, about to explode. We had turned on Forty-fifth, heading crosstown. I realized what was really scaring me. Going back to my apartment, shutting the door, facing the empty rooms — the useless stacks of evidence, just worthless paper now. *Alone.*

I was about to blow. I honestly felt like I could.

We turned onto Ninth. From the corner I could already see my brownstone. This nervous, tightening rush swelled in my chest.

I rapped on the glass. "I changed my mind," I said. "Keep driving."

"Okay." The driver shrugged. "Where to now?"

"West One eighty-third, the Bronx."

Chapter 75

I RANG THE BUZZER repeatedly — three, four times, and I knocked on the door.

Finally I heard a woman's voice. "Just a minute. Coming . . . just a second."

Andie opened the door. She was wearing a robe with a pink ribbed cotton tank underneath, her hair still loose and damp, presumably from the shower. She stared at me, surprised.

My left arm hung limply at my side. My clothes were rumpled. I probably had a wild, crazed look in my eyes.

"Jesus, Nick, are you okay?"

I never answered because I really couldn't at that moment. Instead, I backed Andie inside and pressed her against the wall. Then I kissed her as hard as I could. Whatever came of it, well —

Suddenly, she was kissing me back just as feverishly. I tugged the robe off her shoulders, ran a hand underneath the ribbed tank, hearing her soft moans. She had a sweet, citrusy, just-out-of-the-shower scent that I inhaled deeply.

"Jesus, Pellisante." She sucked in a breath. Her eyes were as wide and flaming as torches. "You don't even give a girl time to breathe. I kind of like that."

She started to pull my shirt out of my trousers. Then she went to unbuckle my belt.

That's when I winced — in pain. It felt like sandpaper raking across my side.

"Jesus, Nick, what's wrong?"

I swung away from her, propping myself against the wall. "Something ran into me today . . . at the courtroom."

Andie gently raised my shirt and came upon the large bandage. Her eyes went wide. "What *happened* to you?"

"A bullet happened." I sniffed, letting out a frustrated groan.

"A bullet!" Andie didn't seem to find that amusing. "Nick, *you were shot?*"

"I was. I guess I still am."

She helped me over to the couch, where I slowly eased myself down — crumpled, actually. She gently unbuttoned the rest of my shirt. "Oh, God, Nick."

"Truth is, it just grazed me. It actually looks worse than it feels."

"Oh, right, I can see that," she said, nodding. She propped up my feet on the coffee table. "You were on the way to the hospital. That's where you were when I called. *Nick,* what are you doing here? What'd the doctor say?"

"He said go straight home and take it easy." I curled a contrite smile.

"So what were you thinking that brought you *here?*"

"I guess I was thinking you might find it sexy. Or take pity on me?"

Andie's incredulous stare burned a hole through me. I guess she didn't find that funny either. She unbuttoned my shirt all the way and ran her hands across the edge of the bandage and shrugged. "I don't know . . . maybe it is a *little* sexy."

"See!"

"You're crazy." She took off my shoes and placed a pillow behind my head. "Can I get you anything?"

"No. I'm loaded with painkillers." I pulled her into me. "*You.* I need you."

"Oh, now I see. You catch a little drug buzz, you knock on the one door where you figure you can get something?"

I shrugged. "So? Was I right?"

She leaned forward and placed a kiss softly on my face; another kiss brushed my lips. "Maybe. A bottle of wine would've worked, though. You didn't have to go and get yourself shot."

"Damn." I groaned, disappointed. "Why didn't I think of that before?"

I pressed my thumb softly into the nape of her neck. "I couldn't go home, Andie. I didn't want to be there right now."

She nodded, brushing the hair out of her eyes. "Just stay here. We don't have to do anything." She rested her head against my shoulder.

I closed my eyes, shutting out the horror of what had happened today, and my anger at watching Cavello escape. My side *was* aching like hell. And honestly, I didn't know *what* I'd been thinking, coming here now. "Thank God," she whispered against me, "thank God you're okay."

"One thing about these Mafia douche bags — they're mean as shit, but generally, they're poor shots."

"Please don't joke with me, Nick. This is very unnerving. Somebody tried to kill you."

I shut up, and I felt a tear, her tear, land on my chest.

"Cavello's gone," I said. "I can't believe it, but we don't know where he is."

"I know," she whispered.

For a while we just sat there. I was starting to get woozy. Maybe from the Vicodin. Maybe from the stress of the day. "I won't let you down, Andie. You know that, don't you? We'll find a way to get him. I promise, whatever it takes."

"I know," she said again.

This time I felt she did believe me.

Chapter 76

THE NEXT MORNING, I found myself on Andie's couch when I woke, a quilt pulled around me, pillows under my head. *I had to leave.*

Andie was asleep in the bedroom. I peeked in. I was about to leave a note, but I sat down on the edge of the bed and stroked her hair. She opened her eyes.

"I've got to go."

"Where?" she said, reaching for my hand from under the covers.

"I made you a promise last night. Gotta go deliver."

Andie nodded, eyes glistening. "C'mere."

She had a sexy, early morning voice that was proving tempting, and my side suddenly felt 100 percent better. For a second I thought about taking off my clothes and climbing into bed with her.

"I owe you one," I said, and squeezed her back.

"One, two, *three* . . . whatever you want. How's your side?"

"Better. All I needed was a little TLC." I raised my arm. But not too far.

"What are you going to do, Nick?" She looked at me, a little more seriously.

I knew what I was going to do first. It was no longer possible to stay on the sidelines. "Cut my class." I smiled. I squeezed her shoulder, got up, and went to the door.

"Pellisante," she called.

"Yeah?"

"Do me a big favor. Try not to get yourself shot. Or even shot at."

"I'll talk to you later." I smiled.

I went back to my place to shower and change. Sabbatical was over now. I was heading down to the Javits Building. On the cab ride I checked in with my buddies at the Bureau.

No sign of Cavello. That didn't shock me. I knew, with the kind of planning they'd had, they'd have a perfect out.

We had located the getaway vehicle, though. The black Bronco was found in a vacant lot on Henry Street, not four blocks from the courthouse. Turned out it had been heisted two days before from a shopping mall on Staten Island. And the Jersey plates were pilfered too. We had the entire Eastern Seaboard virtually closed down. Every airport and bridge. Every port from Boston to Baltimore.

But Cavello could be just about anywhere now.

"There's something else, Nick." Ray Hughes exhaled. "Ralph Denunziatta's sister was found late yesterday. She was shot in her home — right between the eyes. A neighbor who was apparently visiting with her was shot dead, too."

"Christ!"

"Nine millimeter, same caliber that was used at the courthouse. We're checking the ballistics now. But listen, it gets worse."

"Worse? How can it get worse?"

"There was a kid there. The police found Denunziatta's one-year-old grandniece in the kitchen."

"Oh, come on, Ray."

"She's alive. But listen to this. She's got severe burns over her face and hands. Hot-water burns, Nick. What kind of creeped-out monster is this, anyway? There was a note scribbled *on the kid's bib*. The handwriting people are looking it over now."

An explosive, tightening rage balled up in my gut. "What did it say?"

"It said, '*I keep my promises.*'"

Chapter 77

I WAS BURNING NOW, on fire.

I went home and took that shower. The whole time I kept thinking of Ralphie's sister and that poor little one-year-old kid. On top of all the other things I was close to exploding about, now this horror. I sat there in my towel, staring at the photos of that animal Cavello I had stuck on the kitchen wall. The piles of useless accumulated evidence.

Until I couldn't stand it anymore.

I dressed and went and got my Saab out of the lot on Eleventh Avenue. But I wasn't headed to the office.

It didn't matter anymore about what was right or "appropriate" behavior.

I crossed the river through the Lincoln Tunnel and turned onto Route 3, to Secaucus, New Jersey. Secaucus was what came to my mind when they called New Jersey the "armpit of the universe." Miles and miles of drive-in, big-box malls and fast-food franchises, stuck in between a toxic swamp and the Jersey Turnpike.

About a mile down 3, I pulled into the lot of a drab, two-story cinder-block building I knew well. United Workers of Electrical Contractors of New Jersey.

Local 407. Cavello's outfit.

I opened the glass door and went straight past the startled receptionist, flashing my FBI shield. "I'm going up to see Frankie Delsavio."

The receptionist jumped up. "Excuse me, sir, you can't just. . . ."

I didn't even wait for her to finish the sentence.

Two broad-shouldered men, who figured this as their job description, jumped out of their chairs to block my way.

"Don't even try it," I said as one of them stretched an arm out in front of me. My eyes were flashing and probably a little crazy. "You understand?"

"Mr. Delsavio's not around," the goon grunted, looking as if he had flunked the screen test for *The Sopranos. Too fucking large.*

I shoved my ID in his face. "This is the last time I say this nicely. *Get out of my way.*"

I hustled up the stairs, moving on pure adrenaline. Everyone in the building was probably connected. Feds didn't burst in here alone, without backup.

The second floor was filled with union offices. Cavello's people who got the cushy assignments, doing nothing but collecting cash. I went down the hall as the bozos from the lobby followed behind. A few secretaries looked up, trying to figure out what was going on.

Another guy stepped in my way. Dark glasses and an open, wide-collar shirt over a polyester suit. "'Scuse me, sir!" He flipped open his jacket, exposing his piece. I didn't even wait for him to pull it. *I pulled mine.*

I stuck the muzzle under his nose and pushed the startled gangster against the wall. I pressed my FBI ID close to his face. "*This* says, 'yes, I can.'"

People started getting up from their desks behind me. I saw that the two goons who'd followed me from the lobby had their pieces out.

"This is a legitimate, private business," the guy against the wall declared. "Our corporate counsel is down the hall. You're here without an appointment or a legitimate business purpose. Show me a subpoena or a warrant, Special Agent, or get the hell out."

I pressed the gun into his cheek. "I asked to see Frank Delsavio."

"As you were told" — and he looked at me straight on — "Mr. Delsavio is not on the premises. You can't see him if he's not here."

Just then, a door opened at the end of the hall. A heavyset man stepped out, ruddy cheeks, hair combed over, in a short nylon jacket and an open plaid shirt.

"*Agent Pellisante,*" Frank Delsavio said in a raspy voice. "Sallie, why didn't you just tell me it was Special Agent Pellisante? I just came back in. C'mon, step into my office. They musta not known I was here."

Chapter 78

"IT IS STILL SPECIAL AGENT, isn't it?" Delsavio grinned. "Or maybe we should call you Professor. I hear you were teachin' a class."

Frankie was Dominic Cavello's longtime number two, but in the big boss's absence, he was running the show. On the family chart he was known as the Underboss. He'd been married for thirty years to one of Vito Genovese's nieces. Royalty, Cosa Nostra–style. But not exactly one of the Five Good Emperors. He'd probably ordered ten to twenty murders we couldn't pin him on.

I followed Frank into his office. There was a cheap hardwood desk cluttered with pictures of his family. On the walls there were some cheesy prints of Italy and a signed photo of Derek Jeter eating at one of Frankie's restaurants. A few tubes containing rolled-up architectural plans were leaning against the wall. I smiled. I wasn't sure if Frankie Delsavio had ever been near a construction site in his life.

"So you have to excuse me." He motioned me to sit. "I've been out of touch the past few days. Down in Atlantic City, checking out a big site. So tell me" — he grinned, smirking — "how goes the trial?"

"Fuck you, you cockroach," I said, grabbing him by the collar and taking him right out of his leather chair and pushing him against the wall. "*I want to know where he is.*"

A few books and artifacts fell to the floor. The grin on Frank Delsavio's face disappeared. This was not a small man, and no one, not even the cops, pushed him around.

"I invited you in here as a friend, Nicky Smiles. There's about two dozen people out there who don't have much to do in their life. They can blow off your head. You're not even on active duty, Pellisante. You sure you wanna do this now?"

"I asked about Cavello," I said, pushing him harder against the wall.

"How would I know, Nicky? I told you, I've been out of touch. Besides, the Boss doesn't clue me in on every little decision he makes."

"Every little decision." I smiled, the rancor boiling over inside. "You know, Frankie, the only reason I never closed you down was because I thought you had the only sense of humor in this shitbag outfit. Otherwise, you'd be waiting for *your* trial, same as him. But I'll bring you in, Frankie. I could do it tomorrow. There's enough on you, I swear. We'll close this whole operation down. You'll all lose the Beamers, your fat-cat jobs."

"You know what I think, Nicky?" Frankie stared as he spoke. He shook his head at me with a little smile. "I don't think you have the clout to do that right now. I don't even think you're on this case. The only reason I let you in here was out of respect to your past position. Now I'd appreciate it if you'd let go of my shirt — before I call in our lawyer down the hall and he slaps you and the Bureau with a harassment suit. That wouldn't go over well in the classroom, would it, Nicky?"

"We're not talking business as usual, Frankie." I tightened my grip. "This isn't going away. This is like Bin Laden. You don't want to step anywhere near this shit. I'll give you a week, then I'll do what I promised. I'll shut the whole operation down." I let go of his collar. But I still stared at him. "That was a one-year-old kid your boss burned up, Frankie. Coulda been your granddaughter."

Delsavio straightened his shirt collar. "I don't know where Dominic Cavello is. And that's the truth. And just for the record, Nicky, no way that could *ever* be my grandkid. 'Cause I'd never rat him out." Then Delsavio grinned, flexing his shoulders. "But if he happens to call in or send me a postcard, I promise, you'll be the first to know. Even before his own wife and kids, Nicky Smiles." He grinned. "Anything you want me to tell him, you know, if he should write in?"

"Just this." I smoothed out the mobster's jacket. "Tell him I keep *my* promises, too."

Chapter 79

AN HOUR LATER, I was in front of Assistant Director in Charge Michael Cioffi, who ran the FBI's New York office. "I want back in," I said.

Cioffi was my boss. He was the one who had placed me on administrative leave after I beat Cavello. Outside of the politicos down in DC, he was one of the most senior people in the FBI.

"Nick." He leaned back in his chair. "No one holds you responsible for what happened yesterday."

"That's not what it's about, Mike. *Cavello is.* And I know more about him than anyone in the Bureau. Besides, we both know I'm a little too late in the game to ever qualify for tenure."

The ADIC smiled. He stood up, stepped over to his office window. You could see Ground Zero from there, the vast, empty space. Beyond it, the Statue of Liberty. "So how're the ribs?"

"No harm, no foul." I raised my arms. "I get a big fat commendation for being wounded in the line of duty, and I didn't even have to stay overnight."

"That's sort of the problem, Nick." Cioffi smiled again, but this time tightly, his hands against the sill. "You weren't exactly *in* the line of duty. And Ray's been handling this for months now. And right now, the shit's hitting the fan a little."

I stood up, too. "This isn't about Ray, Mike. I'll report to him, I don't care. Just put me back on assignment. You need me." I looked at the boss I had served under for eight years. "*I* need it, Mike."

The ADIC looked closely at me. I couldn't quite read him. He stepped back to his desk and picked up a file. It looked like a field report. "I heard you paid a visit this morning to a certain union headquarters in New Jersey. You're not on active duty, Nick. You can't go wild, on a whim. We've got our people on this, Nick. They can't be looking over their shoulder."

"I understand that, Mike. That's why I want back in."

Cioffi sat back. I was just waiting for the nod. He let out a long, deliberating breath. "I can't."

"You what?" If the ADIC had pulled out a gun right there and popped a couple of hollow-point rounds into my chest, I don't think I would have looked at him with more surprise. "*Mike?*"

"You're one of the best I have, Nick. But you're too close to this case. Way too close. Too emotional. This isn't a witch hunt, Nick, it's an FBI investigation. The answer's no."

I sat there, jaw hanging, the words digging their way into my brain, one by one.

"I'll give you another assignment if you want back in. Wall Street. Antiterrorism. Name it, Nick. *But not this.*"

Not this. I stood there absorbing the blows. I'd tracked this bastard for years. I'd lost two men bringing him in. I didn't want *another* assignment. All I could do was stare back blankly. "Please, *Mike* . . ."

"No." The ADIC shook his head again. "I'm sorry, Nick, you're out. And I won't change my mind."

Chapter 80

RICHARD NORDESHENKO had flown back out of Washington, DC. Right under the almighty U.S. government's nose. Through London, then on to Tel Aviv. Then he drove along the coast back to Haifa.

The acacias were blooming as he piloted his custom Audi S6 up the heights of Mount Carmel to his home high above the Mediterranean. He had burned his extra passports before he left the States; he would never need them again.

"Father!" Pavel gleefully shouted as Nordeshenko stepped through the door. He was two days early. His wife, Mira, ran out of the kitchen. "*Richard!* Is that you?"

"It's me," Nordeshenko answered. He hugged both of them tightly, each in an arm. Three days before he didn't know if he would ever see them again. "It's good to be home."

And it was. Through the glass doors, the deep turquoise

of the Mediterranean was like a welcome, mood-lifting tonic to him. And the tender embrace of his family. He would never deceive them again. He had all the money he needed; his career was over. This was a young man's game, after all.

"Father, come see." Pavel pulled him by the hand. "I've found a defense against Kasparov's Spanish opening. I've solved it!"

"What an Einstein we've raised," he joked to Mira.

"No, what a *Kasparov*," said Pavel.

The boy tugged him into his room. Nordeshenko was exhausted. And not just from the flight. He had dropped Cavello off at a safe house they had arranged near Baltimore. The bastard was to be crated up and put on a freighter. *And to where?* Nordeshenko found some amusement in his destination. Even Interpol would not go there.

He was happy to part ways. The malicious animal killed for sport, not for business or necessity. It was his nature. Back in Russia they would spit and call him a devil. Well, he had done his job. He hoped he would never see that piece of garbage again in his life.

"Look, Father." Pavel dragged him over to the chess set. The boy held up a queenside bishop. "You see?"

Nordeshenko nodded, but in truth, he didn't. He was so incredibly weary. The board was a jumble to him. Chess was a young man's game, too. But he smiled, tousling the young child's hair. "Look in the bag. I've got something for you," he said.

The boy hurriedly undid the wrapping. His eyes grew wide.

World Championship Poker. Pavel's face erupted in joy. "Come," he said, pushing the chessboard aside. "Let's play."

"My little Einstein wants to play poker? Okay. We'll go best out of three. Then I get to sleep for about a week!" Nordeshenko pulled up a seat, recalling his great bluff back in New York, which seemed a lifetime ago. "And I've got quite a poker story for you, Pavel."

His feet felt like twice their normal size. "Just let me take off these shoes."

Chapter 81

FOR A WEEK straight I never left my apartment. I kept replaying the tape from Cavello's escape. The scene in the elevator. I even timed it — exactly forty-seven seconds. I'd watch it over and over. Then I'd rewind it and play it again. And again. And again.

The phone would ring. My doctor checking up on me. My department head from school. The Bureau — there was still an inquiry going on. And Andie — she called my cell phone a couple of times.

Finally, I stopped picking up, even my cell. All I did was watch the tape. Each time it was the same. Cavello lunges out, hits the button. The two marshals try to rein him in. The doors open. In steps the guy with the beard, surprising them. No time to react. He takes out the marshals, flips Cavello the disguise. In a moment they're gone.

I focused on the guy with the beard. Zoomed in on his

face. I tried to memorize every line, every feature. I kept running through the Homeland Security photo books I'd been given. I didn't know what I was looking for. But something. There had to be something.

Cavello was gone. Probably already out of the country by now. You could get aboard a freighter out of Newark or Baltimore; you could hop a private jet to some landing strip in Mexico, without filing a flight plan. Passports could be doctored.

I kept reminding myself I'd been an FBI officer for thirteen years. It had been my world, my life. The vows I took, to uphold the law — these were sacred vows.

But something Andie said had got me thinking.

You can't make the world come out right just because you want it that way, she had whispered to me through the door.

Outside, darkness had fallen again. I took another swig of beer. I rewound the tape.

I remembered what I'd said back to her, through the door.

I can try.

Chapter 82

THE BUZZER RANG, startling me. I thought about just letting it go. *Don't even move. Whoever it is, they'll go away. They always do.* I took another sip of beer and let it go down slow.

The ringing continued. Insistent. Irritating. Then maddening.

"Nick. Come to the door. Don't be a poop." It was Andie.

Maybe I was ashamed to see her because I'd made promises that now seemed empty. Maybe I was afraid to cause her more pain, or drag her in, now that I'd made up my mind what I wanted to do.

The buzzing continued. "Nick, please. You're being a jerk."

Maybe because I knew if I opened that door, I wouldn't be able to close her out again. And maybe that scared me a little. Maybe it scared me a lot.

But she was *sitting* on that damn buzzer.

I paused the tape. Then I walked into the hallway. I stood for a moment in front of the door, still not sure what I was going to do. She buzzed again.

"Hey!" I called out, finally opening the latch. "I'm coming."

She was dressed in a green cowl-necked sweater over jeans. "You look awful," she said, staring at me.

"Thanks." I let her in. "How . . . ?" I started, but she cut me off.

"You look like you've been wearing the same clothes for a week, and a shave sure wouldn't hurt."

"How did you find me?"

She stepped into the apartment, her eyes surveying the place. "You think there's another Nicholas Pellisante who was shot and taken to Bellevue Hospital? You didn't return my calls."

"You'd make a good cop," I said, shuffling into the living room.

"You make a lousy friend."

"You're right. I'm sorry."

"Apology not accepted. This *could* be a nice apartment."

Andie took off her coat and scarf and draped them over a chair. I sat down against the padded arm of the couch.

"I went to the Bureau after I left the other day. I tried to put myself back on the case."

"Okay . . ."

"They told me I was out. Off the case. No way in hell I'd ever get back on."

Andie looked shocked. "Why?"

"Too emotional, they said. Too close. They'll hook me up with any case I want. Just not this one."

"That seems totally unfair. What are you going to do now?"

I looked up at her. Her molten eyes. The sweater, contracting and expanding with her breaths. "I don't really know, Andie."

"You know what?" She came over and stood in front of me. She cupped my face in her hands. "You *are* too emotional, Pellisante. You *are* too close."

She brushed a kiss against my cheek. Then my eyes, my lips. I pulled her in to me. Her mouth was soft and warm, and tasted delicious. This time she kissed me hard. My hand traveled under her sweater. Over her bra. Every nerve in my body was excited, on edge. The hairs on my neck were standing. Andie had very soft skin, very nice breasts.

She kissed me again, unbuttoning my shirt, popping a button. She ran her tongue across my shoulders and chest, licking along the edge of my wound. Then she yanked her sweater over her head. Was this a good idea? Did it matter? Not anymore it didn't.

I pulled her to the couch, undoing her pants. She grappled with my trousers, kissing me again, her thick hair falling all over my face.

"I think we need each other, Nick," she whispered, touching her lips to my cheek. "Whatever the reasons, it's just the way it is."

I slid out of my pants and back onto the couch, and I

pulled her soft body onto mine. I was finally inside her, and it felt right. We started to move against each other, into each other, whatever.

"I'm not arguing. I'm glad you came."

"Not yet . . . but very soon."

Chapter 83

THE FIRST TIME, we made love like two starved people who couldn't get enough of each other, who hadn't been with anyone for a long time. Which happened to be the truth. It was sweaty and frantic, and at that slapping, breakneck pace, we couldn't hold back, and didn't. I think we both came at about the same time, locking hands, locking on each other's eyes, maybe already falling in love.

"Oh, Jeez." Andie collapsed into me, her hair damp with perspiration, her body drenched and spent. "That was long overdue, wasn't it?"

"Yeah," I said exhaling, agreeing, rolling onto my back. "Overdue."

The second time it was a lot more tender. We moved into the bedroom, with a bottle of Italian Prosecco on the night table, Tori Amos on the CD player. This time it was slow and much more romantic, at least my idea of romance. It was like slow dancing. We found this nearly perfect rhythm. Both of our bodies were slick with sweat. I loved it.

The third time, we went back at it like numero uno. Couldn't control ourselves. The hottest yet. Probably the best. I guess it was something we were dying to do for a long time.

The fourth . . .

All right, there was no fourth. We were too empty, too spent. We just lay there, coiled together in each other's arms. Andie's heart was racing against my chest. I loved that too.

"Don't get the wrong impression," she whispered. "I'm not that easy. I usually don't give it up until the second trial."

"Me either," I said, breathing heavily. "Unless we're unable to reach a conviction."

We stayed like that for a while, entwined and exhausted. It took all my remaining strength just to caress the curls of her hair with one finger.

"I meant what I said before, Nick," she whispered. "I know how much you want Cavello. And I know how much it hurts after what happened the other day. I know what it feels like having the thing you want most in the world taken from you."

"I know you do," I said, squeezing her tight.

"What I'm trying to say is, I want whatever happens between us to be in spite of that, Nick. Okay?"

"Andie, I'm not going back to some bullshit job at the Bureau policing corporate tax returns. I can't. I'm gonna get Cavello. With their help or without. For you, for me . . . it doesn't matter. I can't be right until it's done, until it's over."

"And me?" She shrugged. "Am I wrapped up in that, too?"

"You?" I leaned on my elbow and smiled. "I think we're sort of wrapped up in each other right now."

"I'm serious," she said. "What happens now?"

"*Now?*" I didn't have an answer. I was a little scared by this incredible magnetism between us. In fact, I felt myself come alive again. All of a sudden we were at it again — my hands massaging her, Andie making ever-descending circles with her nails just above my crotch.

"*Now*" — I rolled on top of her again — "I guess we go for four."

Chapter 84

ANDIE AND I MADE LOVE a lot over the next couple of days. Four turned into seven, seven into ten, but neither of us was really counting, nothing as rational as that. A couple of times we even got dressed and went out in the neighborhood for a meal or some coffee. But all it took was a look. *That look.* And we'd rush back.

Maybe both of us just needed the thrill of feeling excited again. After our long, inward thaw, I couldn't take my hands off Andie. I couldn't wait to feel her body next to me, merged with me. I didn't want to be separated from her. Cavello could wait for a while, just this once. It was like the tap was wide open and the water kept pouring out. We both needed it. But the reprieve didn't last very long.

I hadn't checked my messages for days. When a call came in, we'd listen to the voice on the machine and pretend it was a million miles away.

Until this one call. The caller's voice froze me with surprise.

"Hey, Pellisante." The smirking Jersey accent was about the last one I expected to hear.

I spun over to the side of the bed and fumbled for the phone. "*Frankie?*"

"Nicky Smiles." Frank Delsavio acted as if he were talking to a long-lost friend. "You know that postcard I was talking about, from that mutual friend of ours?"

"I know who you're talking about, Frank."

"Well, wouldn't ya know, I got one after all. How 'bout that?"

I stood up. "Where is he, Frank?" It was more of a demand than a question.

"Where is he?" Delsavio chuckled, clearly finding amusement in twisting me on a string. "He's at the end of the earth, Nicky-boy! He told me to tell you that." The scumbag started laughing. "That's what he said to say, 'the end of the fucking earth, Nicky Smiles.'"

Maybe he knew. Maybe he knew I was out of the game — that I couldn't touch him, whatever he said or did. I clenched my fists and felt the blood surging through my veins.

"I told him you needed to know and it was urgent," Frank Delsavio said, still chuckling. "He told me to send you his regards. He said to make sure I said that — those exact words. *End of the earth.* 'Come and get me, Nicky Smiles.'"

Part Three

THE EEL

Chapter 85

YOU NEVER QUITE KNOW when the breakthrough comes, that one, case-altering clue. Usually it's not an *ahha!* Just someone talking to someone else, rolling over to escape prison time. Sometimes it's one of those moments, though. A blur in a sky full of shining stars that all at once takes shape and becomes stunningly clear.

For me, that moment came while watching the courthouse tape. Those *forty-seven seconds* I'd been over so many times.

A buddy in C-10 kept me going with updates on the case for old times' sake. A female court employee named Monica Ann Romano had been found murdered the day after Cavello's escape, and they were looking into it. Her mother said she'd been seeing someone. She'd never met him — nor had Monica Ann's friends at work — but she knew he had an accent of some kind. The cops were thinking she may have been blackmailed into planting a gun inside the courthouse.

The getaway Bronco had been ripped apart for prints and DNA. The house where Denunziatta's sister had been killed turned up nothing. The neighborhood around Paterson, New Jersey, was being canvassed. Every toll camera on I-95 and the Jersey Turnpike was being reviewed.

It was the middle of the night when I found it. I hadn't been able to sleep.

I was at my desk on my computer, going through the courthouse tape for maybe the thousandth time. I had printed off the face of the guy with the beard to show to Ogilov, running over what leverage I could apply. Which was basically none.

I'd let the tape roll to the end. My eyes were growing heavy. It was after two in the morning. I needed a little sleep. I made a move to rewind.

Then suddenly, I stopped.

I blinked. It was a eureka sensation, as though I'd just found a cure for cancer or a deadly virus. *There it was.*

I leaned forward, panning in with the remote on the accomplice with the beard. But not his face this time — or the gun or his watch — things that were already burned into my memory.

On the sonovabitch's shoes.

I pressed the remote, zooming in on the shoes. I was wide-eyed now. There was a distinct rubber logo above the heel.

Some kind of circle — with a wavy line bisecting it.

Jesus, Nick! Why hadn't I seen this before?

I knew those shoes.

My chest started to pound. Three years before I had made a special trip to the Middle East, to train inspectors.

The shoes were Israeli-made. For the Israeli Army. *For extra support.*

I had even worn them when I was there.

Chapter 86

CAVELLO'S ACCOMPLICE had to be Israeli. I actually had something.

The frustration of losing that black Bronco was fading away.

It was almost morning. It took another cup of strong coffee to keep me focused, but I started going back through the books of terror suspects I had gotten from Homeland Security. I felt I had something to fix on. The needle in the haystack had just gotten a bit larger. Most faces appeared to be Middle Eastern, but I leafed past those. I was looking for a European. I had an approximate height and weight.

Three o'clock turned into three thirty. Then four. There were books and books of faces to scan through. Hundreds. Pakistanis, Basque separatists, al Qaeda sympathizers, FALN. IRA. All were on some kind of terror-watch radar. All had been thought to be in the country at some time. Many had explosives knowledge. Four started to bump up to five. I never even noticed when the first rays of light hit my window.

Then something made me stop. I came upon someone else. Maybe I'd passed him before. Maybe I'd passed the face a dozen times.

The man had short brown-gray hair and Slavic features, serious, slate-gray eyes.

Russian — and that wasn't all that interested me.

He was an ex-member of the Spetsnaz Brigade. Army Special Forces. He'd been stationed in Chechnya. In 1997 he went AWOL. For a long time he had simply disappeared. He was thought to have gone over to the rebel side.

Remlikov. Kolya.

I pulled out the file.

He'd been implicated in several Mafia-type slayings throughout Russia and Europe. A corrupt police inspector in St. Petersburg. A testifying gangster in Moscow. He was also being sought for questioning in the very public killing of a Venezuelan oil minister a year ago in Paris.

But what really stopped me wasn't just his résumé. Which had promise. Or even those brooding, dark eyes.

It was that he'd been wounded — in Chechnya. His right leg had been struck by shrapnel from an exploding grenade. He was thought to still walk with a slight limp.

I was thinking about those shoes.

I put the small file photo close to the screen, side by side against a frame from the courthouse tape.

Holy shit! It was a long shot, but it just could be.

I glanced at the clock. It was already after five. Nothing

was going to happen here, but that meant it was lunchtime halfway around the world.

I opened my desk and leafed through packets of business cards I had held together with rubber bands. I had a number, somewhere, for the antiterror desk at the Russian Security Service in Moscow. I'd used it when we wanted to extradite a contract killer who had worked for the Russian mob and had fled back home. I frantically searched through my files and found it. Lt. Yuri Plakhov. Federal Security Service. FSS. I dialed the thirteen-digit European number. I was praying to find him at his desk. It was a prayer answered when I heard his voice.

"Plakhov, *vot.*"

"Yuri, hello. You may remember me." I reintroduced myself, reminding the Russian official who I was. It was a bonus to be able to keep this call this far away from the Bureau.

"Sure I recall you, Inspector." Yuri Plakhov's English was well practiced and colloquial. "We tracked down that mafioso of yours. Federev, right?"

"Good memory, Yuri," I congratulated him. "Now I need you to run someone else through your files." I read him off the name.

"*Rem-li-kov?*" He stretched it out. "Rings a bell." I gave him a moment while he punched it in. "A little early back there, is it not, Inspector?"

"Yes," I answered quickly, not into small talk. "It is."

"Here it is, Inspector. *Remlikov, Kolya.* Wanted in questioning with several murders throughout Russia and Europe. Quite a dossier. Among his credits, he's suspected of taking part in bringing down an entire apartment building in Volgo-donsk, in which a government official resided. Twenty-four people were killed."

My adrenaline was pumping. "How do I find this man, Yuri?"

"I'm afraid I'm unable to give you his mobile number, Inspector." Plakhov chuckled. "It's clear here he's used several aliases and passports. Estonian, Bulgarian. Names of Kristich. Danilov. Mastarch. We think he was in Paris last year, when that Venezuelan oil minister was killed. The trail is very gray. I doubt he is in Russia. It says he is known here, Inspector, as the *eh-oop,* the Eel. Very slippery, yes? I can send a facsimile of his fingerprints, if you like."

"Please," I answered. The Eel. A slimy fucking eel. Things were starting to add up. "Where would I start to look, Yuri?"

The Russian paused, scrolling farther down the file. "Perhaps with your own State Department, Inspector. Judging from what I see, they may be better help than us."

The State Department, our State Department. "Why is that?"

"Remlikov's last-known whereabouts. He is thought to be in Israel, Inspector."

Chapter 87

FINALLY I WAS ONTO something. The bearded face now had a name, and a history. Remlikov's prints came in over the fax a short time later, but my eyes had started to close.

I dozed off until nine. Then I shaved and showered, and called a colleague I had worked with at the FBI. I asked if I could meet him around ten.

Senil Chumra was a plump, likable Indian whose office wasn't in the Bureau's official place downtown. He was in a nondescript warehouse building up on Eighteenth and Tenth, overlooking the river. Chumra headed up a specialized area of the department we called CAF.

Computer Assisted Forensics.

These were the guys who could trace e-mails, hack into computers, worm their way through coded passwords, track the complicated movements of cash overseas. I had last worked with him tracking the flow of Cavello's union pay-

backs to the Cayman Islands. Senil's other talent was manip-
ulating digital images.

"Hello, Nick." The techie lit up as I walked through the
door of his lab. The technical guys always liked it when one
of the so-called glamour boys showed up. "Haven't seen you
in a while. What have you been up to?"

"I'm good, Chummie," I lied. "Busy." These technical
whizzes worked in their own little specialized cocoon up
here. No reason he'd know what I was up to — or in this
case, *wasn't*. "You got that e-mail I sent over?"

"I got it." The Indian wheeled over to a Mac screen down
the line, maybe a little disappointed. "Got it uploaded right
here."

Senil touched a mouse, and the image of Cavello's bearded
accomplice jumped onto the screen. "Okay, Nick, tell me —
what is it you want me to do?"

"I want to change around the image, Chummie. See if it
matches someone I know."

He nodded, hunching over the screen and cracking his
knuckles. He clicked the mouse again. A grid appeared over
the image. "Shoot."

"First, I want to lose the beard."

"Easy." Senil typed in a few coordinates, and the image
immediately narrowed in to just a square of the suspect's
face. Then, using a cursor, he outlined the area of the beard.
Gently, he moved his cursor back and forth, as if he was air-
brushing.

"What are you onto these days?" he asked while he worked,
his fingers guiding the cursor like a surgeon's. "Things have

to be pretty hot up there for you C-10 boys, what with Cavello and all. What're you thinking, he changed his face on you?"

"Sort of," I said, not picking up on his inquisitiveness. "Just a hunch."

"A hunch." He sighed, dropping the conversation. "This process is called grafting and displacement," he said, continuing to carve away the facial hair, tracing it around the chin. "Essentially, we eliminate a field: skin tone, a scar, in this case, a beard." In a moment the facial area was blank, and Senil retrieved a section of skin from another part of the image and filled in the space. "Then we just graft onto it." He smoothed out the facial lines. "Cut and paste."

"That's good," I said, leaning over his shoulder. "Now what do you say we try and alter the hair. Make it short and close to the skull. A little darker."

"You mean like this?" He pressed an icon, and a file of various hairstyles came up. Then he chose one fitting my description and basically transplanted it over the newly configured face.

"Now set the hairline back a bit. Around the sides."

Chummie started playing around with the cursor again.

"Yes, like that. Now, can we ditch the eyeglasses?"

"Faster than Lasik." He grinned. "Cheaper, too." It took about a minute of more grafting and displacement.

The man's dark glasses disappeared.

"*Fucking A!*" I exclaimed. The image on the screen almost knocked me on the floor.

"Anything else, Nick? If you're not satisfied, give me the word. I'll make him look like anyone you like."

"No, Chummie." I patted his shoulder. "I think we're done."

I pulled out the file of Kolya Remlikov that Yuri Plakhov had faxed me. I put Remlikov's face side by side against the altered image of Cavello's accomplice.

"Bingo," Senil Chumra said.

We were staring at the same man.

Chapter 88

THIRTEEN YEARS of working my way up through one of the most bureaucratic law enforcement agencies in the world told me to go straight to the Javits Building and drop what I had right on ADIC Cioffi's desk.

There wasn't much doubt that Kolya Remlikov was the man who had sprung Cavello.

I got as far as hailing a cab on the corner. Then something made me hold back. I wasn't sure exactly what.

Maybe it was the thought of handing Remlikov over to the very people who had let him escape. Or the sudden realization of just how difficult this could prove to be — getting through channels, interrogating him. Which agencies would be involved? Would I be involved? One leak and Remlikov could disappear. And with him, Cavello. Then where would we be?

I'd spent so many years doing the right thing. Suddenly the right thing didn't seem so right anymore.

I waved the taxi on.

I just went back and leaned against the building for a while, holding the photos, trying to decide what the right thing was. When it hit me, I told myself, *For a professor of criminal ethics, Nick, you're about to do one very stupid thing.*

I looked up a number in my BlackBerry and placed a call. I asked Steve Bushnagel if he had plans for lunch. Steve was a partner in a private law firm now, but he used to advise the FBI. He was an expert on matters of extradition and international law.

"Lunch? Where?" Bushnagel asked.

"Cheap and fast," I said. "I'm buying."

"How fast?" the lawyer asked.

"Hop into the elevator. I'll be right outside."

When he stepped out of the lobby of the big glass tower on Sixth Avenue, I was leaning on a parked car, holding out a couple of hot dogs. "Ketchup or mustard?"

"Not to be particularly lawyerly about it — but how 'bout *both*."

We sat on a ledge on the busy corner, the lunch-hour crowds streaming by. "Steve, I've got someone I want to get to who's fled to Israel."

"Get to?"

"I need to get him back."

Bushnagel took a bite. "Are we talking fugitive or citizen, here?"

"Citizen, I suspect. He's been there awhile."

"And what you want him for, these are crimes committed in the United States, not Israel, right?"

"We're just talking, right, Steve?"

He waved his dog at me. "I assure you, you're not paying me enough for anything more specific."

I grinned. "Okay. Then we might be talking some other things in Russia and France as well."

"*Hmmph.*" Bushnagel grunted. "The Israelis are cooperative — to a degree. You remember Jonathan Pollard? We arrested him for espionage in 1985 — in the Israelis' eyes, unjustly. They've been trying to get him back unsuccessfully for twenty years. And that electronics guy who fled there? 'Crazy Eddie' Antar? Look at how long it took to get him back. Of course, it all depends on what we're *really* talking here."

"Talking?"

"In the post-9/11 world." The lawyer shrugged. "Do the Israelis want something from us? Are the other governments involved? Look, Nick, I didn't become a complete dummy when I left the government. I know we're not chasing tax cheats here.

"If the evidence is solid, you could definitely get the guy held for questioning. But what kind of access you'd have, and how long that would take, that's all up for grabs. How time sensitive is this?"

"The highest." I shrugged glumly. "Off the charts."

"Always is. Well, factor into this the matters of state, too. Does this have any rhythm for the Israelis? Do they want to make a deal with us? Do they want to make a deal with the Russians or the French before they turn him over? It's *delicate*, Nick — and I don't think that's a word that sits particularly well with you."

I nodded.

"Look, you'd get him held. You get a lot of people involved. But what happens next is anybody's guess. Then there's always the chance they drag their feet, the guy slips away, and you never hear from him again."

"I can't take that risk," I said, shaking my head.

"I understand." Bushnagel nodded. "Problem is, though, it's still the only game in town."

"In the real world, yes." I nodded. I balled up my wrapper.

I knew Steve was wondering why I had come to him. He had left the government long ago. There were plenty of lawyers on staff who could handle this kind of matter. "Just for the record, Nick" — he looked closely at me — "is there any other?"

Chapter 89

I TRACED THE EDGE of my fingernail along the slope of Andie's back.

"Don't." She stirred, snuggling up to me.

I'd been thinking all night. Since I left Steve Bushnagel. In the real world, I knew, I would have Remlikov arrested. I would lead the interrogation. He would give up Cavello, and I would go get him. That was my job. It was just that the "real world" had gotten a lot more complicated lately.

I ran my fingers along Andie's spine again. This time she turned and faced me, resting on her arm. She saw something was serious. "What is it?"

"I may have a line," I said, "on the man who blew up the bus."

Andie sat up, the sleep already gone from her eyes. "What are you talking about, Nick?"

"I'll show you."

I reached over and opened a manila envelope I had on the night table. In a long row on the bed I spread several black-and-white glossies: Homeland Security photos of Kolya Remlikov and the ones Yuri Plakhov had sent me.

"His name is Remlikov," I said. "He's Russian. He's a killer for hire. And a particularly good one. He's got a very bloody résumé. I think Cavello may have gotten him through the Russian mob. I think he's in Israel."

Andie's eyes widened at the photos. I put down the one Chummie had doctored in his lab, showing the man in the elevator without his disguise. They stretched wider. She picked it up and stared at the angular, dark-featured face a long time.

"Why do you think he was the one who blew up the bus?"

"*This.*" I removed two final photographs. The first was one I had given Senil. This photo I had found myself, from hours and hours of plugging through the courthouse security cameras. Not from the day of the escape. But from earlier.

From Cavello's *first* trial.

"Take away the sideburns and the dark glasses." I put a cleaned-up image next to it.

"Oh my God!" She picked it up, jaw tightening, gazing at the face with a hurt, stunned expression. Then her eyes filled with tears.

"Why did you keep this from me?" she asked, her back to me.

"I didn't. I only got these photos today."

"So what happens now? You give this to your people?" she said excitedly. "They go and get him? Tell me that's the way it goes."

"I don't know. It may not be that easy. The Israelis will have to be contacted. It involves governments. Procedures. This sort of evidence is highly speculative. Photos can always be doctored. You never know what will happen."

"What do you mean, you don't know? This man killed federal marshals, and he helped Cavello escape. He blew up the loaded juror bus, Nick. He killed my little boy."

"I know. But it's complicated, Andie. Remlikov is a foreign citizen. There may be other governments involved. Other law enforcement agencies. Then the Israelis have to agree to give him up."

"What are you saying, Nick?" Alarm rose up in her eyes. "They can go get this guy. You know where he is. These are your people, Nick. What does the Bureau think?"

I shook my head. Waited a second. Then I spoke again. "I didn't take it to the Bureau, Andie."

She blinked like a fighter trying to clear his head after a stunning punch. She kept looking at me, trying to read my face. "What are you saying, Nick?"

"I'm saying a man like this would disappear the second he knew people were onto him. And the instant Cavello finds out we're onto them, he takes off, too." I looked at her, eyes clear. "We've lost Cavello twice. We're not losing him again."

I think, at that moment, she knew what I was proposing. The angry flush on her face was swept away, and it was replaced by a look of clarity. When she looked at me again, I think she understood what kind of man I was.

"I told you I was going to get him, Andie."

She nodded. "I'm not even going to ask, Nick. I just want

you to know, whatever it takes, I'm with you. Do you hear me? Do you understand?"

"Not on this," I said. "This is something I have to do alone. You don't want to be involved."

"No." Andie smiled thinly. "That's where you're wrong. I know exactly what you have to do, Nick. And I'm already involved."

"Not like this." What I had to do was in another country — and was way, way outside the law.

"Yes, *like this*, Nick. Like everything." She picked up Remlikov's photo. "I lost my son. I want Cavello, too."

"You know what's going to happen over there? You know what we're talking about, Andie?"

She nodded. "Yes." She leaned her head against my chest. "I know what's going to happen, Nick. I'm praying that it does."

"We're leaving in two days," I said.

Chapter 90

THE REEDY MAN in tortoiseshell glasses leaned back against the park bench and looked at me. "These prints you sent me — where did you get them from?"

Charlie Harpering and I were old friends. We were sitting in a tiny park across from the courthouse: the historical Five Points in *Gangs of New York*. Charlie had spent many years at the FBI. Now he worked for Homeland Security. It was he who had procured all the files for me.

"Never mind how I got them. What I need to know is if there was a match."

Harpering studied me long and hard. What I was asking him to do — to go around all normal channels and procedures, to give me information that he might not pass on to his boss — was a lot to ask, even of a friend.

"You know, I could screw up a well-earned pension over this."

"Trust me." I gave him a big smile. "Retirement's way overrated. This is important, Charlie. Was there a match?"

The Homeland Security man let out a breath. Then he opened his briefcase and set a file on his lap. He nodded. "Yeah. There was a match."

He opened a plain manila file. Facing me was a blowup of the fingerprints Yuri Plakhov had faxed me.

"They belong to an Estonian," Harpering said. "Stephan Kollich. He came in through JFK on a commercial visa, April twelfth."

April 12. Cavello was sprung from the courthouse six days later.

A wave of validation surged up inside me. Remlikov had been here.

"You'll see he left seven days later." Harpering pointed farther down. *A day after the escape!* "Back to London. Out of DC."

"And on to anywhere else?" I asked.

"All she wrote, I'm afraid." The Homeland Security man shrugged. "At least, under that name."

"Thank you, Charles," I said, tapping him on the chest. "Here." I slid over a shopping bag containing the bound Homeland Security files. "I won't be needing these anymore."

He tucked the bag between his legs. "What the hell are you up to, Nick? You know I did this out of friendship. Anyone else, we'd be in a federal office right now. Who is this guy?"

"Let's call it a career move. We'll try and figure out later if it's up or down."

Harpering sniffed, agreeing. "I see what you mean about

retirement. Then I might as well take you the distance, Nick — whichever the hell way it goes."

"What do you mean?"

He took two additional sheets out of his case and slid them into the file. "Kollich's visa application. For old times. And just for the record, it didn't come via Tallinn, Nick. Estonia. It came from Tel Aviv."

I blinked. "Jesus."

"Gets even better." Harpering dropped the file on my lap. "Assuming you're trying to find him, of course. Good luck, Nick." Harpering stood up. "Give the sonovabitch a shot in the balls for me."

I looked down at the new file. There was an address on the visa application: *225 Yehudi Road.*

Haifa.

Chapter 91

RICHARD NORDESHENKO was contemplating a chess move with his son on the terrace when the doorbell rang.

"Get that for me, Pavel." Mira was out shopping. The boy went to answer the front door.

Nordeshenko was enjoying his new life. He had tossed his cell phone into the sea and let the one or two contacts he still trusted know he was out of business. *For good.*

Every day he went swimming in the Mediterranean. He picked up his son after school and drove him to chess. At night he took Mira to the fancy shops and cafés in Carmel Center. He tried to put to the back of his mind that just a few weeks before he had gotten away with a crime covering the front page of every newspaper.

"Father! There's a man."

Nordeshenko pushed himself slowly out of his chair and

went into the living room. It might as well have been a squadron of Mossad he saw standing there.

"Hello, Remi."

"What are you doing *here?*" Nordeshenko gasped. Reichardt. His face went slack and ashen.

"Just a little traveling, Remi. Some sightseeing. Throwing myself on the hospitality of old friends."

He turned to Pavel. "Go and look at the board, son. I moved."

The boy hesitated.

"Go and look at the board, I said." His voice was much harsher.

Pavel swallowed. "Yes, Father."

The boy left, and Nordeshenko turned back to the man at the door, feeling his every nerve grow tight. "Are you insane? Come in, quickly," he said. He looked past Reichardt and up the street. "Are you certain there was no tail?"

"Relax, Remi," the South African said. "I've come through three countries. I've been doing this as long as you. You've got a nice-looking boy."

"It's not *Remi* here." Nordeshenko looked at him sharply. "It's Richard."

Reichardt stepped in and whistled admiringly at the broad, spectacular view. "Business must be good, Richard."

"Business is over," Nordeshenko said. "And you better understand one thing clearly — my wife and son . . ."

"Don't worry," Reichardt said, "I won't be a burden. You said this was the quietest place in the world. It'll only be for a few days. Until the world cools down."

Nordeshenko didn't like this. It violated all the rules of the arrangements. But what choice did he have? There was no way to tie them to the States. No way to tie them together at all.

"All right," he said. "Just a few days."

"Thanks," the South African said. "But, Remi, you are mistaken on one thing."

"And what's that?" Nordeshenko asked, picking up one of Reichardt's bags.

"Our business." The blond killer sighed. "It is never over."

Chapter 92

THE LOUDSPEAKER CRACKLED. "Delta Flight 8976 to Tel Aviv is ready for boarding."

I stood there waiting at gate 77, gazing down the terminal. My heart was racing pretty fast. I glanced at my watch. The plane was boarding. I had to get on it, with or without her.

Where was she?

Maybe she had second thoughts. That would be okay, I told myself. She'd be smart to stay out of this. She'd be smart to let me do what had to be done.

"All rows, Delta Flight 8976 to Tel Aviv."

I didn't have a precise plan. I had no idea how I was going to handle it when I got there. How could I? All I knew was that I was going to find Kolya Remlikov and somehow make him tell me where Cavello was. No professional courtesy here — no Geneva convention. I'd put the muzzle of my gun down his throat and cock the hammer. I'd blow off a kneecap if I had to. He would talk. The question was, *then what?*

A Hasidic family in black rushed past me onto the boarding platform, with loud shouts of relief. They looked to be the last ones on. I scanned the terminal. No sign. I put my travel case over my shoulder and went to board.

It was better this way, right?

Then I saw her. Hurrying toward me. Still a good ways down the corridor.

I felt a warm, glycerin wave of relief surge through me. Who are you kidding, Nick? You wanted her here very much.

Andie was wearing a red leather jacket, her hair tucked under a Knicks cap, *Jarrod's cap,* a travel bag slung loosely over her shoulder. She looked incredibly beautiful to me. And brave. I knew then I probably couldn't have done this thing alone. I wanted her with me. Andie made me believe it was right.

She stopped about two feet away.

"Let's get something straight." I tried to make a joke of it. "If this was the altar, we'd be looking for a refund on the reception right now."

"I'm sorry, Nick. I had to say good-bye. To Jarrod."

That certainly shut me up.

She shook her head contritely. "Actually, I've been sitting in the terminal next to the Burger King for the last hour."

"Second thoughts?"

"I don't know, maybe. Probably. But not about this. I love you, Nick."

I stood there looking at her, her eyes glistening. I nodded, gently placing my hand against her cheek. "That's what I was thinking here. That I love you, too. That I might not be able to board that plane without you."

"I knew that's what you were bumbling around trying to say the other night."

The PA interrupted us — the final boarding call. We stood there another second. The ticket agents were getting ready to close the doors.

"So what are we doing?" I shrugged, shifting, unsure on my feet.

Andie stepped up to me, her eyes moist and strong. She locked her fingers in mine.

"Boarding. We're taking a trip together, Nick. Isn't it exciting?"

Part Four

HAIFA

Chapter 93

IF I DIDN'T KNOW for sure that I was in love with Andie DeGrasse, the flight to Israel removed all doubt. For much of it we just sat there, our hands locked. I felt something steady and unwavering running from her to me. Andie slept, her head leaning against my shoulder. She bolstered me. She gave me the courage to do what I felt was right.

Our first night in Tel Aviv was spent eating dinner in a quiet café on Shenkin Street, and fighting jet lag. Back in the room we made love, trying to forget — for a night, anyway — why we were here. In the morning we would drive up the coast to Haifa.

It only took about an hour and a half. We passed beach towns on the way up the coastal highway. The city's physical beauty surprised me. Haifa rose dramatically on steep mountain terraces above the gem-blue sea. Lowest was the port and the Old Town, with its ancient stone walls built by crusaders.

Farther up was the busy downtown, the scents of bakeries, bazaars, modern businesses. Then higher still, the bustling heights of Mount Carmel, overlooking the Mediterranean.

Up here there were modern hotels, residential streets jutting out over the sea with posh homes and incredible vistas, boulevards of trendy restaurants and stores.

Kolya Remlikov was up here, too.

I was certain that Remlikov wasn't his name here. The name he went by now didn't matter. We dropped off our bags at the Dan Panaroma Hotel. Our twenty-fifth-floor room had a stunning view of the sea.

"It's beautiful," Andie said, gazing out the window.

"It is." I nodded. I placed my hands on her shoulders. "Just remember why we're here."

"It doesn't mean we can't find time to take a swim in the Mediterranean."

"Go ahead." I picked a few things out of my travel case: a set of binoculars, a map, my gun, which was licensed. "I'll be back in a little while."

"Nick" — Andie turned, a worried look on her face — "don't do anything without me. Promise?"

"Relax." I smiled. "I'm just going sightseeing. I promise."

I had our rented Ford parked in front of the hotel. I got behind the wheel, then folded back the map. I had marked out this route many times in advance. I almost felt as if I actually knew the way.

Yehudi Street. 225.

I drove higher up the mountain, on Yefe Nof, a little way past the hotel. Up here was Carmel Center — parks, museums, trendy cafés. Farther up, the road began to loop in ever-narrowing switchbacks overlooking the sea. I turned onto Hayem, then Vashar. Up here, there were expensive homes with dramatic views. I kept on climbing higher. The road clung to the clifflike sides of Mount Carmel. The brilliant blue Mediterranean was a thousand feet below.

Finally I found Yehudi. It was a quiet, residential street with a spectacular view. Number 225 was a few houses down. It was a white, flat-roofed contemporary, down a short stone drive. As I passed it, I felt my blood run cold a little. I drove on to the next switchback, then stopped at a point where I didn't think I could be detected. I got out of the car with the binoculars and looked back down at the house.

Through the lens I could see an expensive house. Murder was always a business that paid handsomely. I didn't see anyone. I didn't see any activity inside. There was a blue minivan parked in the driveway, a European model.

I squinted through the lens.

After a few minutes, I knew I'd better move on. Someone would drive by. The area was affluent, probably well patrolled. I could always say I was up here for the view, but I couldn't keep hanging around.

The garage door suddenly started to open.

A white Audi backed out. I focused closely. The glass was tinted, but the driver's window was rolled down. I could see.

It was him. *Remlikov!* He was wearing sunglasses, but I recognized him immediately. My heart jumped as if it had been jolted with an electric shock.

And someone else was in the car with him. I shifted the

lens. It was a boy. In the passenger seat. He looked about ten, maybe younger. The Audi backed out and turned around in the driveway. I could clearly see Remlikov now.

I found you, Remlikov. I found you, you bastard!

The Audi pulled out onto Yehudi Street and drove away.

I remained there for a few minutes, making notes about the house. Today, I didn't want to follow. I had promised Andie. I got back in the car and drove away.

As I went by the house, I paused for a second in front of the mailbox. I pulled the latch. Quickly, I filtered through and grabbed the most innocuous-looking junk mail I could find. They had junk mail here, too, in Israel.

Back at the hotel, I opened the door to find Andie on the bed taking a nap. She stirred. "What'd you find?"

"I found the house. It's nearby. I'll take you there tomorrow."

Andie sat up. She nodded, a little tentatively.

"And *this*," I said, tossing the piece of junk mail, a solicitation from a local rug cleaner, on the bed. "Souvenir. His name isn't Remlikov or Kollich.

"It's Richard Nordeshenko."

Chapter 94

"LOOK!" NICK POINTED toward the modern, glass-ringed house a hundred feet below. "That's him! That's Remlikov."

Andie focused the binoculars. She spied the man — thin, dark, not so large, not so scary. A surge of anger tightened her chest.

She hadn't known how she would feel when she saw the man who killed her son. And now that it was happening, now that he was only a few yards away, she knew it wasn't what she wanted. It made her stomach cramp.

"I see him." Andie's fingers gripped the binoculars even more tightly. Behind her, Nick squeezed her arm.

"Does he look familiar?"

"No." She wished he did. She wanted to feel deep hatred for him. Revulsion. *Something.* So this was the killer? The man who took her whole world away? She shook her head again. "No. I've never seen him before."

"He lives with his wife and son."

"He has a *boy*?" That, Andie hadn't expected. Did his family know? The terrible things he'd done? When they were sitting at their meals or kicking a ball between them or whatever the hell they did? How could someone with a child do these horrible things?

"He goes out every day around this time," Nick said, gazing through his own binoculars. "At four, he drives his son."

"Nick." Andie put down the glasses and looked at him, teary-eyed. "I don't think I can do this. I know I'm supposed to hate this man. Look what he did to me. I know what we need from him. I know what we have to do. It's just that. . . . *You sonovabitch*," she spat toward the house. She turned her eyes away.

"Just do what you have to do," she said angrily. "You were right. You *are* right."

Suddenly the garage doors started to open again. Nick glanced at his watch. "There he goes."

The man who had killed her son stepped out of a door from inside the garage. He was wearing a white, short-sleeved shirt, tan slacks, and sunglasses. He looked around for a second, then climbed in the Audi and started the car.

"Every day. Same time. There's the boy."

Andie turned and brought the glasses up again. The boy couldn't have been much more than eleven or twelve. A little older than Jarrod. He was innocent, she told herself, of whatever the father had done. "Where are they going?"

"I don't know. I want to follow them. Are you okay with that?"

Andie nodded. This scum. This bastard. *How could he play the loving father when he knew what he had done?*

The boy stepped out of the house and met the car, which was backing around in the driveway.

Andie focused closer. He was carrying a book and what looked like a portable computer. The cover of the book came into view. She didn't know why she was even interested.

Chess.

The boy climbed into the Audi.

"Come on," Nick said. He tossed his binoculars into the backseat. "Let's go. I don't want to fall too far behind."

Andie nodded, about to put down the lens, taking one more sweep of the car backing up to the front of the house.

Then, as if she'd been plunged into an icy pool of water, she exclaimed, "Oh my God, Nick!"

The shock of what she had just seen sent a violent, nauseating force through her. She became covered in perspiration as flashes of the horrible memory invaded her brain. "Oh, Jesus Christ, no."

"What?" Nick put the car back in park.

"Look in the house!" Her jaw tightened, and her mouth was so dry she could barely spit out the words. "You see that man?"

Nick grabbed the binoculars from her.

He saw the man standing near the front window, hands on hips, in sweatpants and a white Guinness T-shirt, watching Remlikov drive away.

"That's him!" The blood drained out of Andie's face. She could see his long blond hair in her mind's eye.

"That's the same man I saw running from the van!"

Chapter 95

THE NEXT DAY, Andie stayed back at the hotel while I tracked Remlikov's movements. I followed him and his son down the mountain to his chess lessons on Hassan Street, in the center of town.

At night, I held on to her tightly. Seeing that man had brought everything back — the bus, the explosion, Jarrod. I saw in her face the same pain as that day in the ER after it all happened: the events suddenly fresh and vivid again.

That night I was sure she was asleep, but she was just lying there in the darkness, wide awake. Once or twice, I felt her shudder, then she turned away from me and buried her head into the pillow. "It's okay," I whispered, and wrapped my arms around her, trying to make her strong. But I knew it wasn't okay. I knew the hurt was fresh and new. This face from the past complicated everything.

On the next night, just before dawn, I was lying in bed

thinking, tracing the first rays of light as they washed over the room.

"Do you know how you're going to do this?" Andie asked, surprising me.

"Yes." I turned to her.

I had a plan. I was just afraid to share it. I knew it wouldn't go over well with her.

We had to get to Remlikov. The problem was, he rarely left the house. I couldn't burst in there, guns blazing. We needed Remlikov alive. I knew there was only one way — one leverage.

The boy.

There was no way around it, and I knew how troubling this would be for her. Also, I needed Andie's help. So I told Andie what had to be done — that it involved the boy.

"It's going to be dangerous," I said, shifting onto my elbow.

I knew precisely what I was asking. The boy was innocent, just as Jarrod was. But we had to get at Remlikov through the one thing that he loved most — just as he had taken the one thing from her that she loved most.

"Nick." She shook her head. "I can't do that."

"We're not looking for a favor from him, Andie. We're squeezing a killer for a piece of information that could get us all killed. It's the only way he's vulnerable. I told you before we came how hard this was going to be."

"Do you know what you're asking? You're asking me to do the same thing to another mother that's just happened to me."

"I know what I'm asking, Andie." I reached for her. "I'm not a killer, Andie. But these people are."

She stared back at me, thinking I was suddenly capable of the same violence and evil that had taken her son.

"I give you my word, whatever happens, the boy won't be harmed."

"Oh, yes he will. *He will.*"

I ran my hand through her hair, pulling a few strands away from her face. "I need you to say yes, Andie. I need your help to get it done."

"And if I don't?"

"Then we walk away. We get on that plane and go back home. We forget about Cavello."

Andie sucked in a breath, wrapping her arms around her knees. "And if I say yes? Afterward, what happens?"

"We let the boy go, Andie. *We let the boy go.*"

She shook her head. "I meant with Remlikov. And the blond man."

I told the truth. "I don't know."

She nodded, and after a while her body just sank into mine. "He can't be harmed," she said. "The boy . . ."

"Of course not." I squeezed her. "I promise."

Chapter 96

PAVEL NORDESHENKO was twelve years old, and he no longer liked that his father still insisted on driving him to his lessons in the center of town.

Other boys his age were riding the Metro. Sometimes, when his father was away on his many trips, his mother let him take the bus lines. He liked to spend a few minutes in the bustling streets of the Old Town, far away from the sprawling vistas of Carmel Center and the heights.

Down here, where Abhramov's academy was, the streets were narrow and busier. *Alive!* The smells were of leather goods and spices and Arab bakeries. The sounds of merchants hawking their goods in the bazaar.

His father was always overprotective. Pavel wanted to go with his friends to the cinema or the beach, but Father always said, "You can't be too safe. Too careful." What was he always so afraid of? Sometimes his mother would let him take a day off, but his father always made him go to his lessons, as if it were religious study.

"There is a tournament next month, in Tel Aviv," his father said as they drove quietly through the crowded streets. "Would you like to go?"

Pavel shrugged. Tournaments meant work, more studying to prepare.

"There will be masters from other countries there. Sergei thinks you are ready. What do you say?"

"I guess." Pavel shrugged. "If he says I'm ready."

The car turned onto Allenby Street. The Baha'i Gardens were in full spring bloom.

"There is a casino in Caesaria. On the way back, we might stop. I'm told they play a little poker there. Just like the Americans. I know a man there who owes me a favor. He might get you in. Just to watch."

"You think?"

"I don't know," his father said, hiding a smile. "I've been known to have a few connections here and there."

They made the turn on crowded Hassan Street. Down here, the traffic was mostly mopeds and small delivery trucks. And taxis filled with tourists making their way up from the port.

Master Abhramov's studio was over a pita bakery. The place always smelled sweetly of dough. Their car slowed in front of the run-down building.

"Study hard." His father winked. "There's a lot at stake."

Pavel gathered up his notebook and computer, and opened the door. He ran inside Abhramov's building, on cloud nine. As he headed for the narrow stairs, a man was standing in his way.

"I'm afraid that I'm lost," he said. "Do you know where Haaretz Street is?"

The man was large and handsome, in a blue shirt and khakis, his eyes hidden by sunglasses. He spoke English like a tourist. American, perhaps.

"Haaretz? I think it's just down there. At the end of the street."

"Can you show me?" the man asked. "I'm not from around here."

Abhramov would be expecting him. They had an hour and a half, and the grumpy old master didn't like him to be late.

"Just here." Pavel pushed back through the door and pointed. "At the end. The bakery. You see?"

That was one of the last things he remembered.

Other than a hand wrapping around his mouth, and the damp, acrid cloth that smelled of chemicals. And the feeling of total weightlessness, of being carried away.

And the fear that his father would be angry when he came to pick him up and he wasn't there.

Chapter 97

"MIRA, LISTEN CLOSELY. *I can't find Pavel!*"

Nordeshenko's heart was beating wildly. The chess instructor said his son had never arrived for his lesson. It had happened a few times before — always when Nordeshenko was away on business. He combed the streets around the studio. He checked the ice-cream stalls, the bakeries, Pavel's favorite places. No one had seen the boy.

"He wasn't there when I went to pick him up at Abhramov's. I was hoping he had called."

"What do you mean?" His wife became alarmed. "He always waits there. He knows not to stray."

"He didn't go to his lesson. Is there anywhere he might go that you can think of? Someplace he's spoken of? A friend?" How many times had he told the boy he had to be careful?

"No!" Mira's voice began to get excited. "Maybe he took the bus. I've let him once or twice."

"He wouldn't let us know?"

Over the years, Nordeshenko had experienced the hollow feeling when a job didn't go right. He had that feeling now.

"We've got to call the police," Mira said.

"No!" *The police!* That was exactly what he could *not* do. Draw attention to himself. Now — with Reichardt in his house. What if they looked into him? He'd have to explain where he'd been overseas. And who this visitor was.

No, he had to think. "You could be right about the bus. I'll follow the line. I'll call you closer to home."

Nordeshenko switched off and wound the Audi through the streets of the Old Town, frantically searching for his son's face amid the crowds. *This is payback,* he thought, *for the things I have done.*

On Hassan Shukri, near Memorial Park, he overtook a city bus and swung the car in front of it to block its path. "I'm looking for my son," he yelled, and pounded on the door for the driver to open. "Please, let me in!"

People would be panicked, he knew. They would think him a terrorist! "Look, I'm not armed." He put out his arms. Finally, the hesitant driver opened the door.

"Pavel!" Nordeshenko jumped on, searching the rows of startled passengers.

Pavel wasn't there!

"I'm sorry, but we must move on," the driver said. Nordeshenko stepped back onto the street.

Mira was right. They would have to call the police. There was no escaping it. Even to delay a minute could endanger his son more. Reichardt would have to leave — immediately.

But surely Mira would mention him. The police would look into him. *This was very bad!*

Minutes later, Nordeshenko pulled into his driveway. He slammed the Audi door and ran into his house. "Any word?"

"No." Mira shook her head, clearly panicked.

"We're in trouble," Nordeshenko said, realizing now there was no other choice.

Reichardt came in from the deck. "What's wrong?"

"You have to leave. *Now.* Pavel is missing. We have to call the police."

The South African's eyes stretched wide. Nordeshenko instinctively knew what the man was thinking. The conversation would turn to their visitor. They would have to explain him — and why he had had to leave so suddenly.

The telephone rang, reprieving them.

Mira covered her mouth. "Maybe that's him."

Nordeshenko ran to the phone. He didn't want to let the South African out of his sight. He swallowed, lifting the receiver.

"Pavel?"

"You have a nice boy," the voice on the line replied. "I'm going to give you instructions, and the degree to which you follow them will determine whether you ever see him again."

"What?" Nordeshenko grunted. So it was some kind of kidnapping. He spoke in English. *Perfect English.*

"I have your son," the caller said again. "The good news is you can have him back safe and sound in a matter of minutes. The bad news is if you don't do precisely what I ask, you'll never see him again."

"Who is this?" Nordeshenko demanded.

"Never mind who it is. What I'd focus on now is which of those two scenarios you see taking place."

Nordeshenko looked at Mira, gave her a bolstering nod. "Let's proceed with the good news. Getting Pavel back."

"That's wise. First things first. I think we're both aware that it's not in either of our interests to involve the police. Do we have an understanding on that?"

"We don't have an understanding on anything, except that you will give me back my son. I want to speak with him."

"I'm afraid that won't be happening. Let's just say he's wearing jeans and a red sweatshirt and Nike sneakers, and he's carrying some chess books and a wallet with a picture of his family in his pocket. As far as the rest, I'm afraid you'll have to trust us on that."

"You don't have any idea who you're dealing with," Nordeshenko threatened into the phone.

"Oh, yes I do. I know who I'm dealing with, *Kolya Remlikov.*"

Chapter 98

IF SOMEONE HAD suddenly burst in and blasted Norde-shenko up against the wall with a shotgun, he would have been no less stunned. No one had uttered that name to him in ten years.

He realized he was dealing with a more serious adversary.

"You hurt him," Nordeshenko said, "you'll be paying for that mistake the rest of your life."

"*Hurt* him?" the American caller said. "I believe that's more your style, Remlikov. You mean hurt him as in the elevator of the courthouse back in New York? Like what you did to those two marshals?"

Whatever color was left in Nordeshenko's face drained.

Who could this be? Who had traced him? Even Cavello's people didn't know who he was. This was worse than a ransom. His whole life was unraveling.

Nordeshenko's mouth was as dry as sandpaper. "How much do you want?" he muttered.

"How much do we want? Not a cent, not a penny. You can have your boy back and go on with your decrepit, lying life. All you have to do is give me a single piece of information."

"Information." Nordeshenko wet his lips. "And what is that?"

"*Cavello*," the caller answered.

Nordeshenko's heart crashed to a stop. He had never once given a client up. He had never traded with anybody, never considered it. The list of people he worked with was sacred.

The American went on, "I'm giving you *one hour.* After that, you'll never see your boy again. Your identity and Interpol dossier will be turned over to the Israeli police."

"And what if I can't help you?" Nordeshenko asked. "What if I don't know?"

"Then I'd start packing."

What could he do? They knew his name. How to reach him. They knew it was he who had helped Cavello escape. And they had the one thing that he valued most in the world in their possession. "Okay," he said.

"Give me your mobile phone number — I'll contact you within an hour. Drive down the hill. Wait for my call. The meet will be quick. And Kolya, I think we both know what a tragedy it would be if the police were involved."

"You've got a lot of balls," Nordeshenko said. "Whoever you are." But he gave the man his number.

"That's quite a statement, Kolya, after what I've seen you do."

The line went dead. Nordeshenko gave Mira a reassuring nod. Then he signaled to the South African.

"Come on, Reichardt. There's work to do."

Chapter 99

WE DROVE THE CAR to an abandoned tobacco warehouse I had scouted in the seedy Hadar section of town. And waited. The boy was sleeping peacefully. I gave him a breath of fresh ether every time he stirred.

Over the years, in the course of my job, I'd done a few things I wasn't proud of. None like this. The boy was innocent, whatever his father had done. We watched him sleep in the backseat. Andie was sitting next to him, calming him. Once or twice she brushed his light-brown hair.

The exchange couldn't come too quickly for either of us.

"Where are we going to meet?" Andie asked, the boy's head resting on her thigh.

"You mean, where am *I* going to meet him? In the Baha'i Gardens. Six o'clock. There's an outdoor concert going on an hour later. The place should be jammed."

Andie nodded.

"I'll need to tape his mouth and bind his hands, Andie. It's necessary. He'll be awake. I want him in the car with you. You can reassure him he's going to see his father in a few minutes. When it's time, I'll call you. You drive up, look for my signal, then you let him go. And you get the hell out of there — you understand? I don't want you anywhere around after it's done."

"Where?"

"Back to the hotel." We'd changed lodgings this morning, out of the fancy Panorama to a smaller pension in the Old Town, where we didn't even have to leave our passports. "We're leaving for Tel Aviv tonight."

"Where are we heading?"

"Paris. Late flight out. Assuming all goes well."

"And after that?"

I opened the car door. "That part of the itinerary is yet to be determined."

The boy stirred. The anesthetic was wearing off. Soon, I would let him wake. I glanced at my watch for about the fiftieth time. The hour had passed. "Time."

Andie smiled bravely.

I got out and called Remlikov on his mobile. I told him the location where we were going to meet. I didn't want Andie to hear what I had to say.

I came back to the car and sat in the front seat. "It's done." I nodded, leaning back with a sick expression, as if I'd been chewing rancid meat.

"You know, I'm okay with this, Nick. *I am.* There's just one thing that doesn't seem right."

330

"What's that?"

"Remlikov. And the blond guy. They're the ones who killed Jarrod. They get off free?"

"We knew that coming over here, Andie. We came for Cavello. He's the one who ordered it done."

Suddenly, I heard the sound of the boy stirring. "Father?"

I got out of the car and opened the rear door. "Here." I tossed Andie a baseball cap. "I want you wearing this at all times. And the sunglasses. The boy cannot see your face. This is when it starts to get dicey, Andie. I want you to be very careful from this point on."

"Yeah, thanks." Andie nodded flatly.

I took the rope and some duct tape. She stroked the boy, as if she were comforting Jarrod. "Sshh . . . it's going to be all right."

"And one more thing." Our eyes met, as close as I could come in this moment to an embrace. "After the exchange, you wait an hour, that's all. If I don't come back to the hotel, you drive to Tel Aviv. You make that flight."

"Assuming things go wrong."

"You won't know. You just take off. Okay?"

She shook her head. "I'm not leaving you."

"Believe me, if I'm not back in an hour, you won't have to worry about that."

Chapter 100

I'M NOT SURE who first decided to build the vast, multi-terraced gardens that climb steeply up the slope of Mount Carmel and are dedicated to the Baha'i faith, but whoever it was had perfect insight into the art of the clandestine exchange.

The grounds were public enough to get lost in and open enough to spot any unwanted accomplices hanging around. It had multiple exits leading to heavily trafficked thorough-fares. Tours were constantly going around, and that Thursday, late in the afternoon, the gardens were as crowded as the lawn at a Tanglewood concert.

If this goes well, I told myself, trying to calm my nerves, *I might even give some thought to converting.*

I got there at 6:45 p.m., a few minutes early, and stood around the statue of someone named Sayyid Ali Muhammad, or the Bab, on the lowest level of the gardens, where I told Remlikov we would meet. I had given him only thirty minutes' warning, not much time to prepare. The elaborate park had eighteen different terraces. He didn't know whether I was at the upper or lower gardens. And with Ben Gurion Street only meters away, it would be easy for Andie to drop the boy and escape.

Me — that could be an entirely different story.

I'd done secret meets dozens of times, but always with the confidence that someone with a listening device and a sniper's rifle was watching my back. Never naked, on unprotected turf — and with the slight complication of having kidnapped some cold-blooded killer's kid.

Crowds were starting to form. Some Israeli folksinger was performing two levels up. The setting couldn't be better. I told myself, just think like it's Madison Square Garden. All I had to do, once the exchange was made, was blend in with the crowd and get away.

At five of six, I took out my cell in front of the statue and gave Remlikov our final call. "Are you here?"

"*I'm here*. What about my son?"

"Walk to the statue of Ali Muhammad off Ben Gurion Street. You know it?"

"I know it. How will I know you?"

"I'll be the one holding the twelve-year-old with tape over his mouth. Don't worry, I'll know you."

Remlikov sniffed, unamused. "It will take me a few minutes. I'm on the upper level."

"Don't bother, then. In five minutes, I'll be gone." I punched off the line. He'd be here. I didn't want to give him a single extra moment to prepare.

333

Chapter 101

I HAVE TO ADMIT, the following couple of minutes were as tense and heart-stopping as any in my life. I tried to focus on the crowds, mostly young people and families heading up to the higher terraces. An occasional policeman wandered by, dangling the ubiquitous Uzi.

I checked my Glock one last time. I adjusted my sunglasses. I tried to calm the riot in my gut.

5:59 p.m. Come on, Remlikov. This has to happen now!

Then I spotted him coming out of the crowd. He was wearing an open-collar print shirt and a black leather jacket. A few people passed in front of us, but he focused directly on me. Must've been the chess book I was holding prominently. He walked right up to me. He removed his sunglasses and took a long look into my eyes. I had seen the faces of many professional killers. There was always a dull glaze in the eye, even when they smiled. Remlikov had it in spades.

"Stand in front of me," I said, shifting my back to the statue. I didn't want any sudden ambush taking me by surprise.

He glanced at the chess book. "I believe that's mine."

I handed it over to him.

"And my *son*," he added as if we were talking merchandise.

"Cavello," I replied.

"You've come a long way on the premise I know where he is." He smiled.

"You're wasting time that could be very valuable. I leave here in two minutes."

"Two minutes." He pursed his thin lips. "I'll take my chances. Neither of us wants to walk away empty-handed. You surprised me today. Surprise is a reaction I've grown used to doing without. I'd take it as a courtesy if you told me how you found me."

"The business in New York or your real name?"

"Any order." He shrugged back politely.

I glanced toward the ground. Then I looked back at him with a slight smile. "Your shoes." He was still wearing them. "Not very high-tech, I'm afraid. But I hear they're all the rage in this part of the world."

"My shoes." Remlikov snorted, at first with surprise, then with a roll of his eyes. He shifted on his bum left leg. "My feet kill me." He shook his head. "Even now."

"You might think about a change of brand, if you plan to continue work."

"No more," he said, "I'm finished."

"Wise. You're a family man. Now, you have something for me?"

"You didn't finish." Remlikov continued to look at me. "Though I have the feeling I can take it from here. If you were able to identify my shoes, you must have seen some kind of security tape of what took place. To link that to me, my history, and find me here, that would take a lot of help. Resources. Governmental resources, I'm quite sure. Homeland Security? FBI?"

"Those are a lot of assumptions," I said with a deferential nod, "for a man who only has *one* minute."

"Not so high-tech also." Remlikov smiled. "I recognize you as the person who shot at us in the courthouse during our escape."

I took off my glasses. Now we were staring at each other face to face. "Paid good money for these suckers, too."

"But more important, I'm wondering why an American law enforcement agent in Haifa has to kidnap my son instead of breaking down my door with a warrant if he knew my whereabouts. And more to the point — for purely selfish reasons — how many other people you might be associated with know as well."

"All good questions," I said, deciding to indulge him a few seconds longer. "And what have you come up with?"

"That you must somehow be a very desperate man. Or, at the very least, extremely passionate in your work."

"Chat's over. Now you have to convince me why I should give you back your boy and not shoot you on the spot for what you did in New York."

A wistful smile creased Remlikov's lips. "Because I have something very valuable for you. Something that could get us both killed, and very probably will one day."

"And what if that isn't enough?" This man had done such horrible things. He deserved to die or at least to rot for the rest of his life in prison. An urge rose up in me, to take out my gun and do to him what he deserved — after he gave me what I needed.

Of course, he was probably thinking the same thing.

"Then, because you're not me." Remlikov shrugged. "How is that?"

I wanted to get this done with. Andie was probably dying with anxiety, wondering what was going on here. "Clock's on," I said.

"What you are looking for is in South America," he said. "Argentina, I believe. Or Chile. At the very bottom, near the tip. Cavello has a ranch there. Sheep, I think."

"Keep going," I prodded. I knew he was holding back.

"How do I know you will not turn my name over to the authorities the minute you have Cavello?"

"How do *I* know you won't alert him as soon as you have your boy?"

We stood there facing each other, looking into each other's eyes. Remlikov smiled. "My son is a chess player. He has a natural gift for avoiding stalemates. But of course, you already know that."

"I don't play chess." I shrugged. "But I was thinking, since we both know something about the other that would be best not to get out, it would probably be a good thing if we never set eyes on each other again."

"I was thinking that, too." Remlikov nodded. "I believe it's near a town called Ushuaia. Close to the tip. The weather is not so good, I am told, but the isolation is worth every penny. Even the *name* is telling."

He told me the name of Cavello's ranch. Hearing it, I smiled. I knew his information was true.

"Now, I think you have something for *me*." Remlikov put his sunglasses back on, our business complete.

Chapter 102

I TOOK OUT MY PHONE and pressed the Send button. Andie answered quickly.

"You can bring him now."

I tried not to glance in any direction. I didn't want to alert anyone, Remlikov or a possible accomplice, as to how this was going to take place. My hands were moist, and sweat trickled down my collar. There was nothing to do but wait, and stare at each other.

"So, who was it, if I can ask?"

"Who was *who*?" I shrugged. I figured he was talking about Andie.

"Who was on that bus? The reason you want Cavello so bad?"

"Consider yourself lucky I don't kill you right here for what you've done."

"Interesting," he said, snorting. "I was thinking the very same thing about you."

I saw him rub the tips of his fingers. I knew this killer wouldn't just let me get away. I looked around. I needed cover. A group of young people were passing by. I spotted two policemen, meandering our way.

Out of the corner of my eye I saw our white Ford pull up on Ben Gurion Street at one of the entrances to the park. Andie held there, just as I told her, waiting for my signal. I shot another glance at the policemen, my insurance.

"My son?" Remlikov pressed. "The minute is up, no?"

Chapter 103

"I WANT YOU TO KNOW, Remlikov, if Cavello's not where you say he is, every law enforcement agency in the world is going to have your name and fingerprints. It's a hard way to raise a family."

"And *you* should know, if there's as much as a scratch on my son, I'll be looking through employment rosters of the FBI for as long as it takes."

I raised my left arm. The signal.

The rear door of the car opened. I saw the boy emerge. Andie would've been pointing him toward us. He shielded his eyes through the waning sun.

Remlikov waved at him. "Pavel, over here!"

The boy started to run to him. The killer looked at me. Andie's car started up, then disappeared into traffic.

"I meant what I said, Remlikov. I wish I could shoot you dead," I said.

Then I cut around the statue — in front of the unsuspecting policemen. Without drawing any attention to myself, I started to jog, fast enough to put as much distance as I could between me and Remlikov.

I hunched into a stream of people heading for the upper terraces. The path was hilly and crowded. I didn't notice anyone following me.

I left the path and started up a small hill, using trees and low branches as cover. I spotted another exit down below. Allenby Street.

That's where I decided to head. Catch a cab. In minutes I'd meet Andie back at the hotel. We had what we needed. Within the hour, we'd be gone.

I never looked back until I'd zigzagged to the top of the knoll. When I did, Remlikov was kneeling with his arms held out. His son ran into his embrace. He peppered the boy's face with grateful kisses.

Then he looked up the hill in my direction. I didn't know if he could see me. Trees obstructed the view. But it felt like it.

For the first time in minutes, my heart rate finally started to calm. I had what I needed. Andie had gotten away safely. I knew where Cavello was.

I almost felt like cheering. We had pulled it off! We were winning this time.

Only then did I feel my neck roughly wrenched backward, and the knife blade digging deeply into my ribs.

"Sorry, mate, it doesn't quite work like that."

My blood froze.

"Now, I'm going to ask you this once," the voice said in a

heavy South African accent, "and if you have any hope of living more than the next few seconds, you'll be telling me the answer. Who dropped off that kid?"

He dug the blade in deeper; the air gushed out of my lungs. I managed to get one look at him, and I knew I was in terrible trouble.

The hair that fell across his face was blond.

Chapter 104

THE TRUTH WAS, I'd been in the FBI thirteen years and had been in a real dogfight only a couple of times. Those were more like takedowns, and not with some professionally trained killer twice my size who had me gagging in a choke hold, with a knife jammed into my ribs.

The guy's grip had me helpless. I couldn't scream. What good would that do? I could barely think. The blade edged into my rib cage so sharply, I wasn't sure if it wasn't already in my chest.

"I can break your neck cleanly, friend, and all you'll do is drift off into la-la land, which I recommend as the way to go. Or, I can play with you a bit."

Oh, Christ!

"Do yourself a favor, mate. Who was the woman in that car?"

A thought came to me. It was from some self-defense course I'd taken at the Bureau years ago. The natural urge in this situation is to struggle harder, to pull away, but to someone who is adept at crushing your windpipe in a second, it only tightens the choke.

Step *into him*, I was told. Go with his momentum. So I figured, what the hell? I wasn't giving up Andie.

So I leaned my weight into Blondie. It threw him off, maybe a step. He didn't release me, just shuffled backward.

It freed my hand enough to reach inside my jacket. I groped for the grip of my Glock. I didn't know if I had it pointed toward him or me. Only that if I didn't fire quickly, it didn't much matter.

The blond killer sighed. "Your choice, asshole."

I jerked the trigger. *Once, twice!* The recoil spun us both back, the closeness muffling the sound. I didn't know if I'd hit something. Or whether it was him or me. But I didn't feel the knife. Or pain shooting through my abdomen. I pulled the trigger two more times.

"Fuck!" The blond guy yelped and staggered backward.

I spun away just as he lashed out savagely with the knife. I rolled on my torso and saw a bloody hole in his thigh, red oozing through his ripped jeans.

"Oh, you are fucking dead!" He looked down, glaring at me with an animal fury.

I still held the gun pointed at him. But I wasn't sure what to do. Now there was nothing to muffle the sound. A group of people was headed toward us. I was an FBI agent, not a cold-blooded killer. But even as FBI, I was toast. I'd be ex-plaining what I was doing here for the rest of my life. From an Israeli jail cell!

"Turn around," I yelled at him. "Open your jacket."

The blond guy eyed the people coming toward us. He slowly opened his jacket. "What are you going to do, mate? Shoot me?"

He had to be armed, but I didn't see a gun. Even worse, these people were coming closer and I was brandishing one. He didn't know who I was. He didn't know where Andie and I were staying. What he *did* know was that if I hadn't already put a bullet through his head, with all these people coming close, I probably wasn't about to now.

"Start walking." I pointed the gun. "Back down the hill. Walk!"

Chapter 105

BLONDIE OBLIGED ME, but slowly, angrily. He cast a cold eye at the approaching crowd, blood oozing from his thigh. I hadn't killed him, and he saw things were working to his advantage now. The asshole had me gauged perfectly.

"Tell Remlikov all bets are off if I don't find what I'm looking for." I started to back away.

There was an entrance to Ben Gurion Street maybe a hundred yards below. People were streaming through the gates by the dozens. I figured that in a crowd, even he wouldn't shoot. I could outrun him. All I had to do was make it that far.

I took off, darting through hedges and trees as cover. I glanced around to see him scamper up the knoll, remove a gun from the back of his jeans, then straighten into a shooter's crouch.

I didn't hear a sound, but a bullet whizzed past my ear, thudding into the trunk of a nearby tree.

He started after me. *It was freaky.* The guy had a .40-caliber bullet lodged in his thigh, and it wasn't stopping him a bit.

I was no longer backpedaling. I ran down to the entrance that led onto Ben Gurion, a busy thoroughfare, where I figured maybe I could lose him. All I had to do was find a cab and make it back to the hotel. That's all!

A boy and his girlfriend were just turning into the park. He was wearing sandals and a Linkin Park T-shirt, and had a guitar slung around his back. I heard something zing past my shoulder. Right in front of my face the kid wheeled around and hit the pavement, his shoulder exploding in red. His girlfriend put her hands up to her face and screamed.

"*Get down! Get down!*" people were shouting.

I stared in disbelief.

An innocent person was down. This was way, way out of control now. I knew I should've stopped and ended it there. Taken him down, waited for the cops, something logical and sane. There were screams and bedlam everywhere. I took a look back for the blond-haired killer. *I had lost him!* Policemen were running up to the scene from Ben Gurion. I didn't know what to do. I made a quick judgment that the kid would be all right.

I took off toward the square.

Concealing myself in the crowd, I tried to put as much distance as I could between me and my assailant. I was praying the police would corral him, but then I spotted him — his blond hair and darting eyes — racing along the perimeter wall, following my path. I pushed deeper into the crowd.

I hurried without a clear destination through the crowded

streets, searching frantically for a cab. I could still get out of this. All I had to do was get back to the hotel. They had no idea who we were.

I found myself racing down a narrow street of bazaar merchants, angling away from the park. Hundreds of tiny stalls — leather jackets, embroidered shirts, baskets, spices — crowded with hawkers and tourists.

I zigzagged through the side-by-side stalls, switching sides of the street as I strained to see if he was still behind me. And he *was* — knocking over racks, pushing people out of his way, gaining. Sirens were coming from the entrance to the park.

This madman wouldn't stop. I was on a crowded street with no cabs. *You don't know where you're going, Nick!* At some point I was going to have to stop and confront him. I should have shot him when I had the chance.

Two more rounds zinged by my head, slamming into a stall in front of me that was filled with colorful fabrics, toppling it over.

I ducked, picking up my pace. The end of the street was fast approaching. The problem was, I was going to get there quicker than I had a plan for where to go next. It opened to a terraced cul-de-sac, maybe twenty feet above a busy street below. I was trapped. Cold reality set in — *Nick, you're going to have to fight this bastard.*

I turned at the corner and just stood there, staring at my options: leaping into the crowded street below or facing him. I gripped my gun. I thought of Andie, the image she had lived with for the past year, the blond man hurrying away from the juror bus.

This was the man who had killed her son.

I stopped behind a stall at the end of the street. Maybe it wasn't Cavello, but this was the man who blew up the jury. I had no real plan. I wasn't a cop or a fugitive. Just someone whose adrenaline was racing. Someone who was about to make a stand.

The blond-haired killer finally staggered into the cul-de-sac.

"Put it down," I said, pointing my gun at him.

"Put it down?" He smirked, coming to a stop. He stared at me. "I don't know who you were, but you're a dead man now, friend."

Chapter 106

HE STARTED TO RAISE his arm, and I jerked off two shots. Both hit home, tearing into his chest. He grabbed the top of a nearby stall, fabric falling all over him as it crashed down. He tried to get up. I saw him elevate his gun hand, frantically tearing garments off himself.

"You blew up that bus!" I screamed.

The blond killer hesitated. It took him by surprise. Then a smile creased his lips, as if he found all of this amusing. "I did." He winked, trying to free his gun hand. *"Boom!"*

I hurled myself at him, smashing my fist into his face. He staggered backward into the railing. I held him by the shirt collar, out of control. I hit him again with everything I had in me. Teeth cracked, and blood spurted from his mouth. But he didn't go down.

"Well, here's a message." I flung him with all my might toward the railing. "Boom your fucking self!"

The killer smashed against the edge, still trying to right his gun toward me, and toppled over, jerking a shot wildly into the air.

Like a dead weight, he landed on top of a parked car below.

I went over to the railing. People were screaming, running out of the way. I was exhausted, out of breath, gasping for air. For a second, I didn't care who saw me. I didn't care if I heard a police siren or if the cops found me.

Then I came to my senses. I couldn't believe what my eyes were seeing.

The crazy bastard opened his eyes. He looked up at me. He wouldn't die. Blood was matted in his hair and on his shirt. He rolled off the car and, with legs like jelly, staggered backward toward the street, somehow still in possession of his gun, arcing his arm upward.

Toward me!

I didn't move. I just stood there staring at him. *"Die, you sonovabitch,"* I said. *"Die!"*

He crouched between two cars. I could see he was having trouble breathing. Then he quickly stepped out and aimed to shoot at me. There was a smirk on his face.

I heard the beep. And the chilling screech of brakes. It was sharp and penetrating, bone-rattling loud.

The killer spun. His mouth opened, but no sound came out. The look on his face was one of disbelief.

The bus careered into him, throwing him fifty feet into the street. His gun flew out of his hand and hit the pavement with a crack that sounded like a shot.

I heard screaming. I took a last look. He was just a crumpled, bloody mound.

This time I wasn't waiting around for another encore. When the crowd looked up, the balcony was empty.

Chapter 107

MINUTES LATER, I was knocking on the door of our hotel room. "Andie, let me in!"

The door opened, and I almost fell through, collapsing into Andie's arms. "God, Nick, I didn't know what to think," she said, throwing her arms around me. She stared at my bloodstained shirt, the black-and-blue marks on my neck.

"Nick!"

"I'm all right," I said. "But we have to get out of here *now!*"

I changed quickly. We dragged our bags downstairs and paid. In minutes we were weaving back through the streets, Andie driving, to the coastal highway, headed back toward Tel Aviv. We had a ten-o'clock flight out of there. I closed my eyes, leaned my head back on the headrest, and blew out an exhausted breath.

"You weren't supposed to stay." I turned my head and opened my eyes.

"What?"

"I said an hour. I was thirty minutes late. I told you to get out of there. You weren't supposed to stay."

Andie stared at me as if she'd misheard. Then a smile creased her lips. "*Braveheart* was on the movie channel . . . I got caught up."

Andie took one hand off the wheel and briefly patted my arm. "I told you I wasn't leaving you, Nick."

We drove a little longer, the lights of Haifa fading into the darkness. I felt as empty and exhausted as ever before in my life.

"Did we get it?" she finally asked.

I hesitated a little. "Yeah, we got it." I smiled.

"So are we headed to Paris?"

"Stopover." I nodded.

"Then where?"

"Still love me?" I asked.

"You scared the hell out of me, Nick. I don't know what I'm feeling."

"You should have been in my shoes." I paused. "No. Not really."

A smile edged across my lips. A wide one — triumphant. I couldn't believe we had pulled it off.

Then Andie was smiling, too. "Yeah, I still love you," she said. "So *where?*"

The end of the earth. Cavello had taunted me. *Come and get me, Nicky Smiles.*

That's what had made me laugh. Why I knew Remlikov

had told me the truth — the name of Cavello's ranch: El Fin del Mundo. *The End of the World.*

"Patagonia," I told her.

"Patagonia?" Andie looked at me. "I'm not even sure I know where that is."

"Don't worry. I do."

Part Five

EL FIN DEL MUNDO

Chapter 108

THE YOUNG GIRL'S pathetic wails echoed through the large stone house. Her name was Mariella, and she was still curled up on the bed, blood on the pillow from the cut he'd opened on her face.

"Shut the hell up," Dominic Cavello finally barked at her, wrapping his robe around himself and stepping over to the window. He threw open the shutters, letting in the afternoon light. "Better me than some ignorant farm boy, don't you think? Or maybe your father, drunk on beer. Or is your father your lover?"

A brown haze had settled over the vast valley outside the bedroom window. Soon it would be winter. Everything would change. The pastures would be blanketed in snow, and a howling wind would lash them for months — frigid and unending. Cavello's skin turned cold just thinking of it.

Still, it was worth it — all that he had given up to be free.

He had the largest ranch in the region. The extradition treaty with the U.S. was weak and rarely, if ever, tested. He had anyone who mattered in the local government on his payroll. He was safe.

And there were no delicacies like young Mariella back at Marion prison.

A couple of bodyguards, armed with machine guns, were lounging on the fence next to one of his Range Rovers, sipping coffee. At the girl's sobs they looked up and met Cavello's eyes. Hard to tell what they thought, and he didn't care.

"I told you to stop whining." He came back at the cowering girl. "You sound like a hen. Is that what you want — to sleep in the barn with the other hens? Or maybe" — he undid his robe, feeling himself come alive once more — "you want to screw Daddy again."

She reared up and cursed at him in Spanish. Cavello rushed forward and slapped her across the face again, slicing open her lip. He slipped off his robe and pushed her back on the sheets. He grasped her by the wrists as she struggled, staring at her perfect breasts, at her young pussy. "Yes, I think that's what you need."

Suddenly, he heard shouting downstairs, and then a loud knock at the bedroom door.

"Who is it?" Cavello snapped.

"It is Lucha, Don Cavello."

"What do you want? You know I'm busy."

"I'm afraid we have a little problem, Señor," Lucha called through the door.

Lucha ran security for him here at the ranch. He oversaw

the men downstairs and the dogs that patrolled at night. All the local law enforcement people in Ushuaia were on Lucha's payroll. He was an ex-policeman from Buenos Aires.

Cavello pulled himself off the girl and belted his robe. He cracked open the door. "You're pissing me off. Not a good idea, Lucha. What kind of problem?"

"The girl's father. He is in the house right now. He is demanding to see her, Don Cavello."

"Pay him off." Cavello shrugged. "Get Esteban to give him a day or two off. I'm busy now."

"Señor Cavello, this one is different," the security man said. "The girl is fifteen."

"Pig! Filth!" The father's angry shouts rang down the hall.

Mariella threw herself off the bed. "Papa!" she screamed. Cavello grabbed her. She tried to break free and run for the door.

"This is not so easily disposed of, Don Cavello," Lucha continued. "If word gets out, it will draw attention."

The farmhand's loud voice could be heard calling him a pig — and his daughter a whore.

"Bring him here," Cavello ordered. "I'll talk to him myself."

"Don Cavello?"

"Bring him here!"

Lucha nodded, and two of his men dragged in the burly, wild-eyed farmer. He glared at Cavello with venom in his dark eyes. He spit on the polished hardwood floor.

"He says he is dead to the world now, Don Cavello. And you as well."

Cavello stared into the farmer's angry eyes, while he stroked

Mariella's slender backside. "He is right, Lucha. It is wrong to leave him in such shame. Give the man his wish."

"*His wish,* Don Cavello?" The security man looked on, unsure of what to do.

"Kill him. Shoot him. Bury him."

"*No!*" The daughter's eyes flared up. "No. Señor, no!" She fell to her knees, pleading with him in Spanish.

The security man hesitated. He was paid well to do as Cavello wished, and he would do what had to be done. "That will take care of one problem, Don Cavello." He nodded toward the girl. "But what of the other?"

Cavello looked at beautiful Mariella, disappointed. He knew he would not find one like this again.

"Kill her, too. Better yet, I'll kill her myself. *Eventually.*"

Chapter 109

IT TOOK TWENTY-TWO HOURS, and three feature-length movies, to travel from London to Santiago, Chile, halfway around the world. Then another four and a half hours on LAN, the Chilean airline, down to Punta Arenas, a gray, ice-free port at the foot of the Andes, at the bottom of the world. We could have flown directly to Ushuaia, but if Remlikov had double-crossed us, I didn't want to be arriving there.

It was autumn in the southern hemisphere, and we were down at the very tip. The sky was slate gray, and a steady wind beat into our faces anytime we stepped outdoors. It took a day to adjust. Remlikov said Cavello's ranch was near Ushuaia, a twelve-hour drive.

"Where the hell is *Ushuaia?*" Andie asked, squinting at the map.

"South."

"I thought we were south." Andie smirked cynically.

I pointed at a dot at the very tip of South America. "All the way south."

For years, Ushuaia was pretty much noted for its remote prison. I had a book on Patagonia by a writer named Bruce Chatwin. He described a fabled and mysteriously remote land. Magellan had stopped there, and all he had encountered were Indians who didn't wear much clothing and huddled around fires in the most hostile climate. The Land of Fire, he named it. *Tierra del Fuego*.

As we sat there on the second morning in our rented Land Cruiser, ready to pull out, Andie said to me, "All I can say is, if Remlikov turns out to be a liar it's a helluva long drive back."

The route south and east was weather-beaten and winding, but the landscape was spectacular. Like nothing I'd ever seen anywhere. We immediately climbed up through the Andes. Craggy, saw-toothed mountains jutted from sprawling plains. Massive ice-blue glaciers nestled between the peaks. The channel coastline was rocky and irregular, as it must have looked a million years ago. As if God couldn't make up His mind between beautiful and desolate. At almost every turn in the road, swirling clouds opened to sudden chasms of the most brilliant blue.

We finally crossed the border into Argentina. The winding road hugged Beagle Channel, islands and peninsulas pushing out into a blue-gray sea that *looked* freezing cold. Occasionally men on horseback with scarves over their weathered faces waved silently from the side of the road. The landscape was barren and lunar.

We eventually came upon a roadside cantina, the first commercial establishment we'd seen for miles. There were gauchos sitting around outside, hearty-looking locals who looked us over and probably wondered if we'd gotten our seasons wrong.

"I get the feeling we ought to stop," Andie said. "The *closest* McDonald's is probably about thirty-two hundred miles away."

The meats at the cantina were roasted on open flames and served smothered in a green *chimichurri* sauce with vegetables on tortillas. Not outstanding, but not half-bad. We took a picture of a sign that read ANTARCTICA, 807 MILES in a dozen languages.

A young cowboy with a multicolored shawl let Andie climb up on his horse. Her smile was one I'd remember until I died. I hoped that wouldn't be too soon.

Andie looked wistfully at me as we climbed back in the car. "I wish Jarrod could have been here, Nick. All the things he missed."

When we came to the outskirts of Ushuaia there were no picture postcards. The last stopover before Antarctica.

The town sloped upward from the sea against a steep mountain, almost a wall. This was the other side of the world from Haifa, and not just geographically. The place appeared to be a pit. Narrow streets rose up from an industrial port, loaded with locals hawking everything from penguin dolls to Antarctica T-shirts. Packs of mangy dogs roamed the streets. The low stucco houses had these strange baskets atop stakes in front of them. The stunning beauty of our drive there came crashing down.

We found a modest hotel near the port called La Bella

Vista that the guidebook said was decent. I shrugged in Andie's direction. "The Ritz was booked."

Our room had a queen-size bed, some pictures of the town as it was a hundred years ago, and a framed nautical map of Antarctica, which was as common down here as a print of St. Peter's is in a hotel room in Rome.

We stepped out on the tiny balcony overlooking Beagle Sound. The clouds were low and dark and swift-moving. Mountains rose from the flat land on the other side of the gray channel. A cold, nasty wind smacked us.

"Don't ever say I never took you anywhere interesting."

Andie put her head on my shoulder. "No, I can't say that about you, Nick."

We both knew the fun was now officially over.

Chapter 110

IN THE MORNING we went downstairs, and after breakfast, we made some inquiries at the front desk. The wavy-haired clerk greeted us as if we were lovers on a holiday, eager to tour the sites. "Would you like to see the penguins?"

"No penguins." I took out our map. "We're looking for ranches outside town. Maybe you can help?"

"Ahhh, *la estancia*," he replied, using the term for the sprawling farms that had been privately owned since the 1800s but were now tourist destinations in national parks.

I handed him the map. "We're actually looking for a particular one. It's called El Fin del Mundo."

"El Fin del Mundo," the clerk repeated, nodding. *"The End of the World."*

"You know it?"

"No." He shook his head. "But it is well named."

If I was here on official business there would have been

dozens of ways I could have located Cavello. But unfortunately, they all involved the local police. I was sure privacy was a guarded commodity down here, and I didn't want to attract attention.

"There are many estancias north of town." The clerk took out a pen. He circled an area on the map. "Here, near the skiing. Or *here*." He circled another area to the west. "You have a car, Señor?"

I nodded. "A four-wheel drive."

"You will need every bit of it." He grinned as if in on a private joke.

We left town, taking a different route from the way we came in, toward the northeast. The road hugged the coast for a while, passing deserted islands. In the distance the mountains of Chile ringed the horizon.

Then we turned at the mountain road and started to climb, *really climb*.

"Let me guess," Andie said, feigning disappointment. "You really *don't* want to see the penguins?"

"After we find Cavello." I grinned. "I'll make sure we leave some time."

We drove up into the high valleys above Ushuaia. The plains were greener here, spotted with vegetation, the mountains sloping and tall. We passed a few wind-battered road signs. BRIDGES ESTANCIA. Another with an arrow pointing the opposite way. CHILE.

The scenery was spectacular — frozen falls shooting down from steep, high cliffs, crevices packed with solid ice. We passed a beautiful lake, craggy mountains curling out of it that were twisted into shapes I had never seen before, bathed in a luminous bronze light.

We spent the next two hours bouncing up every marked road we could find. We passed a few wooden gates. All false alarms.

I was sure we were more likely to find Bigfoot up here than Cavello. On the way back, we wrapped around the mountains and came down to the west through the Tierra del Fuego Park. At some point we saw the biggest block of ice imaginable. It was at least thirty feet tall and covered the top of a valley between two peaks for miles.

We came across three ranches. Each was huge and in a beautiful setting, tucked into the mountains, overlooking barren coastline and sea. None were the one we were looking for.

I groaned, completely frustrated. Who knew what Remlikov meant by 'near Ushuaia'? We didn't even know in what direction.

When we drove back to town around 4:00 p.m. the sun was heading down. It was one of the most scenic days of my life, but that wasn't why we came. We drove back through the seedy streets and pulled up in front of our hotel.

"Señor!" Guillermo, the desk clerk, waved as we came in. "Did you find it?"

"I found the end of the world." I snorted with frustration. "Just no ranch."

He seemed excited. "I asked my wife, Señor. She is Dutch. She works at el pasillo de ciudad. City hall."

I waited for him to tell me.

"El Fin del Mundo. She knows of this place."

I went over and let him fold back the map and indicate a point east of town, nowhere near where we'd been trolling around all day.

"*Here*. It is owned by an old local family. At least that is what the documents say. But my wife says it belongs to a foreigner. An American, yes?"

I patted Guillermo on the shoulder and smiled. "An American — yes."

Chapter 111

WE DROVE OUT to find it the next day.

It was *east* — not near the other fancy estancias but in a remote valley. We pushed the Land Cruiser up the narrow, winding canyon, cut through sweeping, rocky cliffs and overhanging glaciers. There wasn't a single road sign. We only pressed on because of Guillermo's directions.

We stopped the SUV on what I took to be a high sheep path overlooking the property and made sure it was out of sight.

Then Andie and I crawled to a hidden overhang and peered through the glasses. I knew it was Cavello's ranch as soon as I set eyes on it.

"He's here."

The property didn't look welcoming or open like the other ranches we'd seen. There was no sign over the wooden gate. Instead there was a tower and two men — more like soldiers — leaning back on chairs, flipping cards.

"They're sloppy," I said. "That's a good sign. I hope."

Flocks of sheep grazed on land that swept up the steep mountain walls. But the wire that stretched from the closed gate wasn't to keep them in. It was barbed. It was to keep others out.

The men in the tower were armed. Two automatic rifles were leaning against the wall. I spotted four other guards patrolling the periphery with dogs. I wasn't looking at a ranch, I realized, but a fortress.

El Fin del Mundo.

The property was so vast I couldn't even glimpse the main house or the setup. I had no way to determine what the complete security situation was. So I focused on the guards at the gate. The damn thing might be electrified; at various intervals I spotted cameras.

I passed the binoculars to Andie. She took a nervous sweep. I'm sure she never spotted the weapons in the guard tower, but after she surveyed the property, she put the glasses down with a defeated shrug.

"Any idea how we're going to get in there, Nick?"

I leaned back against a rock, picked up a handful of gravel, and flung it loosely to the ground.

"We're not."

Chapter 112

WE WATCHED CAVELLO'S ranch the next day too, from the narrow sheep path about a quarter of a mile away. Each time, we hid the car and huddled in it against the rain and chill, just looking over the ranch, waiting for something to happen.

On the third day something finally did.

The front gate started to open. In the tower, the guards stood up. I zoomed in closer with the binoculars.

In the distance, two black blurs were approaching down the road. I hopped out of the Land Cruiser. Andie sensed that something was happening. "Nick? What's going on?"

I didn't answer, just trained the glasses on the advancing vehicles — maybe a quarter mile away — which turned out to be two black Range Rovers. The guards at the gate picked up their rifles and jumped to attention.

The Range Rovers slowed to a stop at the estancia's front

gate. I couldn't see into them. Their windows were tinted black. One of the guards in the tower waved and said something to the lead driver.

I knew he was in there. Dominic Cavello. I could feel his presence in the pit of my stomach. It was the same terrible feeling I'd had when I saw Manny and Ed lying on that beach in Montauk.

Then the vehicles pulled away, down the valley road, heading for town.

"That's how we're going to do it, Andie." I kept my eyes on the Range Rovers as they bounced down the mountain road toward Ushuaia.

"He's going to come to us."

Chapter 113

WE HAD TO BE a little patient; we'd known that from the start. Twice a week, Cavello emerged from his compound. It was always on Wednesdays and Saturdays, in the two black Range Rovers, and always around noon. Cavello would drive the first car, while two capable-looking guards followed in the second.

On Saturday we waited at the edge of Ushuaia and picked up his convoy as it headed into town. Was this our chance?

Cavello came in to have a meal — always at the same cantina — pick up some newspapers and cigars, and get laid.

We'd learned from a local bartender, and a waitress, that the American ate at a café called Bar Ideal on San Martin Street, near the port. He sat at the same table in the front window. He sometimes grabbed and flirted with a hot little blond waitress there. A couple of times they had been seen going off together, after her shift, to a hotel down the street. Cavello and the girl usually came out after about an hour or so.

Then, like a sated bull, he would wander over to a smoke shop a few blocks away, on Magellanes, his bodyguards a few paces behind. He'd buy a box of fancy cigars. *Cohibas* — Cuban. Then he'd take a *USA Today* and a *New York Times* from a newsstand down the block. Cavello seemed to be fearless here. Who would recognize him? Occasionally he would sit at a different café, order a coffee, open his papers, and light up a cigar. Merchants seemed to cater to him, as if he was an important man.

As I glimpsed him getting out of his car, I felt my insides ratchet tight. All the anger and anguish from so many deaths came hurtling back at me. I could only watch silently, my skin numb and hot.

How was I going to do this? How could I get him alone? We had no bait.

How was I going to get close to Cavello? And then, what if I did?

That night, we stopped to have dinner in a small café outside of town. Andie seemed unusually quiet. Something was weighing on her, and I was feeling it, too. We'd been so close to Cavello — and he was a free man here. Finally she looked at me. "How are we going to get this done?"

I took a sip of the Chilean beer. "He's well guarded. I don't know how to get close."

Andie put down her beer. "Listen, Nick, what if *I* can?"

Chapter 114

ANDIE HAD BEEN THINKING about this for a long time. She had watched Cavello enough that she just *knew*. She'd had this feeling even watching him come into the courtroom that first fateful day. She knew how to get close to him if she ever needed to, and now she did.

"I'm an actress, remember?"

She and Nick began to think out a loose plan, just going through the motions.

She had to make sure she wouldn't be recognized, but Cavello had only seen her during the trial — with her hair long and usually tucked in a beret. So she went out to the *farmácia* and got a dye to lighten her hair to blond. Then she braided it, Indian-style, and put on a baseball cap. With a little orange lipstick and sunglasses, she surprised herself.

"What do you think?"

"I think we take this a step at a time, Andie. I think it's a good disguise."

It wasn't just acting a role now. It was the real thing. It was life and death.

They found a place to lure him easily enough. But with Cavello's bodyguards always around, Nick had to be ready to come in fast. There was always a chance he might not get there in time. And then Andie would probably die. They would both die.

Nick bought a short, serrated blade, a fisherman's knife. And a melon.

"You push the knife in *here*," he said, showing her. He guided her thumb to the soft spot under her chin, pressing into her larynx. "It'll stop him dead, make him helpless. He won't be able to scream. He'll be too shocked, and bleeding too much to do anything. *There'll be lots of blood, Andie.* You have to be prepared for that. And you have to keep the knife in him. Until he dies. You think you can do that?"

She nodded tentatively. "I can do it."

Nick handed her the sheathed blade. "You think so? *Show me.*"

She held it unnaturally. She'd never used a knife for anything except preparing food. She slowly lifted the blade, still in its sheath, to the spot under Nick's chin. Pressed.

"Let me practice on the melon," she said.

"Practice on me. *Harder,*" he said.

Andie pushed the blade with more force . . . into Nick's throat.

He grabbed her wrist. "*Quick* — like *this.*" His hand jerked upward with a violent movement, scaring her, his thumb going right to the same point in her neck.

She let out a gasp.

"*You have to be able to do this,*" he said, applying more pressure, his voice hard. "If he suspects anything or recognizes you, this is what *he'll be doing to you.*"

"You're hurting me, Nick."

"We're talking about killing a man, Andie."

"*I know that, Nick!*"

Nick let her go.

She held the knife until she grew comfortable with it, and it began to fit more smoothly in her palm. She thought of all the times she had wanted to do this to Cavello — in so many dreams that she'd had, over and over again.

She pushed the blade deeper into the spot Nick had showed her.

His head bent with the pressure. "*Harder.* One movement. What if this is all we have, Andie? What if you're in there with him and I can't get there to help?"

Andie jerked her hand and dug the blade under his chin. Nick's head lifted. His face showed pain.

"Better." He nodded and picked up the melon. "Now show me again. I want to see you stab this fruit hard. *Kill Cavello, Andie.*"

Chapter 115

DOMINIC CAVELLO'S Wednesday had turned to shit.

He always looked forward to Wednesdays. By then he usually couldn't take it anymore, couldn't take feeling locked up on the remote farm like a prisoner in his own house.

Wednesday was the day he rocked the daylight out of Rita, the hot little tamale who worked at the Bar Ideal. But Rita wasn't around today. The bitch was up in Buenos Aires, at some spic family thing.

So Cavello just sat there in Bar Ideal, nursing a warm beer and sausages, horny and frustrated as hell. For years he never, ever ate alone. He was always surrounded by his men, his business partners, dozens of them if he wanted, plus an assortment of pretty bodies. All he'd have to do was snap his fingers. Now he ate alone all the time.

He might as well *be* in a federal prison. Well, maybe not.

Cavello was thinking how he missed that sweet little thing

he'd had back at the ranch. Mariella. What a shame that was. He thought of her satiny smooth ass, her baby tits. *At least —* and he chuckled aloud — *I was the only one to do her!*

Soon the snow would start, and it wouldn't stop for months. It would be even harder to find distractions here then. He took another swig of shitty Argentine beer. He felt so trapped and bottled up, he wanted to kick over the table. Times like this, back home, he'd snap his fingers and he could have all the women he wanted. Any age. Or put a gun in someone's mouth and hear him beg for his life. *Yes, he'd done that just for fun!* He could do anything back home. He was Dominic Cavello. The Electrician.

These Incas had no idea who he was.

Cavello got up and tossed a few crumpled bills on the table. He went outside and nodded to Lucha and Juan, who were in the Range Rover across the street. He started to head up the hill in his black leather topcoat, his shoulders hunched against the stiffening wind.

Fuck. This. Shit.

With his bodyguards trailing, Dominic Cavello turned up the hill away from the port and headed toward Magellanes. Two dogs were barking, tearing at strips of meat from a tipped-over garbage can. Pretty soon, they would be fighting each other for the scraps. *That* was his amusement now. He pulled out his gun — shot one of the dogs. Felt better.

Then he turned on Magellanes. What else was there to do today except smoke a fat Cohiba and then go home?

Chapter 116

ANDIE'S CELL PHONE buzzed. She didn't answer. She knew what it meant.

She turned to the short, mustached clerk in the cigar shop who barely spoke English. "These are the best, you say? They're Cuban, right?"

"Sí, Señora, the best in the world. At any price."

Andie nervously held out the two cigar boxes. Montecristos and Cohibas. She waited for the sound she knew would be coming, the little bell tinkling behind her — *Cavello entering the store.* A tingle of nerves danced down her spine. *This isn't some stupid play,* she said to herself. *You're not on stage here. You have to calm yourself and do this right. You have to be perfect.*

Finally, she heard the bell, then the whine of the door opening. Andie tensed but never looked behind. She knew who it was.

"But which is the best?" she kept asking. "It's a gift for my husband, and they're expensive. I'm not making myself clear, am I?"

"Señora, they are *both* the best," the tobacconist pleaded. "It is a matter of taste."

She looked at the two boxes. "Please."

"You won't go wrong with either of those," she heard the voice behind her say. "But for my money, Cohiba is the best."

Andie sucked in a shooting breath, almost afraid to turn and face him. Finally, she did. She saw a man in a dark black leather topcoat and a tweed cap. Cavello looked a little older than she remembered, his face more haggard. But it was still the same man she hated.

"It is like a choice between a Brunello and a great Burgundy. I go with the Brunello, in this case the Cohiba. But Frederico's right, it's a matter of taste."

The tobacco clerk nodded. "Sí, Señor Celletini."

Celletini, Andie noted. She handed the clerk the Cohibas. "I'll go with these." She turned back to Cavello. "Thanks for rescuing me."

"No rescue. Even a connoisseur would find it a difficult choice." He moved closer to her. "Business or studies?"

"Sorry?" Andie said.

"It's unusual to find an American accent down here this time of year. Most of the tourists have gone home."

Andie smiled. "Business, I guess. I'm taking a job on an expedition to Antarctica next month."

"An *explorer.*" Cavello made a show of seeming impressed.

"Not quite. A chef, actually. Maybe more of an escapist than anything else."

"No shame in that." Cavello smiled. "Down here, most everybody is."

Andie slowly lifted her sunglasses. She let him see her face. "So what are *you* escaping?" she asked, wetting her lips.

"At this moment, sheep. I have a ranch, twenty minutes out of town."

"Sheep, huh?" She cocked her head coyly. "That's all?"

"All right, you caught me." Cavello raised his hands as if surrendering. "I'm actually in the Witness Protection Program. I made a wrong turn at Phoenix and headed south. This is where I ended up."

"A man with a very bad sense of direction." Andie laughed, and hoped it seemed genuine. "But don't worry, Mr. Celletini, your secret's safe with me."

"Frank," Cavello said. Now his look bore in a little closer. The crafty killer, the psycho. The Electrician.

"Alicia." Andie lied as well. "Alicia Bennett."

"Nice to meet you, Alicia Bennett." Cavello put out his hand. "Explorer."

They shook hands. His touch was rough and scaly to her. Andie tried not to flinch. She fished in her wallet for money.

"And what about you?" Cavello smiled, keeping up the banter. "What are *you* escaping?"

"Me, I'm a desperate housewife." Andie chuckled.

"You must be very desperate, if you're *here*. But you don't look it."

"I saw this ad." Andie shrugged. "It promised the end of the world. I figured it meant here in Ushuaia, but if I'm buying Cuban cigars and talking to an American about TV, I guess I haven't found it yet. So I'm heading farther south."

"Your husband must be quite a confident man to let you come down here by yourself, Alicia. Or maybe it's *him* you are escaping?"

Andie sighed, a little embarrassed. "Actually, I lied. I'm not married. I was trying to pretend not to be some dumb woman for the store clerk here. The cigars are for the ship."

"Buying them so early?" Cavello looked at her. "You certainly are a prepared little girl."

Shit. Andie flinched. *The first mistake.*

The proprietor handed her the package. Andie took her change.

"You've made a wise choice to go with the Cohibas, Alicia. And as far as the end of the world, I think that's something I could show you. And you may not have to go as far as you think."

"Is that so? What do you mean?"

"My ranch. That's what it's called. This must be fate, Alicia."

"I don't believe in fate," Andie said, smiling once again. She put her package under her arm and slipped past him as he held the door. "But I believe in lunch."

Andie's heart started to quicken. *Stay cool,* she said to herself. *Just a few seconds more. You have him — don't lose him.*

Cavello followed her out to the sidewalk. Down the street, Andie noticed two bodyguards milling around, not paying too much attention. *Sloppy,* just as Nick said.

"I have lunch Saturdays at the Bar Ideal," Cavello said. "It's down by the port. If you care to join me."

"It all depends," Andie called, backing down the street. She could see the gleam in his eye. She had him hooked.

"On what?" Cavello followed her a few steps.

"On what you did to get yourself in the Witness Protection Program, Mr. Celletini. I only go out with a certain kind of man."

"Oh, *that*." Cavello grinned, taking one more step after her. "Mafia boss. Does that qualify?"

Chapter 117

SATURDAY CAME.

Andie was already sitting in the café when Cavello arrived. The two black Range Rovers pulled up down the square, and the door to the lead one opened. Cavello got out looking full of himself as always.

This was no game, no role, she knew. This man would gladly kill her given the chance. But she had to do this, she told herself. She had to stay calm. She had to act!

Cavello looked pleased and maybe even a little surprised as he stepped up to her table. He was wearing the same black leather topcoat and dark sunglasses, the tweed cap. "I'm very happy to see you, Alicia. I see my past occupation didn't scare you off."

"Gee, and I thought we were only playing with each other." Andie looked at him over her own sunglasses. "Should I be scared?"

She had let down her hair this time, and was wearing an orange T-shirt that read BALL BUSTER in small type under her waist-length denim jacket. Cavello read the lettering on her shirt. "Maybe it's me who ought to be scared, Alicia. May I sit down?"

"Sure. Unless you like to eat standing up."

He sat down and took off his hat. Cavello's hair was slightly grayer. His face had barely changed from the one she had stared at with hatred in the courtroom, the day of the new trial.

"You don't seem too sinister to me," she said. "Anyway, how could anyone who farms sheep be so bad?"

Cavello laughed, and she knew that he could be charming when he wanted to. "You know, that's what I've been trying to tell the Justice Department for years."

Andie laughed. They both did.

A waiter came up. He seemed to recognize Cavello.

"The empanadas are like rocks here. But the margaritas are the best north of Antarctica," said Cavello.

"Margarita," Andie said, not even opening the menu. Cavello asked for an Absolut on the rocks.

"So why *are* you here?" She tilted her chair. "They have sheep all over, don't they? You don't seem like much of a farmer, Frank."

"The weather." Cavello smiled, then went on. "Let's just say it suits me here. Desolate. Lonely. Isolated. And those are the good points."

"You know, I'm actually starting to believe that Witness Protection thing." She eyed him with a coy smile.

The waiter brought their drinks. Andie lifted her margarita. Cavello, his vodka.

"To the end of the world," he said, "and whatever hopes and expectations go along with it."

Andie met his eyes. They clinked glasses. "Sounds like a plan."

She took a sip and looked past him into the square. Somewhere out there Nick was watching. That gave her strength, and God she needed it right now.

"So, what sort of hopes and expectations do you have, Frank?" she asked, peering over her sunglasses.

"Actually, I was thinking of you."

"Me?" Andie, nervous again, put down her glass. "What do you know about me?"

"I know people don't come this far because they're happy. I know you're very attractive, and apparently open to new things. I know you're here."

"You're quite the psychologist."

"I guess I just like people. How their minds work."

He asked about her, and Andie went through the story that she and Nick had fabricated. About how her first marriage had crashed, and how some Boston restaurant where she was a sous-chef had failed, how it was time for a change in her life — new adventures. So here she was.

A couple of times she touched his arm. Cavello responded by leaning closer. She knew how the game was played. Andie just prayed he hadn't already seen through her act.

Finally Cavello locked his hands in front of his face. "You

know, Alicia, I'm not the kind of person who beats around the bush."

"No, Frank." She took a sip of her drink.

"*No, Frank?*" He paused, disappointed.

Andie smiled at him. "No, Frank, I never got the impression that you were."

Cavello grinned, too. Under the table she shifted her leg so that it brushed against his.

Cavello sat there staring at her. This was so pathetic — and nauseating.

"You might like to see my ranch. It's not too far away. The vistas are some of the best anywhere."

"That would be nice. I'd love it. When were you thinking?"

"Why not this afternoon? After we eat."

"We could do that." Andie shrugged. "I have another idea, though. My hotel is just a few blocks away. Frank, I'm pretty sure I can give you an equally stunning view."

Chapter 118

I WAS WATCHING the two of them from the cover of the Land Cruiser parked across the square. As Andie and Cavello rose from the table and started toward the hotel, I felt my heart begin to pound. She had done her job. They were heading to her hotel room.

Cavello nodded toward someone in the lead Range Rover, which I was praying meant, *Take the rest of the afternoon off*.

It didn't.

Two men stepped out immediately. One was squat with a shaved head and a mustache, the other tall with long black hair, wearing an Adidas warm-up top. The bodyguards fell in twenty yards behind. This wasn't good.

For the first time since Andie and I planned this, reality smashed me in the face. I knew that just the feel of Cavello's hand must be agony for her. His putting his hands all over her would be sickening, and maybe too much for her to take.

And now there was the issue of the bodyguards. They were obviously accompanying Cavello to the hotel.

I touched the grip of my Glock, loaded and ready in my jacket. Then I stepped out of the Land Cruiser.

The question exploding in my brain — did I try to take them out now?

Chapter 119

ANDIE WAS JUMPY as she turned the key to the hotel room door. Cavello barely gave her time to catch a breath. "Let me," he whispered, close to her ear.

He took the keys out of her hand and, a second later, pushed her up against the wall inside, pressing his body hard against hers. He put his tongue into her mouth.

Andie almost gagged.

Then Cavello had his hand underneath her T-shirt, pawing at her breasts.

Oh, God. This was Dominic Cavello. He was Jarrod's killer.

Andie closed her eyes, then felt his hand slowly slide down her stomach, slipping underneath her panties.

"You're all hot." Cavello pulled away, grinning luridly.

"Yeah. Let's not rush this, though, Frank. We have all the time in the world."

He pulled her denim jacket off, tossed it on the floor. "You know *the second* I saw you I wanted this to happen. I wanted to take you right in that store."

"Does that mean the trip to the ranch is off?" Andie said, trying to be cute.

Cavello laughed again, pulling her in to him, cupping his hands over her breasts again. She wanted to kill him right now.

"I need a couple of seconds." Andie gasped.

"Not right now." He pulled her T-shirt up, started licking her breasts and shoulders. He began to grind against her thigh. Then he ripped her bra off in a violent tug and started fondling her bare breasts.

"Please, I need a second," she said. "The bathroom."

Cavello looked into her eyes. "You don't want to back out now?"

"Who's backing out?" Andie tried to laugh, but Cavello grabbed her by the wrist and flung her onto the bed. He seemed out of control. She tried to calm herself, but she was thinking of the knife. She slid herself up to the pillow, where it was hidden. She'd cut through that melon. She could cut Cavello.

Cavello thrust himself between her legs. He was trying to get her jeans off.

"Slower," Andie said, pretending to help him, shuffling back until the pillow was under her head. She reached behind, feeling for the blade. She stretched out, pretending to enjoy Cavello undressing her. She prayed that Nick would come through the door. *Where was he?*

She felt the handle of the knife under the pillow. She had

to get him a little closer. She fixed her eyes on Cavello's neck —
the spot where Nick taught her to plunge the blade.

"What's the name of your ship?" Cavello said, startling her.

"What? E-excuse me?" she stammered.

"The name of your ship, Alicia." He had her wrists pinned.
She couldn't move. "The one to Antarctica."

Andie froze. She stared back into his eyes. Her heart
thumped as she struggled for an answer.

"Nothing goes out this time of year. They leave in the
spring, not winter," Cavello said. "You're a fox, Alicia." He
dug one hand into her throat. "But now I think it's time you
tell me who the hell you are."

Chapter 120

THEY'D BEEN UP THERE for seven minutes. I knew I couldn't wait any longer. It didn't matter that the bodyguard in the Adidas warm-up was smoking a cigarette in front of the hotel entrance. Or that the other one, with the shaved head and mustache, had followed Cavello and Andie inside.

I had to go in.

Los Pelicanos wasn't exactly a five-star. It was sleepy and quiet, with a tiny lobby and a single clerk behind the desk. A cramped three-person elevator served its five floors.

I went around back to a small alleyway. I couldn't chance going into the lobby. Above me, there was an old fire escape, the kind with the lowest platform hanging from the second floor. I jumped, latched onto a grate, and yanked myself up. The window facing me opened to what looked like a hallway. But the window was locked.

I cocked my elbow back and hit the pane. Shards of glass

shattered all over the floor. I squeezed my hands through the splintered pane and lifted the frame. The window rose. Then I ducked inside the hallway, the Glock in my hand.

In front of me was the elevator landing and a narrow staircase leading to the upper floors. That's where Andie was, on three. I made my way up the stairs.

I stopped on the third-floor landing. I saw Shaved Head leaning against the wall. He had his back turned to me and was gazing out a hallway window.

I rushed him — and he must have heard me coming. In a frantic motion, he fumbled for his gun.

I flattened the muzzle of my weapon against his jacket and jerked the trigger, twice. The retort convulsed him, the sound muffled against his body. He slumped against the wall, his hand still grasping for his gun. He slowly slid down as his eyes rolled back. A crimson stain spread out on his shirt.

I raced down the hallway to 304. I held back at the door for a second; then I heard a gasp — *Andie.*

Chapter 121

"YOU KILLED MY SON!"

Cavello's eyes bulged as he tried to make sense of what she said. Then recognition spread across his face. He reached for the dog tag Andie always kept around her neck. It had Jarrod's birthday on it.

"You're from the trial! You're the one whose kid was on the bus!"

"You pig!" Andie tried to twist out of his grasp, but Cavello held her tight.

"You'll like this," he said. "I wanted to do you all through the trial. Right in the jury box."

Suddenly the hotel room door crashed open. Cavello spun around.

"Get off her!" Nick yelled as he stepped into the room, his gun leveled at Cavello.

The strangest look came over the gangster's face. He was

shocked at first, staring at the gun muzzle. But then he couldn't hold back an incredulous grin. "*Nicky Smiles.*"

"You told me to come and find you. So I did."

"You've been wasting your talents, Nicky. All these years, working for the FBI." He looked at Andie. "And you. You lost out on a really good time."

Without a word, Andie punched his face as hard as she could. "A good time? I had to keep from throwing up. *You killed my little boy!*"

"Well, that really stings, Alicia, or whatever your name is. Tell me, Nick, is this little rendezvous official? How'd you find me?"

Cavello rose from the bed, rubbing his jaw and moving it around.

"El Fin del Mundo. This is it. Remlikov sold you out."

"Remlikov?" Cavello squinted. "Who's that?"

"*Nordeshenko,*" Nick said. "You got a lot to pay for, Dom."

"Yeah, well I figure I got time. The extradition treaties don't move so fast down here. Not to imply I'm not totally humbled — you guys coming all the way down here to take me back."

Nick stared at him coldly. "What makes you think anyone came down here to take you back?"

The color in Cavello's face began to drain. "You're a federal agent, Pellisante."

"Actually, not anymore. What do you think of that?"

Cavello sniffed. "Well, waddaya know. I'm impressed, Nicky Smiles."

In a swift motion, Cavello took the small writing desk by the window and hurled it.

Nick fired. The bullet tore into Cavello's shoulder.

Nick jumped back as the desk crashed against the wall. Cavello made a leap for the window, hitting it with his clenched fists. He crashed through the glass.

Both Nick and Andie ran to the broken window. They saw Cavello writhing on the ground, three stories below. Then he started to rise. He struggled to his feet, clutching his shoulder. And he began to stagger away.

Chapter 122

I BOUNDED DOWN the stairway at the end of the hall, two steps at a time. Then I remembered Cavello's other bodyguard. He was still guarding the hotel entrance, and that was a problem.

I came to a stop on the second floor. The elevator was there. I reached in and pushed the button for the lobby, sending it on its way. Then I backtracked and crept along the staircase, following the clanking elevator down.

I waited for the doors to open to the lobby.

The second I heard the elevator rattle to a stop, I stepped out, my pistol drawn.

Cavello's bodyguard must have heard the commotion upstairs because he had his semiautomatic pistol trained on the opening doors. He heard a noise and spun toward me. I squeezed, popping two rounds into the logo on his mint-green warm-up, blowing him back into the empty elevator car. Then I ran out the front door.

Outside the hotel there was no sign of Cavello.

I took off in the direction of the harbor, back toward the Bar Ideal, where the Range Rovers were parked.

As I turned into the square I saw Cavello. He was limping toward the cars, getting close.

With a glance back, Cavello pulled himself up into the lead Range Rover and started the engine. He jerked it into reverse, did a three-point turn, smashing into a street sign and sending a few onlookers jumping out of the way.

I ran over to my Land Cruiser, which was parked across the square. I pulled out after him. I knew that if he got to his ranch, he was lost to me. At best, there'd be months of red tape and diplomatic protocol, and a lot of explaining about my involvement.

Besides, I hadn't come down here to see him put on trial a third time.

Cavello gunned the Range Rover through the town streets, careening around tight curves, flying through any stop signs and red lights. I followed a few car lengths behind.

We made it to the east road out of Ushuaia — then he accelerated, going seventy, eighty, in the direction of his ranch. I picked up speed behind him. He passed a slow-moving truck, gunning for the narrow space between it and an oncoming bus, loudly honking its horn. Cavello didn't move out of the way. The bus driver hit the brakes. Cavello jerked the car back in its lane, missing the bus by inches.

I passed the truck, doing everything I could to keep

the Land Cruiser on the narrow, weather-beaten road. The speedometer climbed. We both got up to about 160 kilometers, close to a hundred miles an hour. I could make out the back of Cavello's head, checking me in the rearview mirror as I closed on him. His Range Rover began swerving. Once or twice I thought it was going to fly off the road.

Suddenly Cavello's window went down. I saw a semiautomatic.

I slammed on the brakes as bullets ricocheted off the Land Cruiser. I hunched low over the steering wheel.

Up ahead, I spotted a road sign, and a road approaching on the right. DAWSON GLACIER. I hit the gas one more time, making up distance. Then I plowed into Cavello at full speed!

The Range Rover shot forward and spun. This time he couldn't control it. He hit the brakes, screeching into a hundred-and-eighty-degree spin. I thought he was going to roll over, and hoped he would. The Range Rover somehow righted itself and clung perilously to the shoulder, dust and gravel billowing everywhere.

I pulled forward and slammed my brakes, too. When I came to a stop I was blocking him. Our eyes met.

Cavello's only way out was into the canyon. He sent a spray of bullets my way. Then he took off up the road.

You're mine.

Chapter 123

IT WAS A ROCKY, unpaved mountain road, barely wide enough for a single vehicle. If we didn't have SUVs, neither of us would have been able to stay on it for a hundred yards.

And it was starting to climb higher.

I pursued Cavello, my head nearly bouncing against the roof. I didn't know if he knew where he was heading. But I sure didn't, and I didn't like the idea of this ominous-sounding glacier ahead and the unknown terrain. The canyon walls rose above us, overhanging and steep. Cavello's vehicle sped ahead. It was hard to make up distance. Every time I hit a bump or a dip, I clung to the steering wheel as if it were a life preserver.

The land had the look of a primordial world. Vegetation dwindled down to nothing. Ahead, gleaming, snow-capped peaks came into view. Frozen cataracts hugged icy cliffs over-head. It was surreal.

Judge & Jury

We were going fifty or sixty, careering over huge bumps and dips. Any second, either of us could blow a tire and be dead because of it. Cavello fishtailed perilously around turns, scraping boulders and branches.

I had to end this.

Cavello slid around another turn, and I floored the accelerator, ramming his back end. The Range Rover swerved, trying to hold the turn — then its wheels sputtered wildly into a gully.

The Range Rover rolled over, then landed upright in a cloud of dust. I slammed on my brakes and jumped out with my gun ready. I didn't see any movement, and it looked bad.

Suddenly, the passenger door creaked open. I couldn't believe it! Cavello, with a bullet in his shoulder, along with whatever other injuries he'd just sustained, crawled out of the vehicle. He was still holding the gun, and he sprayed a barrage of bullets my way. I moved behind the SUV as bullets pummeled the Land Cruiser, shooting out windows. He kept firing until the magazine was empty.

I called out to him. "End of the world, Dom — for you."

Chapter 124

I STARTED TOWARD HIM, and Cavello began to hobble up the slope toward the ice field, limping horribly. What was with this guy?

"It's pay-up time, Dom. You remember Manny Oliva? Ed Sinclair?" I yelled, and my voice echoed.

He continued to claw his way up the slope, falling back, righting himself, grabbing at rocks and loose gravel. I kept up, maybe thirty yards behind.

Over a ledge ahead of us was a massive block of ice. It was thirty feet tall — and vast — clinging to the valley walls between two mountains. It was breathtaking. Could've sunk a thousand *Titanics*, and Cavello was headed toward it.

He started to slide and fall. This time he cried out in pain.

"How about Ralphie's sister, Dom? Remember her? How about that little girl, the one you burned? What was she, a year old?"

Cavello backed up against an ice-filled crevasse that was maybe twenty feet deep. There was nowhere else to go.

He turned and faced me. "So what do you want now? You want me to kneel and beg? You want me to say I'm sorry? I'm sorry! I'm so sorry!" He mocked me and everything I stood for, believed in.

I was breathing heavily, and exhausted. I reached out the gun, pointed it in the direction of the mobster's chest. He just stood there, at the edge, with nowhere to go. I'd waited for this for so long.

"Go on, Nicky Smiles. You won! It's cold, and who knows what kind of animals are up here in the wild. You want some last words? I'm so sorry, Nick. I really am. I'm sorry I never got the chance to fuck her first before you came in. Quite a piece of ass. There you go, Nick. See how sorry I am! Go on. *Shoot me!*"

I did. I sent a bullet ripping into his leg. Cavello buckled and howled. He staggered backward. I shot again, the ankle this time, shattering it.

Cavello screeched then hobbled back; then his foot slipped over the edge. He began to tumble into the crevasse, scratching at the ice. He landed heavily on his back. Now he was completely trapped — no way for him to get out of there without my help.

For a second I thought he was dead. He was bloody and twisted and barely moving.

Then he stirred, clawing himself up to his knees. His eyes were glazing over. "You think you're better than me? You're done too, Pellisante. You'll be lucky if you don't spend the rest of your life in jail. You get the joke, Nick? You'll give up the rest of your life, just to get *me*. So go on." He spread out his arms. "Get it over with. Shoot! Better that than some wild animal. Make my day."

I aimed the Glock at Cavello, ready to take this pathetic animal out. I was thinking that we were in the middle of nowhere, no one around for miles. He couldn't climb out. The smell of blood would act as a magnet and draw whatever predators were up here. Or maybe he'd just die of exposure during the night.

I lowered my gun.

"Y'know, Dom," I said, "I kind of like your idea. I like it a lot. The part about the animals coming for you."

"C'mon, Nick, do it," he snarled. "What's the matter, you don't have the guts?"

"His name was *Jarrod*, Dom. He was ten years old."

"C'mon, *do it*. Kill me, you sonovabitch. *Shoot me!*"

"You remember what you said to me that night in jail when I came to visit you, the day the juror bus blew?"

Cavello kept glaring at me.

"Well, I just want you to know — I'm going to sleep like a baby tonight."

I watched Cavello for another minute or so, until I was sure there was no way he could get out of there. Then I left.

Chapter 125

ANDIE AND I landed back at JFK in New York two nights later.

I half-expected to be held by the police as soon as we got off the plane, but we breezed through customs and immigration. The terminal was crazy. Families and limo drivers, hands in the air, waving at everyone arriving. Some guy in a slick black suit came up to us. "Need a ride?"

Andie and I looked at each other. We hadn't made a plan, didn't know how we were going to get back to the city. "Sure, we could use a ride," I said.

I gave the driver Andie's address. For most of the ride into Manhattan we just stared at the familiar sights — the fairgrounds, Shea Stadium. I think we were both nervous and scared about what was going to happen next. I wasn't sure I had a job anymore. I didn't know if I would get arrested. And Andie — somehow I didn't see her going back to auditioning for Tide commercials.

We crossed over the Triborough Bridge, and as we got closer to Andie's neighborhood, she just looked at me. Suddenly, there were tears in her eyes. She shook her head. "I'm sorry, Nick, I just can't."

"Can't what, Andie?"

"I can't get out of this cab. I can't go back to my life without you."

I put my hand to her face and brushed away a tear from the corner of her eye. She held my hand tightly. "I can't go back to my apartment and pretend I'm going to start my life over, and that I'm the same. Because I'm not. And if I walk through my door I'll have to face what's there, my stupid life."

"Then don't." I held her by the shoulders. "Walk through mine."

"I can't forget my son, Nick, and I never will. But I don't want the rest of my life to be just missing him."

"Andie" — I put my finger to her lips — *"walk through my door."*

Tears were streaming down her cheeks. I didn't know if they were tears of anguish or joy. "You know what I earned last year?" she said. "Twenty-four thousand six hundred dollars, Nick. That's all. And even *that* was mostly from residuals."

"I don't much care," I said, holding her, caressing her. "I know the truth. You don't have to prove it to me. *The girl can act.*"

Andie choked back a laugh. Her mascara was running. I called up to the driver. "Change of address."

I gave him mine. We were going home, together.

Epilogue

ONE YEAR LATER

Chapter 126

RICHARD NORDESHENKO squeezed a look at his hole cards — a king and a ten of hearts. He decided it was worth it to stay in the hand. He was feeling lucky tonight. He had several stacks of chips in front of him, and he'd looked forward to this evening for a long time.

The American had been true to his word. Not a thing had happened after the abduction of his son. No policemen. No Mossad. No Interpol. No one had ever connected him to Cavello's escape in New York. Or to Reichardt's death in Haifa. He had closed up his business and stopped all contacts with his former network.

A year later, he decided it was safe to put his toe back in. He'd taken another job in America. It involved some desperate men from Iran, but the pay was excellent and had been delivered up front.

This time around he was Alex Kristancic, a businessman from Slovenia. His visa said he was here to sell wine at a trade show in the Javits Center.

All night long, luck had gone his way. His stack of chips had steadily grown. He'd allowed himself two vodkas. He wasn't even counting the money he had made.

Once or twice, he caught the eye of a woman sitting at a table across from him. She was in a low-cut black dress, with thick curly hair pulled elegantly up on her head. She didn't seem to be with anyone, and she was playing at the small-stakes table.

The flop cards showed another king and a ten — matching his hole cards. The luck continued. Another player hung around until the end, which was excellent news. Nordeshenko flipped over his cards. The player groaned, beaten with two low pairs. The gods were still with him.

"That's it for me," he announced, stacking his chips into neat, tall towers. He went to the bar and ordered another vodka, feeling very good indeed. His mood lifted even more when the woman he'd noticed slipped into an empty seat beside him.

"Quite a night for you," she said. "I couldn't help noticing. Like everybody else in the room." Her backless dress was sexy, and she was wearing an exquisite perfume. She had a long, very beautiful neck.

"Yes. The poker gods were watching out for me tonight. And you? I hope you did well."

"Just enough to buy a gimlet and a taxi home. I guess I don't trust the gods as much as you."

"Then let me buy the drink." Nordeshenko smiled, signaling the bartender. "You'll have doubled your winnings."

He introduced himself as Alex. She told him her name was Claire. They talked about the popularity of poker, some about wine, and New York City, where she was in real estate. They ordered another drink. A few times, Claire touched his arm as they spoke. After a while, he found himself doing the same thing. Her skin was soft and smooth. Her eyes absolutely dazzling.

Finally it was past midnight. The card tables had started to thin. He was going to suggest to Claire that they continue their drinks elsewhere, when she put her hand on his arm again. She leaned in close. Her breath was clean and sweet.

"You've already had a good night, Alex. Would you like to make it even better?"

Nordeshenko felt a satisfied glow travel through him. It had already occurred to him this woman might be a prostitute, but what did it matter? She was highly attractive, and she seemed to be available. And he had won enough tonight to pay for several women.

"That would be my pleasure," Nordeshenko said, looking into her exquisite brown eyes. He tossed a few bills on the counter. She put her bag over her shoulder, and he took her elbow as she slid off the stool. "Let's rock and roll."

Claire grinned in surprise.

"My son's expression. He watches American TV," Nordeshenko explained.

"You have a son?" She didn't seem to mind it. In fact — if he read her right — it made her warm to him more.

"Yes," Nordeshenko said. "He's thirteen."

"Is that so?" the woman said. Her eyes seemed to linger on him, perhaps losing a little of their dazzle. "I once had a son, too."

Chapter 127

I KEPT THE NEWSPAPER on the kitchen table and read the article again — a short two-column report on the Metro page of the *New York Post*.

I stared at the black-and-white photo of the murdered man. No matter how many times I looked at it, it was the same.

BUSINESSMAN MURDERED IN POSH HOTEL

The body of a visiting businessman, identified as Alex Kristancic from Slovenia, was found in the victim's Times Square hotel room this morning, fatally stabbed in the neck.

Police investigators placed the time of death at sometime after midnight last night. Hotel personnel recall Mr. Kristancic arriving back at the Ramada Renaissance around midnight, accompanied by an unidentified female guest.

Lt. Ned Rust, of Manhattan's twenty-third precinct, said they are looking into whether the woman might be a call girl, but have received only sketchy details as to her appearance.

"Mr. Kristancic apparently spent the evening at the Murray Hill Poker Club, a private club on East Thirty-third Street, and may have met up with the woman there," Lt. Rust said.

According to Lt. Rust, the crime scene showed no signs of struggle or robbery, indicating that Mr. Kristancic, who had more than ten thousand dollars in cash among his personal effects, may have known the killer.

The lock to my apartment turned, and Andie, wearing jeans and a leather jacket, walked inside.

She seemed surprised to see me home. For the past six months I'd been a partner at Bay Star International, a global security firm. "Nick . . ."

"How's Rita?" I looked up. "You said you were staying at your sister's last night."

"Yeah." Andie dropped a bag of groceries on the counter. "Then I had an audition today."

I pushed the newspaper article across the table. She picked it up and read. Finally she nodded, looked up at the ceiling, then back at me.

"You are quite an actress," I said.

She sat down in the chair across from me. She looked at me, not trying to hide a thing. "He killed my son, Nick. He killed the jury, too."

"How did you know he was in New York?" I asked.

"Your friend, the one from Homeland Security . . . Harpering. He sent you a fax a few days ago. It was about a guy you were interested in a year back. He wrote that the man had reentered the country under a different name. Homeland Security knew where he was staying, the hotel in Times Square."

"So is it finished now? Cavello. Nordeshenko."

"Yes, Nick." She nodded. "It's finished."

I stood up and went over to her. I pulled her up and hugged her, pressing her head against my chest. After a while I asked, "So how did the audition go?"

She shrugged. "Not too bad. It was a *Law and Order* episode. I got a callback."

"Oh. For what?"

"Jury forewoman, if you can believe it," Andie said. Then she smiled. "It's just one line, Nick. The judge asks, 'Madame Foreperson, have you reached a verdict?' And I look at her, a little like I'm looking at you now, and I say, 'Yes, Your Honor, we have.'"

About the Authors

James Patterson is one of the best-known and bestselling writers of all time. He is the author of the two top-selling new detective series of the past decade: the Alex Cross novels, including *Mary, Mary; London Bridges; Kiss the Girls;* and *Along Came a Spider,* and the Women's Murder Club series, including *1st to Die, 2nd Chance, 3rd Degree, 4th of July,* and *The 5th Horseman.* He has written many other #1 bestsellers, including *Suzanne's Diary for Nicholas; Lifeguard;* the International Thriller of 2005, *Honeymoon;* and *Beach Road.* He lives in Florida.

Andrew Gross worked with James Patterson on *Lifeguard.* He lives with his wife and three children in New York.